C0421242

KT-444-138

This item is to be returned on or before the last date stamped below.

13 JUL 1999

26.   AN

16. NOV AN

03 MAY 01 AN   1 0 AUG 2007 EW

11 AUG 01 AN   1 5 SEP 2007 EW

21 SEP 01 AN   2 2 DEC 2007 EW

21 SEP 01 AN   1 7 MAY 2011 EW

23 NOV 01 AN   1 6 MAR 2012 EW
                                        2 5 MAR 2013 EW

09. DEC   1 3 JUL 2013 EW

16 FEB 00   WITHDRAWN   0 6 DEC 2014 EW

5 MAY 00

26 MAY 00 AN   9 JUN 04 EW   APR 2015 EW

23 JUN 00   03 JUL 04 EW   1 6 APR 2015 EW

26 SEP 00   0 6 APR 2005 EW   1 3 MAY 2015 EW

14 DEC 00   1 7 DEC 2005 EW   1 7 SEP 2015 EW

22 DEC 00 AN

7 MAR 01 AN   1 3 NOV 2018

08 APR 01 AN   1 8 APR 2006 EW

                     1 5 MAY 2006 EW

F

Dumfries and Galloway
LIBRARIES
Information and Archives

Central Support Unit: Catherine Street Dumfries DG1 1JB
Telephone 01387 253820   Fax 01387 260294

the silver river

ALSO BY BEN RICHARDS

throwing the house out of the window

don't step on the lines

the silver river

BEN RICHARDS

TF Dumfries and Galloway
    LIBRARIES

    0 8 8 9 6 8   Class F

review

Copyright © 1998 Ben Richards

The right of Ben Richards to be identified as
the Author of the Work has been asserted by him in accordance
with the Copyright, Designs and Patents Act 1988.

First published in 1998
by REVIEW

An imprint of Headline Book Publishing

10 9 8 7 6 5 4 3 2 1

All rights reserved. No part of this publication may
be reproduced, stored in a retrieval system, or transmitted, in
any form or by any means without the prior written permission of
the publisher, nor be otherwise circulated in any form of binding or
cover other than that in which it is published and without a similar
condition being imposed on the subsequent purchaser.

All characters in this publication are fictitious and any resemblance
to real persons, living or dead, is purely coincidental.

British Library Cataloguing in Publication Data
Richards, Ben, 1964-
    The silver river
    1.Journalists - England - London - Fiction
    2.Detective and mystery stories
    I.Title
    823.9'14[F]

ISBN 0 7472 7567 X (hardback)
ISBN 0 7472 7632 3 (softback)

Typeset by
Letterpart Limited, Reigate, Surrey
Printed and bound in Great Britain by
Clays, Ltd, St Ives plc.

Headline Book Publishing
A division of Hodder Headline PLC
338 Euston Road
London NW1 3BH

To my parents

prologue

I am standing on rocks looking out over the ocean. I have yearned for so long for this great immensity of water, the tremendous Atlantic waves, the salt wind in my face.

Behind me somebody calls my name. I turn to see a young girl on the balcony of a hotel. She is smiling. Beside her is a young man, they rest their sandy feet on the wooden rail of the balcony. They wave a bottle at me, inviting me to join them. I wave back and then I turn my face to the ocean, far out to the point where the sky meets the water.

This is the point where my dreams and my memories collide.

roof garden

'Hey! You don't recognise me do you?'

Nick Jordan, caught up in the crush of people trying to squeeze through the door of the building, was irritated by the shouted question from inside. This was no time for people to start renewing acquaintances. Caitlin was behind him; she would be hating this. He could feel his arm still contorted behind him, moulded by bodies, holding her hand as if trying to prevent her from falling from a great height.

'Two at a time . . .' a different voice shouted. 'What's the matter with you people? You're all gonna get in if you're patient. STOP PUSHING OR I'LL CLOSE THE DOOR.'

Over the top of the people in front of him, Nick suddenly saw that one of the bouncers was staring straight at him. But to his surprise, the bouncer's face broke into a friendly smile and he held out his hand encouraging him forward.

'Come on. You're on the guest-list. Just come through.'

Why would the bouncer be greeting him in this way? He wanted to turn to see if somebody behind him was being addressed, but the pressure of bodies made it impossible. He suspected that if he let go of Caitlin's hand, she would turn and fly in the other direction. He gripped her by the wrist and squeezed through.

'Come on, Caitlin. We're in.'

'Don't bother,' grimaced a person coming in the other direction and squeezing to get out. 'It's fucking awful in there anyway.'

1

Nick finally managed to get past the door and pull Caitlin with him into space. The bouncer had clearly got him mixed up with somebody else, but he wasn't complaining.

'Let's go upstairs,' he said to her as she readjusted her clothing and straightened her hair, glaring around her as if she had just been snatched from her normal habitat and was defiantly sizing up her kidnappers.

They had been invited to the party by Nick's friend Karl. He worked as a lawyer in the music industry and the party was being held by the team of graphic artists who designed the album covers of the company for which he was currently working. Caitlin was not particular fond of Karl and had been reluctant to come to the party.

As they passed the bouncer who had let them in, Nick lowered his head and nodded slightly in thanks, hoping that he wouldn't spot his mistake.

'I knew you hadn't recognised me, man. Look at me, Nick. You don't know who I am do you?'

Nick looked up at him. He was a huge, broad-shouldered black man. He didn't recognise him at all. But how did the bouncer know his name? Nick, he had definitely called him Nick.

'I recognise your face,' Nick lied hesitantly, 'but I can't put a name to it.'

The bouncer laughed. It was a funny laugh, a kind of chuckle. It was good-humoured, amused. Nick half-recognised the laugh.

'You go to school with someone, you're in their class, you stop them getting the kicking which they probably deserved, and then they don't recognise you. But I know you . . .' the bouncer stepped forward until he was up close. He was wearing rimless glasses and had small goat-curls of beard on his chin. Behind the glasses, his big eyes were like his laugh, only there were traces of mockery in them. 'Oh yeah, I know you, Nick Jordan. You was a Deli. You remember that, I bet. HEY, DELI! RUN FOR YOUR LIFE!'

He laughed again, and this time Nick could put a name to the throaty chuckle.

'George? George Lamidi? It was the glasses! That's why I didn't recognise you.'

'I've always worn glasses.'

'Have you? I don't remember. This is my girlfriend Caitlin. Caitlin, this is George from my school. We went to school, in the same class and everything. That's weird. What are you doing here?'

'I'm working. Pleased to meet you, Caitlin. Listen, Nick, go up to the roof. It's right at the top of the building as you would expect. Go up there and wait. They might still be stopping people going up 'cause there's a proper bar up there. Tell the geezer that George sent you. I'll be up in about twenty minutes when we've got some of this rabble under control. These people are stupid, man.'

'OK, yeah, sure. We'll see you up there. Come on, Caitlin . . . see you up there, George.'

They began to climb the stairs of the building. It was an empty office-block, bare-bricked walls with chipped purple rails running up the side. The steps were a kind of hard black concrete, finely speckled with minute gold filaments as if a child had been sprinkling glitter from a plastic tube. There were notices tacked on each landing with a felt-pen arrow pointing upwards. People sitting smoking knees-hunched on the stairs surveyed them casually as they passed. The large room on the first landing was half-lit with violet neon, the air thick with cigarette smoke and poppers, while in the corner, cans of lager were being hauled dripping from a dustbin filled with water in which the ice had long since melted. Bodies were silhouetted on the dance floor.

They passed other landings, different rooms, more scraps of paper with purple arrows pointing upwards. A girl was posing on the stairs, hanging from the rail by one arm – face deadpan, arms skinny – while somebody took her photograph. There were promoters, journalists, graphic designers, musicians, artists and directors. And there were publicity, sales and marketing people, there was East vs. West banter, there were the ligger-savants with their bluebottle misbehaviour, and there was a single toilet which could have been an ark given that the preferred mode of entering and leaving it appeared to be two by two.

Nick left Caitlin in a non-moving queue for the toilets while he went to fetch some beers. It was definitely not her type of party – she neither belonged nor wanted to belong to this world, it insisted on far too much conformity than Caitlin would ever be capable of offering; she was too demanding, too unwilling to conceal her impatience. And she did not need to make concessions for company.

He went into a room where people were dancing. At the back of the room was a small queue for beers. Nick felt in his pocket for a scrunched-up note but then remembered that the beers were free. He felt a sudden urge to turn around, grab Caitlin and leave but he knew he just had to ride it out. It was a warm Friday night, it was the kind of night to be out at a party, among people. At the very least he should find Karl. He took his beers, feeling their displeasing lukewarmness against the palms of his hands.

When Nick returned to Caitlin, she was still in the queue for the toilet which had barely advanced.

'Check out the roof,' she said to him. 'It might be cooler

up there. It's too hot. Take my beer and wait for me up there.'

Nick climbed the final set of stairs to find another bouncer waiting at the top. He was rather less hospitable than George had been, with a bored expression and a barely-concealed contempt for the clientele. He was standing with his arm across the door — an ill-tempered St Peter guarding the entrance to paradise. Nick felt awkward clutching the two cans of beer. He had no pocket to put them in.

'Got an invitation?'

'I'm a friend of George. He told me to wait up here for him.'

'George?' The bouncer surveyed Nick as if he had taken an instant dislike to him. 'Which George?'

'The guy on the door. He said it would be OK. He told me to come up and wait for him here.'

The bouncer looked him up and down suspiciously, as if unwilling to believe that somebody like Nick could possibly be a friend of George. 'Go on then.'

'My girlfriend will be up as well in a moment.'

The bouncer barely nodded and lifted his arm slowly like a car-park barrier.

Nick emerged into the soft, mild, evening air. The atmosphere on the roof was far more relaxed, people were sitting on white plastic chairs enjoying the privilege of being special enough not to be packed in with the masses below. Bottles of spirits stood on a low table, a few people were drinking through straws from miniature Moët and Chandon bottles, the music was more mellow. It was a roof patio with a low rail running around it, not nearly secure enough to stop somebody from toppling backwards on to the busy street below. Above them in the dark cloudless sky, there was a bright fraction of moon, and the ruby-tipped wings of planes flashed as they crossed the city in their final descent.

Nick cracked open his beer, sipping quickly at the small exodus of warm foam. He saw the back of Karl's tall figure standing with a group of people. His hand was resting on the back of a slim blonde girl wearing army fatigues and Nikes. Every now and again the hand wandered idly to stroke up and down her buttock, squeezing it occasionally almost absent-mindedly. Nick grinned, glad that Caitlin was not present. She despised men who did that to girls in public. As if suddenly sensing Nick's presence, Karl turned and met his eye. He broke away from the girl, who turned to follow him with her eyes as he approached Nick, his palms outstretched in front of him, smiling.

'Good, you got up here. I was just going to come down and have a scout around for you. I wasn't sure if you would come through. It's much better up here.'

Nick was not small but he still stood a couple of inches shorter than Karl with his long rower's legs, his handsome angular face, his Panzer tank-commander blue eyes, his studied but successful charm. Nick was also fair-haired but his eyes were hazel, he was not as self-consciously blond as Karl, he was slighter and his features were softer, shyer than those of his friend. Neither did he have the faintly aristocratic note that Karl cultivated; the impossible-to-ruffle air of somebody who believed that if everybody would just be a little quieter and a little better-mannered then life would surely be more agreeable. Nick was much easier to agitate.

'Where's Caitlin?' Karl asked now as he saluted his friend.

'She'll be up in a moment. Who's the girl? I think she might be twitching your lead.'

Karl turned back and waved at the girl who was still

watching him. The wave was not an invitation to join them. He shrugged dismissively. 'Oh, I met her last weekend.'

Nick nodded. It was never worth getting to know Karl's girlfriends, because they were so quickly discarded. Karl's idea of a long-term relationship was around three weeks. When people made disapproving comments about this, Nick would never join in. Mainly, because he didn't really care. What business was it of his anyway? He felt that most of the disapproval was envy-fuelled or the result of not having anything else to talk about. Why should everybody be in a long-term relationship? Once, at a party, one of the long-term girlfriends had attacked Karl with a loud and ruthless dissection of his immaturity, selfishness and lack of respect for women. Karl hadn't got angry or even tried to argue but almost bemused that somebody was expending such an amount of energy on analysing his character.

'You're probably right,' he had finally said while courteously refilling her glass with champagne.

Nick told Karl about meeting George on the door.

'From school?' Karl looked puzzled. 'But I don't remember a guy like that . . .'

'No. From my first school.'

'Ah yes . . .' Karl laughed. 'I forgot about your comprehensive days.'

At his first school, Nick had formed part of a small but highly visible core of middle-class children from similar families. They had clustered together, played musical instruments, flouted the rules on school uniform, taken the tube away from the school in the evening, and generally done their best to avoid getting beaten up by the resentful majority who went to the school because they were in the catchment area. When it came to the sixth form, however,

Nick's parents had become worried that he had been spending too much time drinking and smoking in the common room and that the academic standards of the school were not sufficiently high to allow him to get the results necessary for university. So they had carefully tidied away their commitment to the comprehensive system, hauled him out and sent him to a private school (socially progressive but a good success rate with Oxbridge) for his A-levels.

It was at Westdale that he had met Karl. Caitlin claimed that Nick and his contemporaries were more powerful than the *Cosa Nostra*, the Freemasons and the Vatican church, their codes and networks more labyrinthine. The combination of fashionable comprehensive and then social cross-able private school gav ... ... referencing system. To Caitlin, it was all part of the liberal cement that held the bricks of the British establishment together, a diaspora which had re-homogenised at university during the 1980s to form a new model army of journalists, researchers for TV or advisers to Labour MPs. Their names were not up in lights as such, but at the top of newspaper columns, on lists of policy units and think-tanks, or rolling with the credits at the end of documentaries. And they all knew each other.

'When we did PE,' Nick said to Karl, 'one of the options was to go roller-skating in Covent Garden. George and I would go up there on the tube. We used to have a great laugh.'

'Roller-skating for PE?' Karl frowned. 'That's quite right-on.'

'Here's Caitlin,' Nick said as he saw her emerging through the fire-exit door which led on to the roof. She was closely followed by George. Caitlin was laughing flirtatiously.

'Your friend just got me to the front of the queue for the toilet . . .' she remarked, '. . . and you never told me about Delis, Nick.'

'Hi Caitlin, you're looking great as usual . . . What's a Deli?' Karl asked. 'In this context, I mean.'

'Ask Nick. He was one, apparently.'

'I wasn't,' Nick protested. 'A Deli was a kid at our school. It was the name for a certain type. They were the kids who did music when the rest were doing PE, came from middle-class families blah blah blah. They were called Delis because they used to go out at lunchtime and instead of going to the chippy, they used to go to this Italian delicatessen and hang about outside eating little tubs of pasta and stuff. Every now and again, the hard kids in the school started a campaign against them. They used to go about hunting them down, waiting for them in the tube station. Then, basically, they kicked fuck out of them. Carrying a musical instrument was a big giveaway, you might as well have worn a sign saying "kick me" on your back. But I wasn't one 'cause I never did music and I never got a kicking.'

'Only because . . .' George butted in with the huge grin that Nick remembered from school, '. . . only because I stopped them from giving you a kicking.'

And Nick remembered the time walking out of school towards the tube. A group of kids had been cruising about looking for Delis, but had had little luck, given that most of their intended quarry had taken evasive action. Nick had not considered himself a high-risk target, but the kids were bored and needed a victim.

'You're a fucking Deli,' one of them had snarled.

'I'm not.'

'You are. Run, Deli. Run for your fucking life.'

Nick had hesitated. There was no point in running, it

was too humiliating, and they would catch him anyway. One of the boys had been advancing on him fist raised. Nick felt almost calm, knowing that somebody was bearing down on him with the sole intention of inflicting pain. People were walking past in the street, oblivious to the small drama – men in suits with briefcases, old women with shopping trolleys, mothers dragging children. It was a quarter to four in the afternoon, it was as if Nick and the knot of boys around him were just another feature of that dull afternoon. There was nothing that he could do. Then George had appeared.

'He ain't a Deli. What are you wasting your time on him for? Look at him, he ain't worth it. The Delis are all sneaking out of the sixth-form exit and going round the back way. Don't waste your time on him. He's all right. We go roller-skating. He don't even do music.'

The boy with his fist raised had stared angrily at Nick. Nobody crossed George because he was too big and – in spite of his good nature – was reputed to have a violent temper if pushed too far. But the boy wanted to hit Nick now. There had been a fraction of a second when Nick had thought that he still might. Then one of the other boys had said, 'Come on Tone. Stop wasting time. Let's find out where they are.' The boy had held his fist high and then feinted the punch. Nick had recoiled expecting to feel the contact and the boys had laughed and run off to land real blows on somebody else. After that incident, they had just ignored Nick – he was a nothing, a nobody. Which suited him down to the ground.

'But now I know he *was* a Deli,' George continued looking at Caitlin. ''Cause the hallmark, the dead giveaway of being a Deli was that, while people like me stayed on in that shit-hole of a school hoping to get a few decent exam results, the born-and-bred Deli was taken out by Mummy and Daddy and sent to a proper school. It was OK to slum it when they was doing biology O-level or whatever. But when it really came down to it, they were like rats off a sinking ship. People I thought were my mates, who liked having a black friend, they just fucked off and I was on my own.'

Nick was startled by George's tone. They used to tease each other with mock racial taunts. *Honky! Nigger! Snowflake! Coon!* They could take the piss out of all of that. It had all been a laugh. But there was an uneasy edge to George now. He was no longer laughing. Nick watched him pull out a bag of grass and some Rizlas.

'Give me a cigarette,' he said to Nick and Nick handed him one from his packet.

As George began to skin up almost one-handedly, Karl said: 'But if the ship was sinking like you say, then you can hardly blame the rats for leaving.'

George glanced at him. 'Like when the *Titanic* went down it was only the first-class passengers who got lifeboats?' And then as if bored with the metaphor, he added impatiently, 'Maybe if some of them had stayed on, then it wouldn't have been as bad.'

'Ah well . . .' Karl was also beginning to look bored with the conversation. 'It's always been like that hasn't it. Every man for himself and all that. *Sauve qui peut.*'

George put the joint in his mouth and looked steadily at Karl. Although he was silent, his expression was quite sufficient to show what he thought of Karl.

'Anyway . . .' Karl remarked, 'I had better get back and see if Katie is OK. I'll see you later, Nick. Nice to have met you, George.' He winked at Caitlin and was gone.

George followed him with his eyes, the joint in his mouth looking like a blowpipe that might fire a swift poisoned dart into Karl's back. He removed the joint from his mouth and sucked in hard before handing it to Caitlin.

'Wanker,' he said simply, exhaling at the same time so that the word seemed to swirl out with the cloud of sweet smoke. Caitlin laughed. Nick glared at her.

'Anyway, Nick, what do you do now? What are you working at?' George asked.

'I'm a journalist.'

'Yeah? I remember you was always good at English. Good with words and that. So . . . what? You write for a paper or something?'

'Sometimes. I'm freelance though. But at the moment I'm working in TV.'

'Yeah? What programme?' He began skinning up another joint, even though Caitlin had just passed the first one to Nick. Nick paused before answering, watching the skilful way that he quilted the fragile papers together.

'It's a programme about miscarriages of justice. It's called *Reason to Doubt*. It's on quite late. It looks at individual cases where . . .'

'Yeah, I've seen it. You're working on that? What do you do?'

'On the last series I was doing something about somebody who died in police custody. Now, I'm doing some research on a trade unionist who claims to have been set up for embezzling union funds and spending it on whores.'

Nick winced as he thought about Ron Driver. He hated his whiny Midlands accent, his polyester trousers, his thick glasses, his treasured collection of model cars, his dreary rhetoric, his dirty jokes. There was little glamour in championing his cause. It wasn't even that he particularly disagreed with him, he just had no subtlety, no charm. Ron Driver belonged to a world of shop stewards who blew whistles and shouted "All Out!" He gave Nick lectures on the importance of a domestic manufacturing base. Yet there was no doubt in Nick's mind that Ron Driver was innocent, that he had been framed to get him out of the union and that the year he had spent in prison had wrecked his life and destroyed his marriage. It was frightening what they could do when they wanted. They? He sounded like Ron Driver. But *somebody* had wanted him badly enough to stitch him up, somebody had decided that he was more than just an irritant, and that somebody formed part of the fabric of the British state. Anyway, the case was a joke – Ron Driver had gone to prison because of a vicious media and a dumb jury. What did it matter now though? Even if somebody held their hands up and admitted that the case was a travesty, the man was finished. He was never going to stand in his anorak at outdoor meetings and inflame the masses again with mega-phoned demands for free collective bargaining and the need to defend the nation's manufacturing base. The only person who couldn't see this was Driver himself. Nick knew that Ron Driver disliked him almost as much as he disliked Ron Driver, that he too had a clear recognition of his antithesis in this blond-haired media-boy from London. The point was, and this afforded Nick some satisfaction, that Ron Driver needed him.

'Miscarriages of justice . . .' George contemplated Nick slowly. 'I could tell you about a real miscarriage of justice.'

'Yeah? Like what?'

'It's this mate of mine, he . . .'

George was interrupted by the bouncer guarding the entrance to the roof.

'George! George, they need you downstairs, mate. It's only Les down there on his own. They're going fucking spare down there.'

George sighed and handed what was left of the joint to Caitlin. He put his hand over his eyes for a second.

'I'm only doing this party as a favour to a mate. Listen, Nick. Don't go off without seeing me, yeah? Give us your number, at least.'

George turned directly to Caitlin. 'Make sure he doesn't run off without leaving me his number. Nice to meet you, Caitlin. Nick, later, yeah?'

As he strode over to the fire-exit door and disappeared. Nick was annoyed, he wanted to hear what George had been about to say. Maybe it was just some kid alleging that corrupt police officers had planted dope on him. Maybe it was his mum getting overcharged on her phone bill. Or maybe it was a story from the *demi-monde* of bouncerdom – guns and drugs and testosterone. Men in doorways, men counting notes, men in the shadows.

Much more exciting than Ron Driver and the torrid nights that he didn't spend in a Birmingham City shirt on the end of a dog-leash in an Erdington flat with a nineteen-year-old prostitute called Mandy who now admitted that she had never seen him before in her life. *A wanker, yes, but not corrupt.* That was the general consensus on medium-sized Ron from the Black Country and it was a point of view which Nick found incontrovertible.

Nick shuddered as he thought of wet and windy Birmingham – he would probably have to go up some time next week. He saw the sullen permed women pushing the refreshments trolley, could almost hear the conductor's voice – the litany of stops – Watford Junction, Milton Keynes, Coventry, Birmingham International, Birmingham New Street, Sandwell and Dudley, Wolverhampton where this train will terminate.

'He was nice,' Caitlin said slowly. 'That was wicked

grass as well. My head's spinning.'

'Yeah, it was strong. It was strange, you know, seeing him. I was quite close to him at school once. But I just didn't recognise him. And he's sort of changed, he's got this edge to him. Like he's kind of bitter about everything. Even the time we were at school together. Like he kind of sees it differently now. Like he's rewritten history.'

'The point about rewriting history,' Caitlin said, 'is that there's this implication that you're falsifying things. That there's some kind of true original version which gets perverted. But maybe history has to be rewritten sometimes to get at the real truth.'

'It just gets so boring,' Nick said. 'What's the point?'

Caitlin laughed. 'Spoken like a true journalist!'

'I didn't mean it like that,' Nick protested. 'I mean all these people delving into their pasts, realising that the reason they're a fuck-up today is because somebody fucked them up yesterday. It's always someone else's fault. Nobody will take responsibility or think about how *they* are responsible for what they are and how they've turned out. Yeah, it's my fault that he had a bad time at school and works as a bouncer 'cause I'm white and middle-class. Next he'll be saying I sexually abused him in double history . . .'

Caitlin was holding her hand over her mouth to stop herself from laughing.

'Oh no, something's really touched a nerve hasn't it?'

Karl came wandering over with Katie. She was very pretty but had that slightly distant arrogance which suggested that the person to whom she was talking had not demonstrated that they were sufficiently interesting or important enough to merit anything more than the faintest of smiles. She was a researcher for a new TV series which had been launched to look at women's issues in a fresh and irreverent way. Nick blanched when he heard this. Caitlin had watched – with mounting fury – the first episode which had contained features on male strippers, women's rugby and – to provide a little intellectual ballast – an interview with a young representative of the New Feminism who also had a New Book to plug. Caitlin had hurled first a wine cork, then an eyeliner and finally her shoe at the TV in disgust. Tonight though, she simply arched an eyebrow and chose to observe a disdainful silence.

'Nick was just getting slagged because he went to a private school,' Karl told Katie.

'Like that's a relevant issue any more,' she replied with dry scorn.

'I only went in the Sixth Form,' Nick protested.

'Ah now, that's the irrelevant bit,' Caitlin exclaimed impatiently. 'The point being made was that, despite the school being a comprehensive, when it really mattered those with the resources to do so cleared out. And that remains a point of the utmost relevance.'

Katie half-rolled her eyes. 'I just think it's all a bit 1970s that debate about private education. It's here to stay whether we like it or not.'

Caitlin looked at her sharply. Nick waited for the cobra-strike but she just turned instead and held her hands out smiling at Nick.

'Shall we go and dance at least?'

'Are you coming?' Nick asked Karl but he shook his head benignly, steering Katie away with one hand on her back and waving goodbye over his shoulder.

They walked back into the building and Nick felt the sweet, warm air pressing round them again like condensed milk, the corridors closing in, the beat of the music, faces descending the stairway. He felt the hard beat of the music banging in his ears. A saucer-eyed boy lurched up to Caitlin and started jabbering in her ear about the music, lightly pushing at her arm to emphasise each point. Every time he pushed at her arm, she glanced down at it but he seemed quite incapable of taking the hint.

'Oh would you just fuck off,' Caitlin finally said when it was obvious that her patience had been exhausted with this assault on both her ear and her arm. She turned away from him shaking her head and he muttered some dreary insult at her before departing.

'I wasn't really a Deli,' Nick said to Caitlin as he took her by the hand. She grinned at him.

'Of course not, darling.'

'We can go home if you want?'

'No,' she replied, 'we're here now. Let's have a dance.'

childcare

'It's me.'

It was Marianne.

Nick felt stress invading his body as if his veins were being stretched out like liquorice. His head began to throb. Why hadn't he left the answerphone on? He had. Caitlin must have switched it off. He scowled at her but she did not see him, as she was lying face-down on the sofa reading. Caitlin was an astonishing and energetic reader, she read with a taste as catholic as her family background, she read fast but also carefully, and she read books that most people only pretended to have read. In the last months, Nick had watched her ingest Marx's *Grundrisse*, a history of the French Secret Services, and *The Golden Bowl*. She was currently sprinting through a book about the wealth of the Guggenheim family.

'Hi. How are you?' Nick said flatly to Marianne.

'Like you care.'

'OK, I don't care. I was just being polite. What do you want?'

Caitlin turned round on the sofa, having quickly realised from Nick's tone who was on the phone. She began to pull faces, drawing her finger across her throat and then mimicking a noose, sticking her tongue out like a hanged person.

'Are you alone? Or is that woman there?'

'Yeah, she's here. She lives here. Look, Marianne, what do you want? Let's not waste time with pointless insult swapping.'

'I want to know if we can change our arrangement for the weekend. I want to know if you can have Rosa on Saturday instead of Friday.'

Nick drew in his breath. He knew what Marianne's reaction would have been if he had phoned with the same request.

'Why?' He realised that he was clenching the phone so hard that his hand was becoming sore. He relaxed his grip and reached for a packet of cigarettes, pulling the phone extension as far as it would go so that he could reach the ashtray as well. The phone clattered off the table. He picked it up.

'Are you still there?'

'Yes. Look, I don't have to tell you why, Nick. Just give me a straight answer.'

'You're asking for a favour. I've already arranged something for Saturday night. So yes, I do think I'm entitled to ask why.'

'A favour! You are joking aren't you? Spending one night a week with your child and you're doing me a favour.'

Caitlin was kneeling up on the sofa now, frantically shaking her head and wagging her finger. No, she was mouthing. No, no, no, no.

'I'm not trying to get out of any responsibility. But we had an arrangement . . .'

'OK. A friend has bought me a ticket for the theatre. As a surprise. It was expensive and I don't want to let her down. All I want is to change the days. I don't think it's so much to ask.'

'All right.'

Caitlin rolled her eyes in despair and flipped on to her back. She lay on the sofa with her knees pulled up and her arms by her side, staring at the ceiling.

'But, Marianne. You can't keep doing this you know. Or at least you have to give me some decent notice.' He tried to stretch for the ashtray again and the phone slid to the end of the table. He gave up and flicked the ash on to an old bank statement. Caitlin got up and stalked out of the room. Nick almost laughed – all that was lacking was a tail to swish with irritation.

'I would just remind you, Nick, that you're the one who has it easy. So don't start giving me lectures about what I should or shouldn't do.'

'I'm not going to get sucked into this argument again. What time on Saturday?'

'I'll drop her off in the afternoon. About four thirty.'

'Shouldn't that be a question? Like, "Is four thirty OK?" Yeah, all right then. But, Marianne, you come in, you say goodbye to Rosa, you go. That's it. You don't come in looking for an argument, you don't start making snidey comments in front of Rosa.'

'You're a bastard Nick. And it isn't just me that thinks so. I was talking to Judith . . .'

'Marianne? I couldn't give a flying fuck what Judith thinks. I'll see you on Saturday.'

He put the phone down and sat down on the sofa rubbing his eyes until they were almost sore. He looked up and stared at his reflection in the mirror on the opposite wall. It was amazing, he thought, how things turned out. How he could feel such hatred and contempt for somebody with whom he had experienced such intimacies – somebody with whom he had laughed, with whom he had shared things, with whom he had made love. Love! It was as impossible to imagine now as infinity. His hatred was a process of distillation, it grew stronger, purer, more potent as time went on. There was no escaping her though, she had him harpooned, there was no breaking the bond between them now. His daughter Rosa, the daughter he had never wanted, the undeniable physical proof of their past, of their love.

He had never wanted Rosa. He loved her now, but he had not wanted her to be born. No doubt, one day, Marianne would inform Rosa of this fact, if she hadn't already done so. Did he still wish she hadn't been born? Given the option, would he set the clock back, relinquish Rosa and the time that they had spent together? Sitting with her in the park by the lake, watching her run jerkily after ducks and geese, her mouth in a wide O, while he waited for the momentum of her body to send her tumbling forwards, picking her up and dusting her down, kissing the tears from her red-cheeked face, making her laugh. She had her whole life in front of her.

Nick looked at his adult face in the mirror and thought of when *he* was six years old, little flashes of memory: a birthday cake train standing on chocolate finger rails, the fairy lights around the crib scene in the window at Christmas; golden-winged angels and sheep fleeced with curly wood shavings; tiny champagne bottles filled with bubble-bath in each year's stocking; late one night being woken by the sound of his mother screaming, doors slamming louder than he had ever heard a door being slammed before. Perhaps Rosa would remember the afternoon in the park, wrapped in a bright red scarf, chasing the ducks and the geese. Yes, he was glad that she had been born, he loved her. But he hated Marianne.

Caitlin also hated Marianne, was hard-line about her, said that she was a disgrace to women. Nick was relieved about this because he knew that Marianne did her utmost to present herself as the injured party – the wronged woman

abandoned by the callous man, left holding the baby while
he got away from his responsibilities scot-free. This version
of events, which he knew was tacitly accepted by many of
his acquaintances, omitted several key facts. Firstly, that
Marianne had wanted a baby while he had not. Secondly,
that Marianne had come off the pill without telling him.
Thirdly, that she had done this at a time when it was obvious
that their relationship was coming to an end. Fourthly, that
when she had told him about it, she had also informed him
that the decision over whether to go through with it was one
which she – and she alone – would make.

So Rosa had been born and, for a time, it appeared that
things might work out. He had moved out, agreeing a
financial contribution and times when he would look after
the child. The honeymoon period, however, did not last long.
Especially after he had started seeing Caitlin. They had
begun to get phone calls late at night where the receiver was
simply put down after a long silence. Sometimes, Marianne
would start screaming abuse, a couple of times she even
turned up and began hammering on the door. *Bastard,
bastard, you fucking bastard in there with that slut, open the fucking
door you cowardly bastard, come out you whore.* Nick's great fear
was that one day Caitlin would respond to this invitation
since she would be more than a match for Marianne. Mostly,
though, she put the pillow over her head and muttered "Get
rid of her" through gritted teeth.

Nick had once sworn to himself that he would never
behave in front of his own children in the way that his
parents had behaved in front of him and his brother and
sister. But once when he was collecting Rosa from Marianne's house, they had started to argue and she had flown at
him, nails clawing at his face. Wrestling with her in the
living room, spinning her around, holding her hands away

from his eyes, *you mad bitch, you crazy fucked-up bitch*, he had waltzed round to see the little girl standing in the doorway, fat tears rolling down her face – *stop it, Daddy, stop hitting Mummy, don't hurt Mummy* and he had dropped Marianne's hands and she had stood by his side panting with the exertion and her own furious rage, while they both looked at the small figure that they had brought into existence.

Gradually, the violence had ebbed away and, lately, he had been able to relax things somewhat. It was a sullen hatred between the now, a mutual bitterness. He felt that he had been tricked; she felt that she had been let down. Their hatred had matured, had developed from infancy to childhood, but it too still had its whole life ahead of it. And neither of them knew where it would go next, what troubled adolescence lay just around the corner.

He got up and wandered to the window. The rain falling was so soft that it did not have sufficient downward momentum to reach the ground, it was being tossed against the glass pane by the wind. This was his flat – Caitlin lived here with him, sure, but it was his flat. His dad had given him the money for the deposit, arguing that he should buy while the housing market was still in recession. In the end, he had found this flat off the Stroud Green Road about ten minutes from Finsbury Park tube station. It was a bit of a nowhere area but it was still North London and he liked the flat, especially the back roof garden which looked out over a small city park where people kicked balls, flew kites, contemplated their troubles, walked dogs – and which, in summertime, would be lit up by the lingering remains of the dropping sun. He was finally away from Marianne; she could lay no claim to him here; he would never have to leave anywhere again if he did not want to. It was his flat.

Caitlin came wandering back into the room eating a

piece of toast and marmite. She didn't say anything to him, began to rifle through some papers on the desk, sticking the piece of toast in her mouth so that she could use both hands.

'We didn't have any plans for Saturday, anyway,' Nick said. He felt suddenly depressed.

Caitlin contemplated him, chewing and then swallowing her toast.

'We can always get *Babe* out again,' she said. Nick wasn't sure if she was being sarcastic. She had laughed more than Rosa at the mice singing "Blue Moon". While Caitlin hated Marianne, she was affectionate towards Rosa and sometimes seemed positively pleased to be landed with her as it meant that she didn't have to go to any parties or social occasions. It was not that Caitlin was antisocial – she liked company – but she hated crowds, discomfort, and queues. Especially when the crowds and queues were made up of media people, a class of human being for whom she reserved a deep contempt. Caitlin was always categoric in her likes and dislikes; she rarely made exceptions or recognised ambiguous cases. Her disapproval was also eccentric at times: she would get up and stalk out of the room if a film contained a car-chase and could never be persuaded to return. All car-chases were boring and all films containing car-chases were bad, just as the Central Line, science fiction, and musicals were bad. Equally, what Caitlin liked was objectively good and not a matter for negotiation. People who said they did not like Shakespeare were simply fools in Caitlin's opinion and she would not waste her time on them.

It was this kind of certainty that made Caitlin so good at her job as a Welfare Rights adviser. If she decided that Mrs X was entitled to a disability allowance, or that Mr Y had been given the wrong advice on his housing benefit entitlement, then she would pursue the government agency involved with a systematic determination which usually resulted in their weary and graceless submission. Meanwhile, Caitlin would return home with bunches of flowers and boxes of chocolates from grateful clients.

Nick had met Caitlin when he was working on a documentary about people jailed for non-payment of the poll tax. He had fallen for her at once – he liked her terrier-quality, the fact that she was second-generation Irish in contrast to his undiluted Englishness, the way that she was so good at what she did, the flirtatious way in which she mocked his ignorance and political naivety. He liked the way she could look either austere or beautiful depending on her mood and the amount of effort she could be bothered to make. She came from a working-class background but had no interest in flaunting it in order to gain points. It had taken him a long time to get anywhere with her though. Nick was clever enough to realise that there was little point in trying to adopt a persona that would not suit him, and that he would be better off playing to his strengths. He had been charming; he had paid her a lot of attention; he had taken her out. Caitlin had continued with her mocking tone both towards him and the world he inhabited but when he finally plucked up the courage to take her by the hand and ask her to come back to stay the night at his flat, she had laughed, kissed him and said "I thought you were never going to ask."

'If we're babysitting Rosa on Saturday,' Caitlin said now, her hands on the back of the desk facing Nick, 'then I want to go out on Friday and not with Karl or Will or anyone like that. Just you and me.'

Before he could answer, however, the phone rang again. They both looked at it and then Nick picked it up. If it was Marianne phoning to pick a fight again, then he was just going to put the phone down on her. But it was not Marianne.

'I bet you don't know who this is.'

'Who is it?'

'It's George. George Lamidi.'

'Oh right, excellent, erm . . . you said you wanted to talk to me. Something about a friend of yours?'

'Yeah I do. But not on the phone, it would be better if we could meet up somewhere this week.'

'OK. Fine. What about Thursday evening?'

'Thursday. Yeah. Where?'

Nick had no idea where George lived nor where he was likely to hang out. He had once lived in Vauxhall. In town would be the best bet. But he didn't want to go anywhere so crowded that they would not be able to talk.

'It's got to be somewhere we can talk,' George said as if reading his mind.

'There's a place in Russell Square, a big hotel that's got a bar. It's always half-empty. Why don't we meet there?'

'Let's meet at the tube-station first. That'll be easier. It's got lifts hasn't it?'

'Yeah.'

'At the top of the lifts then.'

Nick put down the phone and stared at it for a moment.

'It was that guy from the party,' Caitlin said, stating a fact rather than posing a question. 'He might, you know, have something pretty good for you.'

'He might,' Nick assented. 'But, then again, he might not.'

'It's quite likely . . .' Caitlin mocked him now, '. . . to be one or the other.'

mi cielito lindo

I am invisible but I am not empty. Time and space jostle inside me, memories shift like kaleidoscope patterns; history and geography, names and places, odours and melodies, things long gone but not forgotten.

Let me first tell you about my house.

Montevideo is a leisurely city of turrets and cupolas, of old Cadillacs, of a long avenue winding around the coastline, of beaches with wavelets breaking on the shore where at night you can see the tangled silhouettes of young couples. It is a port and, therefore, also a city of brothels and bars, of young sailors on shore leave. Montevideo is the capital of the República Oriental de Uruguay (pronounced Oor-u-guay not Your-u-guay) and lies on the Río de la Plata (rather more melodious than the River Plate with its suggestion of chipped crockery), where a German battleship was scuttled in a long-ago war. And there is light and colour: the sun above the harbour in the late afternoon, the startling purple of the jacaranda trees in spring, the soft greys of the ageing buildings.

But it was about my house that I was going to tell you. Nevertheless, as Benedetti, our most famous poet, said about the city of Montevideo: *Esta es mi casa* – This is my house.

The problem with telling you about my house is that . . . the problem with talking about my house is that . . .

Perhaps it is better – and by no means an irrelevant digression – to go back to Tupac Amaru, the great Inca

Cacique who rose up in bitter rebellion against the Spanish. Unsurprisingly, he was betrayed, handed over to his enemies, and had his limbs torn apart by horses in the main square of the city of Cuzco in what is now Peru. Neither was it particularly good news to be a relative of Tupac Amaru, since the Spanish decreed that the contamination of his bloodline should also be extinguished and set about this task with systematic and characteristic enthusiasm.

Ah but the poetry of rebellion! The symbolic value of defeated revolts! Because, of course, the Spanish failed – failed utterly – since Tupac Amaru, regardless of his real story, the efforts of historians to point out that he was also not averse to a little indiscriminate slaughter, Tupac Amaru bequeathed his name and his memory like a breeze around the continent. So that when some Peruvian military officers, some Japanese businessmen, some Gringo diplomats realise in horror that their waiter is not offering them another whisky or vol-au-vent but instead brandishing an AK47, that the Ambassador's party is taking a strange and unwelcome twist, then it is interesting to note that these Peruvian guerrillas disguised as waiters operate under the name of the Tupac Amaru Revolutionary Movement.

And that is why, a couple of decades earlier, in the leisurely city of turrets and cupolas that is Montevideo, a group of dedicated idealists fought against a corrupt and ultimately brutal government invoking once again the name of the leader whose final agony had been played out for the populace in the great square of Cuzco. We were the Movimiento de Liberación Nacional – Tupamaros. We would lead the country to happiness. We would create the NEW MAN.

Of course, the legacy of Tupac Amaru is one of pain and defeat and those who appropriate his name must join the

ranks of the vanquished, the ever-swelling army of defeated ghosts. Our disguised waiters were playing football when the bomb exploded beneath their feet, when the special forces burst into the embassy and ministered the coup de grace to a couple of remaining terrified teenagers. Tupac Amaru – it's not, on the whole, a lucky name.

Tupamaros! Urban guerrillas! How you must thrill to it, to all its associations of tempestuous dark-haired women and Guevara-handsome men with black berets and poetic souls. How unfortunate, therefore, that so many would share the agony of the leader whose name they revered. Not, however, beneath the hot sun and arrogant gaze of the parasol-twirling bourgeoisie, but writhing in their own blood, shit and vomit in a dark cell within the very same city of beach-winding avenues and jacaranda trees, or falling drugged from a plane into the freezing waters of the Río de la Plata. I knew some of these people. They were El Negro, La Paloma, El Flaco, La Gaviota. The women often took the names of birds which makes me shudder when I think of how their wings were clipped. Some of these people had stayed in my house.

My house was in fact a flat at the top of an old building not far from the historic centre of the city. We painted the doors and the shutters bright green but the rest was white. It had a balcony with bougainvillaea and white chairs and on spring evenings we would sit out and watch the slow progress of the ships on the great sun-glistening river while the wind from the Atlantic blew the newspapers off the table and my young son would chase after them. Of course, the memory of the exile (if one can any longer use such a word), like sexual memory, is a tricky thing because dull rainy days are excluded in favour of the sweet pain of Spring evenings.

When I first became involved, my house was a safe-house. The connecting hyphen is important because, as a safe-house, it was very dangerous. So much so that I lost my house with the green shutters, lost it at the moment when it stopped being even a safe-house, at the moment when I awoke to find drawers being ransacked and a gun at my head, at the moment when I realised that, like Tupac Amaru hundreds of years previously, we had been betrayed.

So the problem with telling you about my house is that sometimes when I think about it, and notwithstanding the idealising memory of the exile, sometimes when I think about it I feel that there is inside me some intensely fragile and vibrating part – perhaps if I were religious I might call it my soul – and that it is yoked to great horses which are all galloping in different directions.

And so I came from there to here, stopping in a few places on the way. Until I became invisible. Because anyone searching for the art of invisibility has only to take up a mop and a bucket. Not that this is always a bad thing. I have enjoyed my invisibility sometimes. I have cleaned toilets and swept floors in tube stations, banks, newspaper offices and universities. I have even cleaned the office of a university teacher with a big map of Uruguay on the wall and several books with the history of our own glorious Tupamaros. At present, I work in the office of a television company which is easy (although not much better-paid) work because I am a supervisor, and sometimes, at night, I clean the toilets of a nightclub which goes under the hugely misleading name of Sublime.

I do have the pleasure of working with a compatriot, a fellow Uruguayan. Like many young Uruguayans he does not live there any more. Nevertheless, we are not common here, hopelessly outnumbered by Nigerians and Colombians, so it is a pleasure to work alongside Francisco Gonzalez or, as the Colombians cruelly but humorously call him, Pobre Pancho. Poor Pancho is so called because of his reason for being here. Nothing to do with politics but with love. Poor Pancho made the mistake of falling in love with a young English girl at the beach in a very beautiful place called Punta del Diablo which lies on the coast just south of Brazil. And this girl – overwhelmed no doubt by the sun and chilled wine, the great Atlantic waves crashing in on the shore and the charming hotel on the beach – fell in love with Pancho. *Ay qué lindo!* She was a student doing her year abroad, writing a thesis on human rights and impunity in Uruguay. Among the souvenirs with which she returned to London – the shark-tooth necklace from Punta del Diablo, the leather bag, the collected works of Benedetti – she also took with her a new and exotic boyfriend – Francisco 'Pancho' Gonzalez.

Yet something happened in London. Illusions dropped away; things took on a new light; Poor Pancho's novelty wore off. For a start, only being able to say 'Eet is a door' or 'Sugar pleese' is most charming in Latin America but somewhat less so in this great city where he was like any other stupid, confused immigrant. And then the only job he could get was washing dishes and cleaning offices. (This was also difficult for Pancho who came from a wealthy part of Montevideo where he had enjoyed, among other things, the services of a maid.) Things started to go wrong: she started to snap at him, to complain about money, to run her hands distractedly through the blonde hair that had so ensnared Pancho's simple heart and say that she felt confused about the way things were going and that she felt undermined by his Latin American *machista* attitudes.

It was the slippery slope and now Pobre Pancho is working in cleaning jobs, unwilling to return to his house in Pocitos and admit his failure, unwilling even to admit to himself that the relationship with Sophie – who has still generously recognised his assistance in the Acknowledgements of her thesis – is as dead as Tupac Amaru. And the Colombians tease him and take him to salsa bars and tell him to forget about these frigid, uptight lesbian Gringas and get himself some nice *chicolita* who knows how to *mover la colita*. But Pobre Pancho doesn't want a *chicolita* of any type: he wants Sophie, and the Colombians pretend to slit their wrists, put their hands over their hearts, dance fake tangos with their mops half-swinging *Ay Sophie, rompacorazones, mujer traidora, porqué no vuelves a tu Pobre Panchiiiiiitoooo?'*

And Poor Pancho smiles sadly.

He is not at all political my poor young compatriot. Sometimes, during our break, he says to me. 'Don Orlando. You were mixed up in all that crazy Tupamaro shit. What was it all about anyway?' it makes me laugh when he calls me Don Orlando: it is so typically Pancho. Besides, I am not as old as I appear. And yet when one of the Chileans only half-jokingly referred to me as *Ese Supervisor Uruguacho, Tupamaro Conchasumadre* Pancho went berserk and threw a metal bucket at him, cutting open his forehead. It nearly degenerated into a total free-for-all since the Colombians, despite their teasing of him, treat Pancho like their lucky mascot, and then the Nigerians joined in wanting to fight the Colombians because of ongoing rivalry about who had the best football team, and the Chileans promptly divided according to political faction and started fighting among themselves. I was not sure whether Pancho had been offended by the insult to me or to Uruguayans in general, the only thing he said afterwards was, 'You know, Don Orlando, I have never been able to tolerate the arrogance or *la boca sucia* of Chileans.'

'It's a good thing then,' I replied, 'that we don't have any Argentinians working here.'

'Why?' he asked.

He can be a bit slow sometimes, Pobre Pancho. Something which, undoubtedly, Sophie has had plenty of time to learn.

My son – who works with computers – sometimes asks me why I do my job, explains – patronisingly – that I would be better off on the dole with housing benefit. I tell him that I like my job, which is partly true. I do like being around all these people. How else would I know the story of poor love-struck Pancho? I don't tell him, however, how lonely I would be without it, that without it I would be dependent for human company on his occasional trips to my house to eat *asado* when he wants to prove something to his girlfriends. 'At least you could get a better job,' he says. 'You are an educated man, you could do better than cleaning offices. You used to be a journalist for God's sake.' And I just smile and I say nothing because in his own way my son can be as stupid as Pancho sometimes. I used to be a journalist and now I am a cleaner. I do not see this transition as one of the tragedies, the ironies of exile. I no longer want to be a journalist, I no longer could be. I come into work, I talk to Pancho, I perform my shift, I go home. I look after myself. I am not one of those symbolic Professors of Marine Biology reduced to driving a taxi by the heavy hand of censorship or the skeletal caress of neo-liberal economics.

There is a song I sing to myself. I sing it to calm my nerves, I hum it as I clean up the toilets of the Sublime Club or empty the bins on the corridors of the TV offices. When I sing it I remember somebody – somebody it breaks my heart to think of – as painful a memory as my unsafe-house with its green shutters, I sing it on the 73 bus and walking to my house late at night on the cold, wet nights that are the speciality, the great talent of this city:

> *Cielo, mi cielito lindo,*
> *Danza de viento y juncal*
> *Prenda de los Tupamaros*
> *Flor de la banda oriental.*

banged up

Nick Jordan had aspirations to courage and commitment. He would look in awe at photos of flaming martyrs who had doused themselves in petrol and ignited themselves, wondering what super-impulse could override the natural drive for self-preservation and the fear of pain. He thought of torture victims spitting defiance through agony-clenched teeth and his fear was that the only things that he would be spitting were the names and addresses of all his comrades. Even in less extreme cases, he was not sure what the limits of his courage were. He admired greatly the Irish journalist who had faced down the Dublin criminal fraternity and paid for it with her life. Some people were now saying that she was not so heroic but he did not care to hear this.

He concluded that his central problem was that he wanted to be heroic but not heroic and dead. Obviously, few people actively desired this combination but some were prepared to allow it – or at least suffering – as one of the necessary hazards of courage. He remembered seeing a photo of a war in a Central American country where a young guerrilla was kneeling and firing beside the body of a dead comrade. And now that young soldier had memories and stories and maybe even nightmares, while his colleague was just dust. But it would be impossible to be the surviving soldier without risking, without at least countenancing the possibility of being the other, the corpse with its hand still trying to clench the rifle that lay uselessly by his side. Nick was not sure that he was even prepared to take the risk and yet he was depressed in the face of this cowardice which he considered a horrible and debilitating weakness, especially for somebody in his profession.

When he talked to Caitlin about this, she argued that courage and cowardice were not fixed quantities. Nobody knew when they might be brave but everybody had the capacity for bravery and it might emerge at the most surprising moments. Perhaps he had not been tested properly. She reminded him of her friend Derek who was frightened of everything: planes, lifts, tubes, pigeons, small spaces, large spaces, cancer, crowds, children, cinemas, thunderstorms and dogs – and these were just his primary obsessions. Yet Derek had had his nose broken and two teeth knocked out on the tube when he had intervened to help an Asian man with vitiligo who was being tormented by several drunk Sunderland supporters making their way back to Kings Cross. This was all very well, Nick thought, but would he have done what Derek did or would he have pretended not to notice and got off at the next stop?

Did his desire for courage, his longing not to be weak represent some existential yearning to cover up other deficiencies in his identity? He was not from the world of extreme privilege but he was from a world which was privileged enough and the flow of his life had been predictable as a result. Sometimes, he felt an acute desire to break free of the restrictive banks, to disrupt the neat and seemingly pre-ordained structure of things, to feel that he was really living.

Nick was sharp enough not to be complacent about either himself or the world that he moved in. While he was not particularly fond of Ron Driver, he did not think much more highly of some of his peers and colleagues who only tempered their ambition with cynicism, and who were permanently preoccupied with their desire to climb the greased pole as quickly as was compatible with maintaining the all-important show of dignity. Without that you were finished, there was no substitute for it and few opportunities to recover it when forfeited.

He nursed a desire to pull something off, to do something audacious, a bold stroke which would not only be his test but also allow him subsequently to warm himself in the approval that deep down he knew he craved more than anything. Again, he was not unaware of the egotism that lay behind this; he was prepared at least to face it honestly. And yet – just as honestly – he had to concede that recognising a fault did not make the fault any less. Life should be rich, life should be passionate, life should be exciting but how many of his chips should he throw down in order to achieve this? He had a comfortable and mostly pleasurable life, perhaps it would be more honest to settle for that. And yet he still cradled his ambition, still longed for something more challenging, the feeling that he had placed his stake and watched the wheel spinning. He did not feel that he had exhausted all of his possibilities.

These thoughts had been reinforced by the meeting with his old friend on the roof of the party. Their lives had parted but had now strangely converged and he was making his way through Bloomsbury to meet somebody who had been practically forgotten only a few days ago, somebody he had never really expected to meet again. It was dusk, and overseas students stood outside their neon-lit hotels contemplating maps of the city, couples clasped hands with the tight, nervy grip of adulterers on the park benches of the squares, through the lit windows of the colleges and institutes he could glimpse students in varying degrees of attentiveness. Nick felt a certain trepidation about the meeting; he had been unsettled by George's edge on the roof garden and he was not in the mood to be retrospectively weighed-up again.

George was late as Nick had half-expected him to be. Just as Nick was checking his watch again and contemplating returning home, he saw George coming towards him grinning and holding out his hand. They walked to the hotel making the slightly uneasy conversation of people who no longer know each other very well.

'This hotel's pretty horrible,' Nick said. 'We could still go to a pub or something if you would prefer?'

'I'm not bothered really. As long as we can talk.'

'Oh yeah, we'll be able to talk.'

The bar of the hotel was on the corner of the street and was empty apart from a Japanese man at the bar who was alleviating his boredom by chatting to the pale, bow-tied barman drying glasses. The hotel was decorated in pink and grey, forgettable pictures on the wall in a variety of pastel shades and large plants whose leaves were being sprayed by a small Filipina woman in an apron. Muzak drifted vaguely through the bar – *You fill up my senses* curled like smoke around the tables and ashtrays. The barman looked relieved to be able to serve somebody else and escape from the conversation with the Japanese.

'So,' Nick said as he placed the beers carefully on the table in front of them, 'that was strange meeting you like that the other night. How's your dad? Does he still work in the Post Office?'

'He's retired and gone back to Lagos. That's one fucked-up city man. It's out of control. My dad doesn't get a plane that will get in at night 'cause you can get held up on the drive from the airport. He spends thirty years working his bollocks off in this shitty country and has to worry about somebody stealing his money when he goes back to his own.'

Nick nodded. 'What was that stuff he was always saying I would have to eat if I went to Nigeria?'

He remembered sitting in George's living room, the way Mr Lamidi would roar with laughter and threaten to take him to Nigeria and make him eat . . . what was it again?

'Gari . . .' George laughed. 'A bowl of that would sort you out, mate.'

'You sound just like him.'

'I suppose that's not surprising.'

There was a pause broken suddenly by the sound of George's mobile ringing. He took it out and flipped it open.

'Yeah? Oh right . . . No . . . I don't know . . . Well, that ain't really my problem is it . . . you'll have to try Jason won't you . . . Look I'm in a meeting . . . yeah 'bye.' He said all of this in the same slightly weary, slightly impatient tone of voice and then snapped the mobile shut and placed it on the table in front of him, staring at it for a second before lifting his glass again. And suddenly Nick realised that George was unhappy. Not just now but in general, with life. His edge, his bitterness was part of some more general suffering that he would never probably acknowledge, certainly not to Nick. It was there though in that air of weary impatience, in that slight ennui of a frustrated intelligence.

'So have you been doing this bouncing thing for long?' Nick asked him nodding at the barman who was replacing their ashtray.

'Too long. I should take you out one night, Nick. I'll open doors for you. You and your girlfriend, Caitlin. I like that name. You'll have to be prepared to really go out though. I could show you some things . . .' he tailed off as if already bored with the idea.

41

Nick nodded. 'And this thing? The one you said you wanted to talk to me about?'

There was a pause. 'Have you got a cigarette?' George asked.

Nick handed him one and put the packet on the table. 'Just take one when you want . . .'

'You must have met lots of people in prison for things they never done?'

'Yeah, a few.'

'That must be the worst thing in the world. Banged up, staring at the walls, sharing a cell with some nutter who wants to give it to you up the arse. And all for something you never done anyway . . .'

Nick nodded. The thought of prison had always terrified him, innocent or not. It was the length of time involved, the loss of control, the total removal of will and individuality. *Banged up* – there was a kind of appropriate violence in the expression. He supposed that that was one of prison's functions, to terrify enough people into not doing whatever it was they were not supposed to do, to keep the number of people prepared to accept the risk of going to prison for their activities down to a manageable minimum.

'I've got a friend, a good friend. He's inside, he's doing life. For something he never done.'

'For what?'

'For murder. But he never done it.'

'What happened?'

'He was a bouncer. Worked in some club out East. That's a mad scene out there – it's worse than fucking Lagos. Anyway, my mate worked this club. And one night this kid got a kicking outside. It was bad. He was in a coma for a couple of months and then they decided to turn the life-support machine off. My mate had thrown the kid out of the

42

club and he got charged with killing him. But he never did. It weren't him.'

'But he was seen chucking him out, taking him outside? There were witnesses?'

'Yeah . . .' George said impatiently. 'There was plenty of witnesses. But like I've told you, it wasn't him.'

'But what did the witnesses say they saw? Just that your mate took him outside, or that they saw him giving him the kicking?'

George lowered his head and was silent for a moment. 'Some said that they saw him do it. But I know he didn't.'

'How do you know?'

'I know him. He wouldn't do that.'

'He should have called you as a character witness,' Nick said surprised at his own sarcasm and George glanced at him sharply.

'No, but . . .' Nick continued, '. . . I mean that's not exactly much to go on is it? There's some bloke in prison for killing someone, he admits he took the kid outside, there are witnesses who saw what happened, but it should be referred straight to the Court of Appeal because his mate says that he didn't do it 'cause he wouldn't do that sort of thing.'

George was silent, staring at Nick solemnly but without aggression.

'I wish I could get more out of him. He's gone weird now which ain't so surprising when you think that he's going to be inside for the next ten years at least. He won't say much about what happened although I'm trying to find some Scottish geezer he's mentioned. It's tricky 'cause he ain't working in London any more.'

'Who?' Nick asked absentmindedly and then felt remorse at his lack of attention because George's look contained both reproach and disappointment.

'The Scottish geezer.'

There was another silence. Nick also felt disappointment oozing through him. It wasn't that he wasn't interested but he could already feel that there was nothing to go on.

'What do you think I could do about it?' he finally asked.

'That's your think innit? People who've been punished for things they never done.'

'Yes. But you have to have lots of stuff. Other evidence: witnesses who weren't called, legal incompetence, something that shows they couldn't have done it. And you have to be sure of that stuff before you could even think about making a programme.'

'Well, even if it wasn't a TV programme. You write for newspapers as well. You could write for one of those newspapers that likes this sort of stuff. You could look into it.'

There was a tone of desperation creeping into George's voice which only served to convince Nick that this was a lost cause.

'But you've given me nothing to go on. It wouldn't be a very long article would it? I went for a drink with an old mate from school who says he knows someone doing time for something he didn't do, and he trusts him so completely that I am also now absolutely convinced of his innocence . . .'

'Why are you so cynical, man? Even if you're right, how come you don't even care if what I'm saying is true or not? You're the fucking journalist, that's your job to come up with something. You know, even though we haven't seen each other for years, if we had met and you had said to me "listen George, I'm in trouble; there's some geezers after my mate and I need a bit of help; I need twenty mad fucking niggers in cars to sort them out", I wouldn't have asked you nothing about whether these geezers had some just cause to be after your mate, I would have done it for you without asking.'

'Why?'

'What?'

'Why would you?'

''Cause I fucking would, man. 'Cause we was at school together. 'Cause I used to think you was funny and 'cause we used to go roller-skating together and you used to come round my house sometimes and 'cause I ain't all fucking twisted and cynical and I wouldn't demand any evidence like some sort of deposit for it.'

Silence. The sound of George's raised voice had alerted the attention of the Japanese man. He turned from the bar, his head over his shoulder, grinning at them. They both glared back at him and he turned back to the barman.

'Look, it's not like you're asking for a favour. But it would be stupid for me to promise that I can do something when I can't. I'll look into the case and find out what I can about it. But you've got to try and give me a bit more. Do you know who did it?'

George shook his head slowly.

'I don't know the details. And Chris won't say much. There's a girl involved, I know that. He won't talk about her and she's the key to it all. I can try and find out some people for you though. There's this geezer I know who works up there. Didn't work there at the time though. But he might be a good person to talk to. I'll get hold of him. I don't think it's, like, a complicated story. It's just a matter of talking to people.'

Nick nodded again. The Japanese guy was collecting his cigarettes and lighter, shaking hands with the barman. Outside in the street, people were hurrying past, some glancing in at the pinkish light of the bar. His mind began to wander, he was thinking about Rosa on Saturday and whether he could get somebody else to go and pick her up. A muzaked version of 'Yesterday' began to play. A couple of tourists came and sat down at the table next to them. They were talking in a language which Nick didn't recognise and he wondered whether they were Israelis. The woman had a startlingly beautiful face.

'Why are you so interested in this case? Why do you want to help him so much?' Nick asked George, trying not to cast sideways glances at the woman.

'Sometimes you just have to do things and that's it,' George replied. 'It ain't right that he's in there. He done me a big favour once and I ain't gonna forget that either.'

He picked up his mobile and began to slide his arms into his jacket hanging from the back of the chair. The couple who might have been Israeli began to argue, trying to keep their voices low, almost a frenzied whispering. A tear began to roll down the woman's face, she played distractedly with a strand of hair. The man was angry, he was gesticulating. This was the only part of their drama that Nick would ever see or understand. He tried not to stare at them and turned back to George.

'Where are you off to now then?'

'I'm going to see my kids.'

'How many have you got?'

'Two. Chereece and Samuel.'

'Sounds like Sam got the better deal when it came to names.'

George laughed. 'Yeah, well, Chereece – I never got any say over that one 'cause I wasn't living with the mother then. She loves all those stupid names. But Samuel, the oldest, I wanted to name him after my old man. What about you? I bet you ain't got kids?'

'I have as it goes. Rosa, she's four.'

'What? With . . .'

'No, Caitlin's not the mother. I hardly see her any more. The mother I mean. I still see Rosa though.'

'I love my kids,' George said. 'I never wanted to leave them you know. But me and their mum – when we was good we was very good but when we was bad . . .' he breaks into fake patois 'it was murder, you know what I'm saying.'

'Yeah I do. The last bit anyway.'

The woman at the next table got up and walked away from her partner wiping her eyes. The man sat playing with a piece of paper tearing it into little shreds.

'This club,' said Nick reaching for his own jacket, 'what's it called?'

George stood up and put his mobile into his jacket pocket, watching the back of the departing woman and raising his eyebrows at Nick in appreciation.

'It's called Sublime,' he said.

three dead sharks

I spent my honeymoon in Punta del Diablo – the same place in which Pobre Pancho met Sophie. At that time, there weren't as many tourists as there are now and besides it was not really the tourist season, although it was still hot enough to make you feel that the night sky might crack.

We stayed in a small residence which overlooked the beach and at night we lay beneath starched white sheets listening to the thump and hiss of the Atlantic waves rising and breaking on the sand below us. It was basic but elegant with a cool tiled floor that became sandy from our bare feet and the owner was a wiry Yugoslav who loved talking. He used to sit with us while we ate in the small dining room, drinking glass after glass of rosé wine and giving us lectures on the evils of communism. His wife – who was also the cook – would pause to wipe her hands on her apron and roll her eyes at us from the doorway into the kitchen. In the late afternoons, through into the evenings, we would sit drinking on the balcony, hypnotised by the crashing waves, feet up on the wooden rails, while the ice in our bucket began to shrink and return to water.

Punta del Diablo is a fishing village where the principal catch is shark. Apart from the sale of the meat, the villagers make artefacts out of the teeth of the sharks and from shells. They also sell the jaws of the sharks, with their layers of overlapping pointed teeth. My wife did not like the shark jaws so I bought her a smiling seal sitting on a rock made out of pebbles and shells.

One afternoon, as we were walking along the beach, we saw a group of people standing around a catch that had recently been landed. Overhead, the birds waited with anticipatory beaks. We wandered down to take a look and saw a trio of dead sharks on the beach. They weren't very big but they had the unmistakable snout, fin and tail of the shark. One of them was bloody around the gills as if it had thrashed and struggled against its entrapment. Their mouths were torn by the hooks. A dog began to sniff at them and one of the fishermen shooed it away before dragging a shark up the beach by its long tail, leaving a trail in the sand behind them. It was strange to see the dumb dead heaviness of the fish – rough bodies pressing down into the warm sand which had once navigated the ocean far beyond the breaking surf, which had once twisted and turned and flicked with lithe determination in search of their own prey. Dead fish, waiting birds, the fisherman's oblivious calloused hands.

It is equally strange to think, as I sit here now drinking Cuzco beer at the table of a newly-opened Latin American restaurant in Dalston, that the waves are still beating on the shores of Punta del Diablo, the fishermen still landing their catch. My son – who is sitting beside me talking to Pobre Pancho and a Mexican girl whom Pancho met in a *salsateca* – was conceived on one of those honeymoon nights in the small fishing village. The fact of my honeymoon is one which I have not communicated to Pobre Pancho as I do not like to remind him of his doomed love for Sophie who still appears to exercise a mermaid-like charm over him. He persists in a hope – without reason or logic – for their ultimate reunion.

Adolfo, the Argentinian owner of the restaurant, is teasing the fiercely patriotic Pancho about Uruguay, claiming that it is no more than a province of Argentina. Pancho responds by reminding him that the great tango singer

Carlos Gardel was born in Uruguay and not Buenos Aires. Adolfo denies this vehemently. My son is trying to impress the Mexican girl by talking about the globalisation of the world economy. Pancho has told me that she is from Mérida on the Yucatán peninsula – which is famed for the beauty of its women – and that she used to be a stripper in the Zona Rosa of Mexico City. The same old migrant story: provincial teenagers taking off their clothes in Third World capitals, Latins and Africans cleaning offices in European cities. The girl nods politely at my son, pretending to be impressed. She has very beautiful blue-black hair, long and shining. Her stripping activities, however, did not include any acting lessons because it is a pitiful attempt to feign interest, and only somebody as unobservant and uninterested in the reactions of others as my son could fail to notice this.

The restaurant is open to the warm early-evening air and a few people are sitting out drinking Peruvian beers or Chilean chardonnay. A young Hackney couple with earnest white faces are making a great show of ordering their food in Spanish and calling Adolfo by his first name. Like most English people, they have tremendous difficulty with the letters *r* and *o* and even more difficulty when they are conjoined. 'And I'll have the *cordero*, Adolfo,' says the man. The words hang for a moment in the air as if trapped in a speech bubble and Pancho raises his eyebrows at the Mexican girl who – breaking her attention away from my son's fascinating lecture on world financial power-centres and the worrying decline of the Tiger economies – giggles softly and examines her hands.

Perhaps I am too harsh on my son. He might have been different if we had stayed in Uruguay. He had no choice over the range of circumstances that brought us here although he made the choice to stay when my wife and daughter went away to live in Holland. My son who was conceived to the beating of waves; my son who chased the wind-blown newspapers on the roof-patio; my son who was part of our flight from country to country and finally from continent to continent when it seemed that every new asylum was more dangerous than the point of departure. The same confident man who is talking now about the limitations on political action which are imposed by the freedom of capital to roam around the world. And I remember a little boy in shorts vomiting on buses and planes; I remember the pale sleeping faces of my children against rain-streaked windows on the long dark nights of travel that brought us from there to here.

There was a time when I was prepared to die for a cause. At least I thought that I was. I was prepared to die for a host of abstract concepts: Liberty, Justice, the NEW MAN. These were concepts that others had died for, were dying for: Che Guevara christlike in Vallegrande, Allende in the burning remnants of La Moneda, even students on North American campuses caught full in the face by the bullet of a National Guardsman while protesting the bombing of Cambodia. And there were closer deaths as well: there are people that I will never see again; they might also have sat here on a warm London evening drinking Cuzco beer and growing old, listening to the chatter of their children, smiling at love-struck Pancho and the pretty girl from Mérida. I am here and they are not, my memories prickling like the tiny hairs left under the shirt-collar when the barber has held the mirror to the back of your head.

Adolfo asks us if we would like a shot of something on the house. The Mexican girl asks for a tequila, so Pancho and my son ask for the same. I ask for a Havana Club rum. The Mexican girl asks for lemon with her tequila. She flicks salt expertly on to her thumb joint, sucks the lemon and sips her tequila. My son tries to do the same and spills salt everywhere. They are big lemons not the little lime-like ones that they serve you in Mexico. As my son sucks on his lemon, he screws up his face in exactly the same way that he used to when he was a little boy.

Yes, I am too hard on my son. He is just defined – like everybody – by the time that he lives in. He is more interested in his computers and global finance than laying down his life for his beliefs. Or killing somebody else for his beliefs. But the passion with which we held such beliefs also led us into a world of clichés and simplicities and easy answers and stereotypes and the dismissive arrogance of youth. There was a mystique about being a Tupamaro but not everybody could make the grade, not everybody had the right revolutionary qualities. 'The revolution is not a game, comrade.' Somebody once said that to me. At least my son doesn't fool himself – as we did – that the world can be changed by the right rhetoric and a few guns. We are both here, after all, father and son on a lazy evening in Dalston, whatever we do or do not believe.

After we have paid the bill and left the restaurant, my son comes back with me to the house. He notices that I am walking slightly awkwardly due to the fact that my right knee has been swelling again recently.

'Why are you limping?' he asks.

'Oh, it's nothing. Just my knee again. Sometimes it gets quite stiff.'

My son sighs and looks up at the sky.

'You should take some time off,' he observes finally. 'Rest it for a while. It's madness you doing those two shifts as well. No wonder you get ill.'

There is impatience in his voice as if through some kind

of perverse masochism I have deliberately caused my knee to stiffen, as if it is some kind of symbol of my general obstinacy.

'You need to take some time off,' he repeats grimly when I do not reply, 'you're getting old. You can't go on like this. Go to the doctor's and get him to sign you off.'

My son inhabits a world in which sick pay is simply taken for granted. Nobody in our company gets full sick pay. One of the Colombians was recently admitted to hospital with peritonitis and spent more time worrying about his loss of wages than his life-threatening illness.

'I can't afford it,' I say simply.

'What do you mean?'

'We don't get sick pay. I've got to pay the rent and the bills and everything.'

'And you've got to pay for all the booze you drink. That's another thing. You ought to cut down a bit. That can't help your joints either.' He exhales impatiently. 'If you need some money to tide you over while you rest for a while, you know that I'll give it to you.'

It is a source of enormous irritation to my son that I will not accept retirement at his expense.

'You know, Claudio, I don't want to lie about at home and do nothing. As for the money, thanks but I can manage. Also, you are far too young to be giving people lectures about their drinking habits. Maybe you should drink a little more, you know.'

'I drink twenty units a week on average.'

'What?'

'Twenty units. If you drink more than twenty-five then you will start having health problems. You should start counting your units, it might give you quite a shock.'

'You count them?' I am incredulous. 'Like tonight, when

you had a tequila you were thinking about how many units you had had?'

This is pretty extreme, even by my son's standards. He, however, does not seem in the least bit ashamed of this obsessive and dreary behaviour. It is so typical of him that he drinks five units less than the allowed maximum.

'I don't count them exactly, but I always have a pretty good idea. I never forget what I have drunk,' he adds pointedly, giving me one of his significant looks to ensure that I have not missed the point either.

We walk along in silence for a while as I am not particularly interested in pursuing this depressing topic. I reflect on the fact that my son is the same age as some of the young people in the Sublime Club. I almost laugh out loud as I imagine any of them counting their units as they disappear in couples into the cubicles. I sometimes wonder about collecting up the fragments of white powder in the toilets when I clean up and hoarding them, like the pennies I keep in a big whisky bottle at home, to resell later.

Of course, in the ideal society young people would not need to take drugs – this is another of those truths that I have absorbed over the years and which I am coming increasingly to doubt. How bitterly we used to condemn the self-indulgent hippies who listened to American music and smoked marijuana rather than join the struggle to change society. The paradox is that my son is far from representing the NEW MAN and yet views drug-taking with all the contempt of the most perfectly trained cadre. I would not wish for Claudio to take drugs but I do wish that he had a passion for something: something, at least, unrelated to bits and bytes and fax-modems and RAM and ROM and the World-Wide-Web.

When we return to the house, I ostentatiously pour

myself a big glass of whisky while Claudio equally ostentatiously fights not to show his disapproval. I am about to tell
him that the whisky was a gift from Zamorano at work, who
got it duty-free after taking the football team he manages to
Belgium for a Latin American tournament. The team did not
return in great shape after various punch-ups, marathon
drinking sessions and trips to local brothels. They did not
win anything either. I decide not to tell Claudio, however, as
it would appear like an excuse and also an admission that he
has the right to instruct me about what I can and cannot
spend my wages on.

'Want one?' I ask sarcastically.

Claudio pretends he hasn't heard me and turns the TV
on for the news. And then they report the discovery of some
bodies at a deserted airstrip in Bolivia and that it is virtually
certain that one of the skeletons is that of the legendary
guerrilla leader Ernesto 'Che' Guevara. The camera trails
past a group of officials and forensic scientists and there,
mixed up in the dirt, trailing fragments of tattered cloth is a
skull and some bones. The journalist reports that several sets
of remains have been found but that what is exciting everybody is that one body lacks its hands. Because after they had
captured, interrogated and executed Che in the small school
building of La Higuera, they cut off his hands and preserved
them in formaldehyde.

From outside, music beats selfishly from an open car. It
is still light and sun-edged white clouds fill the sky above
London, just as they fill the sky above any city. Fragments of
music thumping with relentless normality from a car, just as
they might escape from the bar where a young girl removes
her clothes for overweight men drinking overpriced
imported whiskies. Or tired workers drinking beers on
street-corner bars with cheap radios crackling out familiar

tangos – *y todo a media-luz, y todo a media-luz*. I grip my own glass so tightly that I feel it might splinter in my hand. Che Guevara's remains found after thirty years in Bolivia along with those of his less famous colleagues. Common graves, shallow graves and watery graves – down in the dirt or cast to the bottom of the ocean. A city of winding avenues and cupolas and jacaranda trees. Three dead sharks with ripped mouths lying in the sand. A young half-drugged woman dragged blindfold to the open door of a doorless plane. The wind screams past her face, beads of rain cling to the doorway, a last word is spoken and she is sent tumbling through the darkness into the water below.

inter-city west coast

Nick Jordan was not sure why the train he was travelling on was part of the West Coast Line, since it was nowhere near the coast; it was in fact about as far from the sea as it is possible to get in England. Since working in Birmingham, Nick had also had to suffer appalling delays travelling to and from meetings caused by a multitude of reasons, the most terrifying of which was locomotive failure. The trains were so old and defective that sometimes they just broke down in the middle of the countryside. In summer, this could mean the train becoming an oven in which its passengers slowly roasted for hours until a relief engine arrived.

Because Nick had had an important early morning meeting that day, he had not risked the train and had spent the previous night up in Birmingham in the soulless single room of the Traveller's Rest Hotel reserved for him by his production company. Nick loathed staying alone in hotels which were not made, as far as he was concerned, for solitude and he jokingly speculated as to whether he might have got some kind of bargain deal from Mandy the cheerful Erdington prostitute, the Brummie tart with a heart who was saving up to do an aromatherapy course. Perhaps he should have made her a business proposition after interviewing her again in the Ron Driver case. She lived in a block with three other prostitutes, all of whom put their names on pieces of paper embossed with childishly-drawn felt-tip flowers on the front door of their bedsits – Chantal, Michele, and Mandy.

Above the English countryside, the setting sun was turning the sky rose and lemon like Turkish delight, an occasional patch of bright blue breaking through the cloud-cover. They were passing moored canal boats, nearing Watford Junction, a dreary place for which Nick had, nevertheless, developed a deep affection. It represented the first announcement of proximity, the gateway back into London. From then on, it was twenty minutes of growing relief; speeding in through the suburbs of Harrow, past Wembley's domes, into the NWs, through Willesden junction with its sullen freight lifters, slowing down by Camden's canal, crawling finally towards the Post Office Tower and London Euston.

He had bought a book to read on the train but it lay unopened on the table in front of him and he had spent most of the journey with his eyes closed, in a strange half-sleep which allowed hallucinatory images and odd narrative patterns to flicker rapidly across his consciousness. When he had drowsily opened his eyes, he had thought about George Lamidi, and his friend doing life for a crime he had never committed. If George said that his friend was innocent, then it was highly probable that this was the case. Working on this series of *Reason to Doubt* had given Nick first-hand experience of the nature of the judicial system and the combination of circumstances which could get you sent down or let off in flagrant opposition to everything which common sense might dictate.

Nick sometimes thought that the general public were remarkably protected from the judicial atrocities which kept innocent people behind bars, suffering the anguish not only of their incarceration but also the knowledge that they had never committed the offence for which they had received the ultimate sanction. People went serenely about their business, and only a few had their conscience troubled by a series which went out well beyond peak time and was not likely to win any battle of the ratings. The programme had, nevertheless, caused questions to be asked in the House of Commons and initiated enough media attention for a couple of cases to be returned to the Court of Appeal.

As far as George Lamidi was concerned, however, the problem remained the same as when Nick had parted from him in Russell Square – absolutely no evidence. Nick could hardly go to his series producer and try and interest her in a miscarriage of justice where the only lead was the friend of the victim. Besides, his hands were tied with the Ron Driver story and there were five other programmes well into their research stage. These included a case of false-memory syndrome, a university lecturer sacked for alleged sexual harassment, an armed robbery for which a black man had been given ten years despite a more than credible alibi and ample witness statements testifying to the robber's whiteness. All good stuff, all more or less cut and dry, but George Lamidi's tale of a framed bouncer – interesting as its context made it – just did not seem to be a runner.

There was something about it though; something that would not let him go. It was to do with George and his reminder of their roller-skating days, when they were just kids whirling round and round the rink at Jubilee Hall, learning the skate backwards, and then on Saturday nights at the Electric Ballroom, eyes popping at the girls flying past – wheeled temptation for two adolescent boys. He hadn't seen George for about fifteen years until the night at the roof-garden party. He was not just an old friend with whom Nick had lost contact – he was also Nick's childhood gazing back at him; he was the reminder of a lost era with wholly different parameters from those which existed now. And

Nick – however unwilling he might be to admit it – knew that their destinies had divided according to the fault-lines of race and class. He certainly wasn't going to indulge in a liberal guilt-trip about it, but there it was staring him in the face and he had to admit that he found it interesting. They were no longer – could never be again – the two boys on roller-skates living the now battered and undermined dream of comprehensive education. Nick felt that even if George had cast his line with something approaching desperation, the hook had caught and it had fastened – he couldn't just forget about it.

The train began its crawl into Euston, Nick craned his neck to see the red neon of the Kennedy Hotel, and people began to reach up for their bags and coats. He took a cigarette out of his packet ready to light as soon as he hit the platform. He had to drop into the office to collect some papers and then he was meeting his friend Will who had finished working on a documentary about ten years of club culture. He would have to remember to ask Will what he knew about Sublime. Nick wasn't particularly interested in clubs or the culture in which they were supposedly enveloped. It was all taken – and it took itself – far too seriously, trying to pretend that something which was fundamentally about fashion and money was of enormous social and political significance. Clubs were for drinking and dancing in, not writing PhD theses about.

Nick took a taxi from Euston to Kentish Town. It was late afternoon and there were few people around when he arrived. Mark – one of the researchers – was sitting with Adidas Gazelle-clad feet up on the desk, reading a copy of *FHM*.

'Hi,' Nick said unenthusiastically as he dumped his bag on his seat. Mark was a pain in the arse, nattering away on

Monday mornings about the weekend's football, the minutiae of Chelsea FC, and how many points he had collected for his fantasy team. Nick liked football, but people like Mark always made him wish that he didn't.

'How was Birmingham?' Mark peered at him over the cover of his magazine which had its standard picture of a young actress blowing a faux-slut kiss towards the camera, her breasts bursting out of the top of a wonderbra.

'Yeah, OK. Did you follow up that journalist who had looked into the Scargill case?'

'Yeah. We're meeting him next week. And I've got a copy of his book for you.'

'Ah . . . good. Thanks. There's another thing you could do if you get time tomorrow. I want to find out about a murder. It's somewhere near Ilford. If you get the time, I want you to get in touch with the BBC cuttings library and check out the local papers. It was about three years ago.'

Mark frowned. 'What's that got to do with Big Ron?'

'Nothing. It's something else. Some bouncer who kicked a kid to death outside a club.'

'Well he deserves everything he got then.'

'That's the point. He would if he had done it. But I think we might have . . . reason to doubt. You remember the name of the series.'

Mark scowled and returned to his magazine. The cleaners were starting to come in. It annoyed Nick when they came and swept around him and started emptying his bin when he was still working. Mark's head popped up again.

'Oh yea, I forgot. Your bird rang. She wants you to call her back at home.'

Nick raised his eyebrows and dialled his home number.

'Oh you got my message then,' Caitlin said when she picked up the phone.

'I think so. I was told my bird had rung so I assumed it must be you.'

Mark blushed and Nick felt a little guilty. He was far too easy a target to start picking on. The cleaner had arrived at his desk and was emptying his bin. It was the Paraguayan guy who occasionally spoke to Mark about football. Most times, the cleaners didn't – or couldn't – say anything to them. But this cleaner spoke good English and would sometimes talk to Mark about his football team. To give Mark his due, his trainspotter approach to football allowed him to accumulate a vast store of knowledge so that he could chat easily about Latin American clubs of which Nick had never heard. When Nick had replaced the receiver, Mark and the cleaner were talking about the famous victory of Peñarol over River Plate in a Latin American cup final at the end of the 1960s.

'4–2. And Peñarol were 2–0 down at the end of the first half.' The cleaner went to take Mark's bin and he swung his feet up on to the desk again.

'Peñarol?' Nick joined in. 'They're from the capital of Paraguay?'

Mark snorted and the cleaner laughed, but not illnaturedly.

'They are from Montevideo. Which is the capital. But of Uruguay.'

The cleaner had an oddly clipped accent as if he had learned his English from a young age in an expensive overseas establishment. But if he had, what was he doing now working as a cleaner? It was Nick's turn to feel embarrassed and Mark's to look smug.

'Yeah, easy mistake to make . . .' Mark rubbed it in

spitefully. 'After all, they've both got – *guay* on the end. Anyway, Orlando, you don't support Peñarol, I thought you supported Nacional?'

'I do,' the cleaner grinned at Nick: 'that's another Uruguayan team.'

'I'm sorry,' Nick said stiffly. 'I thought that you were Paraguayan. I must have heard wrong.'

The cleaner shrugged as if to indicate that it was a matter of complete indifference to him whether Nick thought that he was from Uruguay, Paraguay or darkest Peru. Nick felt a surge of dislike towards him. Fuck off and stop bothering me when I'm working. Then he felt guilty about it. He was always a bit uptight like this after staying up in Birmingham and then the train journey and the stress of worrying whether the train was going to wind down and stop for five hours just past Rugby. The guy was, after all, only doing his job and making a bit of conversation.

'I'll come back later to hoover,' the cleaner said and turned to smile at Mark who gave him a cheerful thumbs-up.

'Anyway, man, what's the name of this club?' Mark asked.

'Oh some nonsense. Delicious? Splendid? No, I know really, it's called Sublime. It's out in East London somewhere . . .'

Nick paused because the departing cleaner had suddenly looked up at the name. But it must have been something else because he just slid the bins back under their desks and returned to where an African woman was laughing at something one of the other cleaners had said.

'Yeah, of course I know that club,' Will remarked as they sat in a pub in Camden later on that evening. 'It's out East. It used to be called something else. It attracted all sorts. Then they closed it down and relaunched it with a new upmarket image. We actually went there when we were doing this feature on safety in clubs. It's got this owner – what's his name again? – anyway, he's this young sort of entrepreneur type. Slippery. But you've got to admit, he turned it round. They did a major PR job – smart dress, ventilation, running water, just say no kids – the works. Of course, it's bollocks that there's no drugs in there, but he knows how to give it all the patter. He's well-connected apparently. Dad knows the right handshake and all that. Shit, what was his name again?'

'There was a murder there.' Nick could still be impressed by Will's encyclopaedic knowledge of whatever topic he chose to tackle. 'About four years ago. A bouncer kicked some kid to death outside. Only I think there might be more to it than that.'

'Yeah, I heard something about it. I never knew the details though. Well, that was about the time that they sort of relaunched the club. About four years ago, they were just starting up again. It had got so mental, people weren't going any more. It must have been about the same time.'

'That's interesting. 'Cause on the one hand, it might look quite bad a death outside the club just when they're turning it around. But on the other hand, if they give the cops full cooperation, hand over a body – apparently, several people from the club testified against him – then that could earn them a few Brownie points.'

'Yeah, maybe,' Will frowned and flicked froth from the neck of his beer bottle. 'But if they're saying it was a bouncer, then the likelihood is that it was. There are some right animals you know. Why do you think it wasn't him?'

This of course was the question. Nick did not want to

start explaining to Will about George Lamidi and his conviction that his friend had been framed.

'It's just a hunch at the moment. A few whispers that there's more to the murder than meets the eye. I want to nose about a bit. See if there's anything to it.'

Will nodded. 'Well, you know what to do on a case like this. Check the local papers. Have a chat to the officer who investigated. Get down to the club. I could help you out a bit there. I think the owner will remember me. You could make out you're doing kind of follow-up. Something that'll make them look good. At least that'll get you some access.'

'That would be excellent. You don't mind if I use your name?'

'Nah. I've finished with that place anyway. We're about to start on that series on mafias operating in London. I've drawn the short straw and got the Nigerians. You know they advertise Hackney council flats in Lagos newspapers?'

Nick thought about George Lamidi and his dad who had worked in the Post Office for nearly thirty years, sitting laughing together after school in the kitchen of their Vauxhall council flat. Will regarded him steadily.

'But Nick, go careful you know. If it's like you say, then they're not going to welcome some journalist nosing about. They might have cleaned up their image but this is a murder case not some dodgy tax returns. Don't let them get a sniff of what it is you're really after. Don't trust anybody.'

'Of course,' Nick replied frostily, not particularly welcoming the suggestion that he didn't know how to go about his job.

'I know you know that but I'm just pointing it out that's all. It's another world. One for the road?'

'No, you're OK. I've got to get back. I haven't seen Caitlin yet.'

After leaving Will, Nick caught a cab from Camden back to his flat. It was still quite early and the streets were full of people heading out for the start of their evening. He felt relieved to be going home and experienced an even greater surge of relief as the cab pulled into his street. He knew that Caitlin would hear the throb of the engine ticking over, the heavy door slamming, the unmistakable sound of a taxi outside the house. Sure enough, when he looked up after paying the fare, she was at the window waving and grinning.

She had been swimming before sitting down to work, her black swimming costume was hanging over the radiator like an abandoned skin. Her real skin smelled of chlorine, her hands of the satsumas she had been eating as she worked. He buried his nose in her neck inhaling the mixture of swimming-pool chemicals and the shampoo from her hair. She took his hand and slid it down her hip and under her skirt. He brought it up between her legs, touching wetness straight away instead of cotton. She began stepping backwards, pulling him with her towards the sofa.

'Should I shut the curtain?' Nick said.

'Forget it. They shouldn't be looking into our flat anyway.'

'Did anybody phone?' he asked her lazily when they were lying later on the sofa drinking a bottle of white wine.

'The bitch left a couple of messages. Then she made Rosa ring. So I spoke to Rosa just to show that I hadn't been picking up the phone because I knew it was Marianne. Your mum rang. My mum rang. Karl rang to see what we were up to at the weekend. And some guy who wouldn't leave his name. Said he was a friend of that bouncer we met at the roof-garden party. But he was quite determined not to leave his name with me.'

'Did he leave a number?'

'No. He said he would call you again soon. I gave him your work number. Every time I asked him for information which he obviously considered surplus to requirements, he would just go "don't matter".' Caitlin giggled as she imitated him.

Nick frowned up at the ceiling. He could feel wheels beginning to turn. Whether he liked it or not, the death at the Sublime club was assuming importance, stealing into his life like smoke under a door. He knew that the next step was to go down there and check it out.

the revolution is not a game, comrade

The player puts the ball on the corner-spot which recent rain has made a little muddy. A policeman strolls behind the goal observing the crowd rather than the pitch, keen faces on the terraces draw in breath as the corner-taker looks up for the big centre-forward. A strand of hair obscures his view, he brushes it from his eye, the ball leaves his foot, the number 9 leaps and the crowd writhes in ecstasy as the ball crashes against the back of the net.

That was over twenty-five years ago during the championship season of 1971–2. I stare at the TV which shows a poignantly nostalgic combination of football clips, fragments of news and hit records from the period. It looks both long ago and not long ago. The hairstyles and kits are different as are the fashions. But the player brushes a strand of hair from his eye, the breeze flutters the corner-flag, the policeman ambles as if it were happening right now.

In 1971 the Tupamaros went on the offensive. In 1972 we were fleeing for our lives.

Confidence had risen after the biggest prison escape in history, when one hundred and ten inmates crawled and scrabbled through the sewers from the Punta Carretas prison. My son used to look it up in the *Guinness Book of Records* and show it proudly to his friends.

At the time of the prison escape, I was in Buenos Aires having exchanged detention under State of Siege for exile. But I was back in Montevideo by April 1972 which was when the full fury of the state was unleashed against us and

71

the State of Siege was replaced by a State of Internal War. Revolutionary rhetoric is of little use when the organisation begins to fall apart and nobody knows who has fallen, who will be next, where to go for assistance. People were walking the streets, sleeping in parks, not knowing whether their house was the next to be raided.

There was only one place to flee to in 1972 and so I began my journey again, escaping first to Buenos Aires and then across the *cordillera* to Chile and the welcome of the socialist government of Salvadore Allende. It was nearly winter when I arrived in a Santiago convulsed by revolutionary fervour, counterrevolutionary violence, and the smell of cold air and paraffin heaters, the bright smell of winter that I have never experienced in any city outside Latin America. I began working in the Ministry of Agriculture, assisting in the agrarian reform programme. And I remember the graffiti on the walls – *Ya viene Jakarta* – Jakarta is coming; a reminder of the Indonesian massacre and a warning from the right of the ultra-violence which would shortly be unleashed.

But in 1972, Santiago was a paradise for leftists from across the continent. There were Brazilians, Bolivians, Argentinians, Dominicans, Paraguayans, Panamanians, Venezuelans and, of course, Uruguayans. Everybody had a different story, different political allegiances, everybody was running from something. Between 1970 and 1973, Chile became a home for thousands of exiles and revolutionaries and a few general misfits. And it was in Santiago, a city encircled by the snowpeaks of the Andes, that I first met Silvia – also from Montevideo, also a Tupamaro.

How do I start, where do I begin? Dreams and memories are almost inseparable now. Was it really me who arrived in the city with my wife and tiny son and daughter? Did any of this really happen?

Silvia had arrived in Santiago shortly before I did. She had had to abandon her studies in Montevideo and join the outflow of Uruguayans escaping their imminent arrest. She had begun working in collaboration with the Chilean MIR with whom our organisation had strong links and which was similar to our organisation insofar as it also contained a large proportion of very young, very impatient people. They were usually from privileged backgrounds, relative to the down-trodden of the earth whose cause they were espousing. Silvia was just such a person and was living at the time with another such person – an arrogant and sarcastic Chilean student from the Technical University.

The Revolution is not a game, comrade! Fighting to create Popular Power! Advance without compromise! A country for all or a country for nobody!

What would she have been at any other point in history, this girl of such generous humour and proud intellect? What would she have been had she reached her maturity in the 1990s, had she been born at the same time as my son, instead of during the turbulent decades when our struggle would guarantee that, whoever else there would be a country for, there would not be one for us?

At the time I met her, Silvia had a job working for the Chilean Ministry of Housing, struggling to fulfil its promise to build houses for the masses and cope with the land occupations that were flaring up across the city. The people's government could hardly repress its own supporters and Silvia would travel to negotiate with the leaders of the new settlements and try to secure water and electricity for their inhabitants – something which the occupiers reasonably interpreted as permission for them to stay where they were. She would take the bus out to the margins of the city, through the working-class districts of San Miguel, Conchali, and Pudahuel to the flimsy new settlements on muddy streets with their Chilean flags raised above precarious shacks, announcing that these people too were part of the nation.

When we met, we were sitting in a flat in the San Borja housing project. The Chileans were drinking tea and the Uruguayans *mate*. She passed me the *mate* and smiled at me. Somebody was holding forth about the political situation, how without guns the revolution was lost, whether the rank-and-file of the army would divide and support the people. It was a chorus I had heard on countless occasions and I studied my new acquaintance who was sipping at the *mate*, laughing at the black Chilean humour, sometimes pitching in with a brief comment or observation. She was chestnut-haired, small and graceful with an air of quiet humour and self-possession about her, clutching a leather handbag as if it contained everything important in her life. She was never without that bag. I watched the tendons in her neck as she turned with little movements to follow each speaker, Jorge, her Chilean partner, was handsome with a shock of black curly hair and unfeasibly long eyelashes. He was engaged in a monologue (his favoured form of discourse) about the objective balance of forces in the country, the role of the organic intellectual, and he kept one hand on Silvia's shoulder as if he feared she might suddenly shake her wings and take flight.

I can't remember what heretical or facetious comment I uttered, but it certainly sealed my fate with Jorge. He turned and glared at me and uttered his famous statement. *The revolution is not a game, comrade.* And I felt the laughter bubbling inside me, my almost automatic reaction to pomposity and self-importance. I managed not to laugh, bowing my head in deference and, when I looked up, Silvia was watching me sharply and she flashed me a conspiratorial smile and passed me the *mate* again. I would get to know that smile well over the next few months. It was a generous, inclusive smile, often filled with sceptical amusement. It was like receiving a present.

The revolution is not a game, comrade.

We used to repeat this to each other in our subsequent meetings, sitting in a small bar near the Ministry of Housing on the Alameda, the main avenue which runs through the centre of Santiago up to the wealthy areas, the *barrio alto* of Providencia and Las Condes. *Civilisation begins at the Plaza Italia* was a saying of the Chilean upper classes who were fighting tooth-and-nail to defend such frontiers. I suppose that I was in love with Silvia even at that time, but it was the kind of love where just being with the person was sufficient; I craved her presence and I missed her when she was absent. I was a good person for her to let off steam with, partly because of our shared nationality and humour but also because, when she was with me, she was out of the watchful and restraining hand of Jorge. I have often encountered this phenomenon of women who permit – even encourage – teasing of their partners' obvious faults and yet remain loyally with them.

We talked and joked about everything. We spoke with homesick longing of our own country – of walking on the *ramblas* on warm Spring evenings in Montevideo, of the old city of Colonia where the boats leave for Buenos Aires, of the Atlantic coastline which runs up to the frontier with Brazil, of Cabo de Polonia with its plump whiskered seals rolling in the surf and Punta del Diablo with its shark-fishermen. And we spoke about the Uruguayans and Chileans and Brazilians who made up our strange society in a country where something had to give, where political opponents fought pitched battles on the streets, where clouds of tear gas filled the main roads, where the wheels of history seemed stuck but were in fact turning inexorably, where the very walls of the city announced our fate – *Ya viene Jakarta* – chronicling a past massacre and the massacre still to come. And we laughed with the exuberance of youth, and she would turn to me, waiting for me to say it in the Chilean accent which I had by now perfected – *The Revolution is not a game, comrade!*

The political and economic situation got worse and our organisation started to arrange to get its members out of Chile. It was obvious that a coup was coming but people moved as if in a trance, there was almost a serenity in the face of the impending catastrophe. And despite all the shortages, the political violence, the sense that the country was in crisis, the March congressional elections came and went, and the government increased its share of the vote.

Silvia was living in a shanty-town in the south of the city which was a stronghold of the MIR. She worked incessantly, organising the supplies of food and participating in attempts to set up popular courts to administer justice and resolve disputes in the settlement. She was also pregnant. My wife talked about returning to Uruguay, about separation. We had been teenage lovers, now we were amiable companions and it was not enough for either of us. Silvia and I continued to meet in the bar on the Alameda or in the central market where we would eat *sopa de mariscos* as the afternoon sunlight filtered through the wrought-iron on to the upturned bellies of sea-bass and pyramids of ebony mussels on the stalls below. She was still working closely with the MIR, although she now spoke openly about her troubled relationship with Jorge. I remember one cold night, huddled around the paraffin fire in their flimsy wooden house drinking *mate*. Silvia's family had fled Spain after the Civil War and she was singing old songs she had been taught by her father from that time, one of which was a sad and bitter lament from the eve of defeat:

> *Ya se fue el verano*
> *Ya viene el invierno*
> *Dentro de muy poco*
> *Caerá el gobierno.*

And even Jorge fell quiet as the prophetic words filled the freezing air.

In June of 1973, a tank regiment rose up and took over the centre of the city. There was fighting in the street and the revolt was suppressed but the real plotters drew some valuable lessons from the event. They learned:

That in the event of a coup the workers would be called to their factories to defend the government.

That, herded together in their factories, it would be easy to identify and massacre government supporters because: The workers did not have any guns.

During the day of the failed test-run coup, a young cameraman filmed his own death. On the footage, an irate army officer turns and aims straight at the camera, straight at you, it is as if he has suddenly spotted you the onlooker and put you in his sights. And as he fires his pistol, you become the young cameraman, your vision suddenly blurs, you are spinning round chaotically, you are looking up at the grey winter sky, you know with a kind of perverse intimacy the last thing that cameraman ever saw in his life.

After the attempted coup, I was instructed to leave Chile.

I delayed for as long as I could and in the end only just managed to get out before the real coup. I saw Silvia for the last time in Chile on the day a million people paraded before Salvador Allende in the *Plaza de la Constitución* in front of the Presidential Palace that he had sworn they would never take him from alive.

Allende, Allende, el pueblo te defiende!

Silvia was not expecting to leave for a while but I was confident that I would see her soon in Cuba – my next destination.

'What do you think of all of this?' I asked her that evening.

She was sad and exhausted, her face pale and pinched.

'Many of those people marching today will be dead soon. Everybody knows there is going to be a coup but they don't seem to realise how bad it will be.'

I knew that she was right. Certain Latin American countries like to pride themselves on being the Switzerland or the Britain of the continent because of their history of parliamentary democracy or their established middle class, or the fact that they wiped out most of their indigenous population at an early stage in their development and replaced them with European immigrants. Both Uruguay and Chile shared this snobbish perception and few of the angry young people, the children of the 1960s impatient for change and for justice, anticipated exactly what cruel fate lay in store for them when the veneer of civilisation was brutally ripped away by the new domestic *conquistadores*.

We watched in silence a few stragglers from the march making their way home. They were young, like us; they were from Quinta Normal or Recoleta or Macul. They were going home, back to their houses and their families, their cousins and nieces and nephews, to kitchens where the tea-cups were on the table and the bread was in the basket covered by a cloth, they were trailing their flags and banners like peacock-tails behind them. It was September and, although it had been a cold winter, the first faint signs of Spring were in the air. Silvia sat with her hands over her belly which only faintly betrayed the presence of her pregnancy. She was excited by the thought of her first child, we talked about names and she said that the child would be named after a poet rather than a political icon. If she were a girl, she would be called Gabriela and if he were a boy then he would be called Pablo.

'For Neruda?' I asked, stating what I thought to be the obvious.

'No,' she replied impishly. 'For de Rokha.'

We both admired de Rokha not so much for his poetry but because he had had an adulterous affair with the beautiful wife of a highly influential foreign communist during the 1930s. Summoned before a disciplinary committee of the Communist Party on some invented charge of violating party discipline he defiantly told his male judges that their disapproval was motivated by jealousy and that each of them would have done the same given the chance. This hindered de Rokha's career in the Party and was the prelude to a literary feud between himself, Neruda and the aristocratic poet Huidobro which was fought with cantankerous vigour and which provoked one of Neruda's more direct and less lyrical pieces – I piss on you.

I told Silvia that she should not work so hard and inwardly cursed Jorge for the selfish, arrogant bastard that he was. She smiled at me with the amused face and I still remember so well and said *The revolution is not a game, comrade*. But this time, neither of us laughed and I took her hand across the table and she dropped her head. I was going away and there was so much uncertainty and it was the beginning of Spring, in the month when Chileans celebrate the independence of their country by sending hundreds of little kites into the skies above the city. Sometimes, the kites would have glass-coated string, aerial duels would be fought, and we would sigh for the loser as it looped slowly above the rooftops and down to the ground.

Two days later, I left Santiago for Havana. Silvia was also expecting to leave soon and we had promised to meet as soon as possible. I knew that we had made an unspoken declaration. I knew that in Havana things would change between us and I was impatient.

The Andes glittered like teeth as our plane soared out of Santiago, my son vomited into a paper bag provided by a benevolent stewardess, my wife held his hand. We did not talk much. And as I looked down at the peaks, I thought of the incredible incident the previous year when a plane carrying young Uruguayans had crashed into the mountains. How could anyone, anything, live for any time in that total isolation of rock and snow. They were only meant to be flown over, those mountains, it was no place for warm-blooded human beings. Yet we have a knack, a gift for survival even if it means resorting to such extreme measures as devouring our dead comrades.

Six days later, the navy steamed out of Valparaiso on supposed manoeuvres with the United States. They turned round, however, came back and seized the port. The army moved into the centre of Santiago, Hawker Hunter jets streaked in from the north of the city, and by the early afternoon Allende was dead in the smoking ruins of La Moneda and along with him the Chilean Road to Socialism. And those men who had fought in La Moneda with Allende – the various economists and sociologists and doctors, as well as the young elite of the *Grupo de Amigos Personales* – they were taken away to army barracks and tortured to death with a savagery that defied belief. In Chile! In the England of Latin America with its fine tradition of parliamentary debate! Jakarta had come as promised and bodies floated in the Mapocho River.

Reports of the massacres were quick to reach Havana, especially because the military carried out various attacks against Cubans and Cuban property. It was not just Chilean leftists and Cubans who were at risk, but all foreigners and particularly Latin Americans. To be Uruguayan or Brazilian or Argentinian could be as bad as a death sentence and certainly merit a trip to the National Stadium – the scene of Peñarol's great glory on a rainy night in 1966.

All of this certainly happened. Yet even in Havana, my memories and my dreams collided just as they do now, mixing and blurring scenes and faces, seducing and mocking me; what happened, what really happened, how did you get from there to here?

I was not to meet Silvia again for another two years. The turmoil of the 1970s brought us together in Buenos Aires. Meeting again in a street café, she told me what had happened after I had left.

She had been fortunate to be staying with a friend in a wealthy area of Santiago on the night before the coup so that she was not in the shanty-town when it was raided. The people of Providencia celebrated what they perceived as their salvation by hanging flags out of the window. Because of Silvia's presence, the friend also hung a flag so as not to attract attention. They sat dumb with misery after Allende's last speech – *Probably Radio Magallanes will be silenced . . .* – and the announcement of his death, watching the little starred tricolour fluttering forlornly in the breeze. *It does not matter. You will continue to hear me. My memory will be that of a dignified man.*

After a few days, Silvia ventured out and took a bus across town to try and find out what had happened to Jorge and make contact with some of the other Uruguayans. Jorge had been in the Technical University when the military stormed in and it appeared that he had been taken to the Chile Stadium – an old boxing and basketball arena near the University. The Chile Stadium was not really a stadium like the National Stadium, it was more like a theatre. It was the scene of unspeakable brutality in the few days after the coup as prisoners were held pending execution or transfer to the National Stadium. Silvia did not know this, of course, at the time. On the way back to Providencia, the bus was stopped and searched. Having no documents and completely unable to imitate a Chilean accent, she was arrested and taken first to a police station and then to the National Stadium.

Silvia was held in the women's section of the National Stadium with two other Uruguayan women who had been captured as they attempted a desperate escape across the mountains into Argentina. The guards forced them to undress so that they could leer at them and make obscene comments. Following several kicks to the stomach, Silvia also suffered a miscarriage. There was to be no Gabriela nor Pablito, just a young woman on a cell floor looking up in agony and clutching her stomach.

The release of the Uruguayans from the National Stadium was as miraculous as Peñarol's recovery against River Plate. It was due to the work of one of those strange figures that history sometimes throws up, usually Scandinavian. Harald Edelstam was a Swedish diplomat who dedicated himself to saving lives – his tall figure stalked the stadium haranguing the jailers and assuring them that they were

Nazis and that like the Nazis their crimes would not be forgotten. Having been told that the Uruguayans were scheduled for execution, he negotiated with the officers in charge to save their lives. He urged the second-in-command at the stadium to release them into his custody where he would undertake to send them to Sweden.

Major Lavandero must have had some degree of humanity intact because he was impressed by Edelstam and agreed to release the Uruguayans. Fifty left the National Stadium – including Silvia – to be transported to what had been the Cuban embassy, which Edelstam had taken over on behalf of the Swedish government and turned into a refuge. While awaiting their exit documents to Sweden, they learned that fury at their release had been such that the ill-fated Major Lavandero had been shot. He too had been swept into the tragedy, showing mercy and receiving none.

Silvia arrived sick and depressed in the city of Stockholm. I see her; I see her now; I see her stamping her feet and shivering, her leather bag over her shoulder, clapping her hands as her breath blows like smoke outside the airport, waiting to be taken to some unknown destination. There was a little group waiting for them at the airport with a sign reading *BIENVENIDOS*, people who would offer their food and homes to the tired, bewildered arrivals.

Silvia was a long way now from Montevideo, swept by the convulsions of history, the invisible forces that had left a young cameraman staring at the grey skies and a career soldier shot in the concentration camp he had been given to administer – it was not a good time to be a dignified man.

And she told me of another victim – of an arrogant young student with long eyelashes who was the father to her child – the Gabriela or Pablito kicked prematurely out of her by army boots. Jorge was indeed detained on the day after the coup when the soldiers stormed into the Technical University. Five days later, his burned, beaten and bullet-ridden body was identified by his grieving mother. The temporary, the potential family that Silvia had created in those tempestuous months between 1972 and 1973 had been totally destroyed.

The revolution is not a game, comrade.

The Silvia I met in Buenos Aires was obviously not the same person I had left in Chile. She smiled less, she was distracted. She had been a vibrant, a unique personality in a delicate frame and she had known that. She had taken pleasure in herself as she had every right to do. The cold city of Stockholm, the grief and confusion of the exile community, could not hold her and she had taken flight again for Buenos Aires. And the complex webs of history were still spinning as footballers placed the ball and prepared for the corner, as a wily old Argentinian politician returned with a nightclub dancer for a wife instead of a saint, and young people prepared welcome banners that would soon be stained with their own blood as the bullets sang around Ezeiza airport.

I too prepared to move. I left the warm city of Havana, exchanging the Caribbean waves beating on the harbour walls for my own Río de la Plata and the winds of the Atlantic, just across the water from my homeland. We fled from one defeat in Chile to analyse our own tremendous defeat in Uruguay. Had we failed to understand the mood of the masses? Were we insufficiently Marxist-Leninist in our theoretical approach? Did we underestimate the middle-class reaction to our belief that a system based on violence could only be overthrown with violence? It was all so earnest, so irrelevant to what was happening. Following the assault against the Tupamaros in April 1972, the armed forces had declared war on just about everybody on the left. Unlike Chile, the coup took place in slow-motion until the army grew tired of even the façade of democracy and got rid of the pathetic President Bordaberry and his sham legislature to take openly the power which had been theirs for the last few years.

Argentina was also in crisis, its institutions in decadence; rotting timbers held up the democratic façade. Buenos Aires was a long spasm of violence – the Montoneros and ERP were fighting the corrupt government of Isabel Perón, and the Triple-A death-squads were leaving their victims hanging from trees as a warning. But the city was filled with Uruguayans and Chileans fleeing far worse situations and I met her again. It was a painful, an awkward reunion, it was even embarrassing, with its hint of destiny-crossed lovers that neither of us wanted. She was damaged; some of her brightness had gone. But we were together again in the same city and, although I knew that everything was changed, that was all that mattered to me.

You will continue to hear me. My memory will be that of a dignified man.

The train creaks out of Liverpool Street station as I make my way towards my shift at the Sublime Club. We crawl out through Bethnal Green and the East End. The memories of that year in Chile bring to mind fragments of Allende's last speech – *Much sooner than later, the great avenues will open through which free men will pass to build a better society.* The train rattles along and, in my head to the rhythm of the train, I hear the words repeating themselves – the great avenues, the great avenues, the great avenues, the great avenues. From the window of the train, all that I can see are the dark and cramped streets of the city which has now become my home.

carpathia

'So Noddy Holder, right, he's shopping for some new gear in Wolverhampton shopping centre. Right?'

Nick glanced up at Mark who had just finished a long personal phone call involving a lengthy analysis of Roberto Di Matteo and the "wall-to-wall totty" that he had witnessed at the Hanover Grand a couple of nights previously.

'This had better be short. And it had better be funny,' Nick warned his research assistant.

'Yeah. So Noddy's after some flares, right? So he goes to the shop assistant . . .' Mark broke into a passable Black Country accent '. . . he goes, "I'd like a lovly pur of flurs playse", and the shop assistant goes, "I've got just what you're looking for, Nodday". So Noddy Holder tries on these massive flares and he goes, "thayse are smashing thayse are, I'll take them". The shop assistant sticks them in a bag and he goes, "yow'll be wanting a kipper tie to go along with those, Nodday" and Noddy goes, "Oh ta very much, two sugars playse." '

There was a second of silence from both Nick and Emma the new receptionist who had paused by their desks to hear the joke. Then Nick laughed. Emma looked puzzled.

'I don't understand,' she finally wailed. 'I never get punchlines.'

'That's 'cause you're too young to remember the 70s and you're too fucking thick,' Mark responded with what he clearly took to be flirtatious aggression but which made Emma blush and walk away with a hurt expression.

'You got it didn't you, Nick?' Mark continued, oblivious to the impact of his rudeness.

'Yeah, yeah, very funny.'

'You can tell it to Big Ron next time you see him.'

'Mmm. Perhaps. I don't think your comment went down very well with Emma by the way.'

'Yeah? That's a shame. I was going to invite her out for a drink. She's got really exotic breasts.'

'Exotic?'

'Yeah, haven't you noticed? They're kind of cone-shaped.'

'No, I'm afraid I haven't noticed Emma's cone-shaped breasts, Mark.'

'Well, check 'em out, man. They're weird. But in a good kind of way. Good weird. Not horrible weird.'

'Well carry on with your charm-offensive and you'll probably be getting first-hand experience of them.'

'Do you reckon?'

'No. I'm being sarcastic. I suggest you apologise to her. What's happening about those cuttings I asked for?'

Mark looked puzzled.

'You've had all the cuttings on the Ron Driver case. They're on file. You never asked me to get them out.'

'I'm not talking about Ron Driver. I'm talking about the murder I mentioned. The bouncer. Remember?'

'Oh, right, yeah. I did call up but we haven't had anything yet. I'll give 'em a bell to remind them.'

Nick nodded and sat thinking for a while. He didn't expect that there would be that much in the nationals about the murder or subsequent trial. He had fixed up a meeting with the local newspaper for the following day, where at least he could find out the identity of the detective who had been responsible for investigating the case. Then he needed to both visit the club itself, talk to the owner and also speak to George Lamidi's friend who still worked there and whom Caitlin had christened Don't Matter or DM for short.

'What's biting you about this case anyway?' Mark asked.

At the other end of the office, Nick could see Emma indignantly recounting Mark's rudeness to Xenia, one of the young female researchers working on the False-Memory Syndrome case. Xenia pulled a face and made a rapid gesture with her hand to indicate the term which summed Mark up best. She also appeared to be attempting to persuade Emma into some course of action, a strategy which seemed to be paying off as Emma was staring at Mark with eye-narrowing contempt. Nick grinned and was almost tempted to point it out to Mark.

'Nick?'

'Oh, sorry, yeah. Well, there's going to be another series. And it's obviously a good thing to have a few ideas knocking about.'

This was partly true. At the end of his contract, Nick had nothing lined up. He wasn't too bothered about this since he could do with taking a couple of months off, especially after all the hassle of commuting to and fro between London and Birmingham. There were a few other options – Will had mentioned something about a new youth travel programme which sounded too attractive to be plausible. Somebody had called him about a documentary exploring the problems faced by asylum seekers which sounded worthy and dull. What he was definitely not going to work on was a three-part series that had been suggested which involved going 'inside' Battersea Dogs Home. Nick was amazed there were any institutions in Britain left for TV to go 'inside' – the cameras had been inside opera-houses, hospitals, hotels, airports, docks, football teams, and all the emergency services, with the most interesting result usually being footage of somebody making an idiot of themselves or swearing in front of the camera. There were few work situations where a shrewd camera-crew wouldn't be able to capture that at some time or another and Nick certainly wasn't going to get involved with another plodding behind-the-scenes-at-the-national-institution, let alone one that involved going inside an emporium for doomed dogs.

He was also pretty sure that he would get something on the next series of *Reason to Doubt* even though there was no guarantee that there would be enough meat on George Lamidi's story to justify a programme. But he might do an article on it: there were some promising ingredients – murder for a start. Clubland was also good and so was Essex. The club might only just be in Essex but that didn't matter; he could bring in the whole angle of the morally delinquent county – the voyeur-drawing, Thatcher-induced, Ketamine-edged suburban anarchy of Sierras and Sunday League and Sex. It wasn't the underclass, it wasn't poverty, it was no sink estate in Tyne and Wear with burning cars and plucky women forming credit unions. This was what went on beneath the surfaces, it was about subtly shifting boundaries of social order, it was C1 attitudes, it was alley-cat sexual moralities.

If this could also be tied into a miscarriage of justice then it might be quite a breakthrough for Nick. He felt his palms begin to tingle with the excitement of his instinct that there was something there. How strange that George Lamidi, his roller-skating protector, should have re-emerged to influence his life again. And although Caitlin was right about the incestuous nature of Nick's world, surely the reappearance of George suggested that there was more to this than simply the constant re-coagulation of people from similar back-grounds.

'You're a wanker!'

Nick jumped as his train of thought was interrupted by Emma who was standing in front of his desk but with her back to him, addressing herself to Mark. She had obviously been brooding and had decided to return and translate Xenia's gesture into concrete and confrontational words.

'Chill out. What's up with you?' Mark looked extremely uncomfortable.

'What you said. It was really rude. You think you can talk to me like that just because I'm a receptionist.'

'No I don't. I was only joking.'

'Yeah well it wasn't very funny. So watch your mouth in future you immature little twat.'

Emma stalked off leaving Mark looking like a wounded goldfish. His cheeks puffed a couple of times and he glanced nervously around to see who had heard, blushing even more intensely when he realised that the entire office had wit-nessed his humiliation. From the coffee machine, Xenia grinned at Emma and gave her a thumbs-up. Nick fought between his instinctive sympathy for the victims of public mortification and his knowledge that Mark deserved his punishment.

'Bit of a red card for you there, Mark.'

'Come on, Nick, you heard me. I was only joking. It wasn't that rude.'

'I'm afraid as I told you at the time, it did sound extremely rude. I still think an apology might be in order.'

'No way. I obviously didn't mean it or . . .'

'OK well whatever. Can you get on to the BBC library again and see about those cuttings. Otherwise, it's going to have to be Colindale.'

Towards the end of the afternoon, the phone rang.

'Is that Nick Jordan?'

'Who's this?'

'It's Trevor.'

'Who?'

'It don't matter. I'm George's mate. I said I'd call you. I work at the Sublime Club. He said we might want to meet up. I can't tell you much that he hasn't.'

'Well that's not much good. He hasn't told me anything.'

'I mean I can't tell you directly. Do you know what I'm sayin'?'

Nick assumed that this last was a figure of speech rather than a direct question so he waited for the speaker to continue. There was silence.

'Hello?'

'Yeah, I'm still here. You know what I'm saying' then?'

'Not really.'

Nick heard a sigh as if Trevor were silently remonstrating with George for having forced him to speak to somebody so remedial in their understanding.

'I wasn't working there when all that business happened. I've heard rumours of course. But I ain't saying nothing about that. I can tell you about the club, how it works, who's who. If you get in there, I can point you in a few directions. I don't know you. I'm doing this as a favour to George.'

'Why?'

'Don't matter. Can you meet up this evening?'

Nick paused. It was Karl's birthday and he was having a dinner in an exclusive Soho restaurant. Caitlin had been moaning about having to go all week, until his patience had snapped and he had told her that he would rather go without her anyway, at which point she announced that she was going for certain, but only for the food. Nick was worried that this actually meant for the food *and* the possibility of misbehaviour. Caitlin was fully aware that the evening would throw up an array of characters who occupied a high ranking in her to-be-lined-up-against-a-wall-and-shot-after-the-revolution list.

'I can meet you early,' Nick said to Trevor, reluctant to lose impetus. 'Where do you want to meet?'

'Don't matter to me, mate.'

'I've got to be in town later. Somewhere in Soho?'

'Sweet.'

After Nick had arranged to meet him in Wardour Street, he called Caitlin and arranged for her to come later so that they could go to the restaurant together. He also called Will to make sure that he was going to Karl's dinner as he wanted Will to accompany him to the Sublime Club at the weekend. Will was both going to the restaurant and agreeable to the idea of the club and Nick resolved to make sure that they got to sit next to him at the restaurant. He was one of the few of Nick's acquaintances that Caitlin had any time for: she liked the way in which he responded to her fierce certainties with amused, flirtatious teasing.

Nick sat in the pub in Soho trying to hold a seat back for Trevor or DM as he had now become in Nick's mind. Nick didn't like being in pubs on his own, he always drank his bottle of beer too fast and then had to wrestle with his need for another one and his desire not to lose his seat going to the bar. Some people looked natural and relaxed on their own in pubs, and some people looked like Billy-no-mates. Nick always felt that he belonged in the latter category, although at least he had never sunk to starting conversations with people who quite clearly resented the interruption but were too polite to say so. He tried not to smoke too much but thinking about smoking immediately made him light another one.

A tall, lean black man came into the pub and Nick knew at once that it was DM, just as the man knew instantly when his eyes lighted on Nick that he had found his point of rendezvous.

'Trevor,' said DM, holding out his hand. He was wearing a leather waistcoat and had an expensive smell about him. He looked as if he never made a clumsy gesture, never had dirty fingernails, could sit in a pub on his own all day without a trace of awkwardness.

'Nick,' said Nick.

'Drink?'

'Vodka and tonic. Thanks.'

DM slid effortlessly into pole position at the bar, gliding past several people who had been waving their notes enthusiastically at the bar-staff like flag-wavers at a royal walkabout. He immediately caught the attention of the barman. Bar queue-jumping was another art that Nick had never been able to master: he always felt too guilty at the reproachful looks by his side and usually surrendered to his belief that queues were the fairest way of determining access to services. But when he really thought about it, he knew that it was the visibility of jumping queues for beer or buses that disturbed him. If there were some clandestine way of doing it, his conscience would be less troubled.

'So,' Nick said when DM had returned with the drinks, 'you work as a bouncer at Sublime?'

'No.' DM sipped at what looked like fizzy mineral water.

'You don't? I thought . . .'

'What makes you think I'm a bouncer?'

'I suppose I just assumed . . .' Nick suddenly felt fed up with being up the defensive. '. . . I just assumed it 'cause you're big and you're black and you'd block a doorway better than most.'

DM laughed. 'That's better, man, that's better. I do work at Sublime but they ain't got no rules against a black man working at the bar. Which is what I do.'

'A barman.'

'Barman, Bar Manager, don't matter really. I wasn't working there when Chris was there. I told you that.'

'Chris?'

'George's mate. The one who's marking off days on the wall of a Wandsworth cell.'

Nick reached in his bag and took out a notepad and pen.

'Do you mind if I jot a couple of things down? You can see any notes that I make.'

'Nah, don't matter. This ain't classified information.'

'Well, I'll respect your confidentiality of course. Obviously, it's important that nobody down there knows I'm looking into the murder.'

DM nodded with mock sagacity as if they were exchanging some vital bond of trust.

'So what happened with Chris?'

DM frowned.

'I told you I couldn't give you much on that. There's rumours. Some people say he was being a naughty boy, serving up in there and so they fitted him up. George don't think so. He thinks it's something to do with some bird who you'll see if you go down there.'

'Surely, he's told George?'

'Then George would have told you wouldn't he? No, this geezer is not opening his mouth apart from to tell George that he never done it. But in those situations the range of possibilities ain't that wide. And the gossip goes around. He pissed somebody off. He paid a price.'

'And do you have any ideas who that somebody might be?'

DM hesitated and poked about at the slice of lemon in his glass.

'You'll find there's a geezer down there called Terry James. In fact, you might be mistaken for thinking that he owns the club.'

'And what does he do?'

'He owns the security firm. Argos Security 'cause his favourite film is *Jason and the Argonauts*. Never stopped to think that it makes him sound more like part of an electrical goods chain.'

'And the bouncers control the sale of drugs in there?'

'Of course. But this story, it's much more than drugs man. Or maybe it's much less. You'll be making a big mistake if you go down there on that angle, anyway. I've seen those stupid programmes you make with hidden cameras, showing some bouncer offering to get some pills or a gramme of coke – some poor, gullible minnow in a big jam-jar. Yeah, wow, big breakthrough. Fucking Bernstein and Woodward reveal to a horrified nation that you can buy drugs in clubs and some sucker loses his job.'

'It must make you wonder what you pay your licence-fee for.'

Nick glanced quickly up from his scribbled note. Fortunately, DM laughed again.

'Yeah. I'm thinking of writing to *Points of View* about it. Why oh why are journalists such a bunch of cunts.'

It was Nick's turn to laugh.

'I'll just say in my defence that *I've* never made a programme like that in my life. But I take your point.'

'That's mighty white of you.'

DM's eyes were glittering with intelligent amusement and Nick knew that the banter was not particularly malicious.

'I'm coming down on Friday, probably, to take a look around. I'll be having a chat with the owner. What's his name again?'

'Richard Irvine? I was well relieved when they gave out those stories about mobile phones giving you cancer 'cause that man should have one big fucking tumour on his ear if it's true.'

'And this girl you mentioned. What's her name.'

'Ah, Joanne, Joanne Sullivan. The lovely Joanne who gives most men a boner from a hundred yards. Yeah, she's the golden fleece, man.'

'The what?'

'She's the It Girl of Brentwood. She's Forbidden Fruit. She belongs to the big chief of the Argonauts. You'd need the protection of some pretty powerful gods to get anywhere near her.'

'So she's Terry James' girlfriend?'

'Razor reactions. You'll be picking up your Pulitzer no worries. But girlfriend is one way of putting it. Property might be a better description. Like most people, he's careless with his property. Leaves her lying around. I suppose he knows that nobody would take the risk of trying to steal her. Not many people, anyway.'

Nick put his notebook away. He didn't know what George had told DM but it was time to establish a few salient facts.

'Look, I'm not necessarily doing anything on this case. Like you, I'm just sniffing around because George is a mate . . .'

'You consider him a mate, then?' DM laughed and Nick sensed uncomfortably that George's background details to DM might not have been altogether complimentary.

'Well, we were mates at school. It doesn't mean there's

anything going to happen. It might provide something, it might not. I'm just doing a bit of . . .'

'Research?' DM laughed again.

'Yes. Research. George wanted me to have a look at this and so I am. I'm not doing it for myself.'

DM drowned his drink and looked sceptically at Nick.

'Then you're almost unusual man, Mr Journalist. 'Cause I ain't never met anyone who isn't ultimately in it for themselves. One way or another. Hello, we've got company.'

Nick glanced up to see Caitlin standing in front of them. She was looking very pretty, wearing a short black skirt and black boots. Her hair was tied back from her face. DM rose taking his jacket from the back of the seat and offered his chair to Caitlin.

'Are you going?' Caitlin asked, producing her purse from her jacket. 'Won't you have a drink?'

'No, don't matter, angel. I'm Trevor by the way.'

'Yes, we spoke on the phone I think. I'm Caitlin. Nice to have met you, Trevor. Nick, would you like a drink?'

'Get Mr Journalist a large vodka and tonic, Caitlin. He's had a hard day researching. If you come to the downstairs bar on Friday, Mr J., I'll give you a large one of those. Catch you later.'

And DM slalomed out of the bar which was full now, and suddenly techno began to blast out over the heads of the various punters who were struggling to get to the bar, or through to the toilets inconveniently situated at the back down a narrow stairway, or simply out of the swing doors and into the swarming street outside.

'What was he like?' Caitlin asked when she returned with another vodka and tonic and a bottle of Becks.

'He was OK,' Nick shrugged, 'plenty of attitude.'

'Good,' Caitlin's eyes shone, 'I like people with attitude.'

'I learn something new about you every day,' Nick clinked his glass to hers.

Karl's birthday was being celebrated in a private club down a narrow alleyway just off the Charing Cross Road. They were slightly late in arriving which meant that Nick was not able to carry off his plan of sitting next to Will. He was disappointed to see that the only seats left were next to Bella at the end of the table. Bella was part of a Labour Party think-tank on welfare reform and partner of a well-known tipped-for-Cabinet MP. The daughter of a respected Marxist political analyst, she was so New that she was still in her packaging. If it were announced that Tony Blair walked on water, healed the sick, and could feed the masses with a couple of loaves of bread and some fish she would have been concerned that he was not getting the credit he deserved. Nick knew that it was imperative that he should sit between her and Caitlin. He failed in this objective because Karl caught his arm to tell him something and Caitlin sailed through and sat down.

Karl was in a good mood because the video of a pop group he was working with had just been banned from national TV. The video involved a lesbian dwarf in domina-trix gear, snorting cocaine from the naked back of a school-girl while strangling her with her own school tie. Karl poured Nick some champagne.

'Yeah, it's great. They're going to try and show it on some late night arts programme and stage a big debate on it.'

'Great,' murmured Nick insincerely. He loathed that type of programme; big armchairs stuffed with the self-satisfied arses of self-important, self-appointed, over-opinionated camera-sluts. Nick might float around this scene, he might come to clubs like this for his friend's birthday, but he did not feel that it defined him; it wasn't part of the essential structure of his life. Sometimes, he had to admit that his feelings for Karl were not that strong: he was just part of the hand of acquaintances that Nick had been dealt, he seemed to have stuck somehow. Nick glanced over at Caitlin who had put on her glasses and was studying the menu with total absorption, moving her finger down the items with the solemnity of a child.

She smiled at him at he handed her a glass of champagne.

'I'm going to have wind-dried tuna and then sea-bass,' she announced cheerfully.

During the meal, Nick chatted to the man opposite. He was extremely vague about his occupation and Nick suspected that he might be one of Karl's dealers retained for the evening to ensure a smooth flow of drugs. Nick was tired from his meeting with DM so he was happy to let the man do most of the talking and eat his gazpacho with salmon mousse into which the chef appeared to have also hurled an entire head of garlic. Nick wondered idly whether this was taste or vindictiveness on the chef's part. It was probably fortunate that Nick was prepared to adopt the role of listener to his opposite number because the man was a genial arsenal of theories and opinions, ranging from the existence of parallel universes to the imminent world takeover by the Chinese. All Nick had to do was sit and nod and murmur from time to time, making pink spirals out of the salmon mousse in his soup.

'So if I were to take this fork and threaten to stab you in the eye with it, what would you say to me?'

Nick was startled by Caitlin's voice rising suddenly. Several other people also heard and forks paused halfway to mouths. He turned to see that she was talking to Bella the Blairite.

'I would ask you not to, obviously.' Bella regarded Caitlin with contempt.

'Right. But if I then said "I'm sorry, I'm not going to make promises I can't keep" and gouged your eye out, would I be applauded as a girl of high principle or condemned as a dangerous psychopath?'

'That's a facile analogy.'

'It isn't actually. It's perfectly appropriate. I can't think of any other situation where somebody would make an inability to promise anything a sign of great virtue.'

Karl leaned over to join in the conversation.

'They have made *some* promises.'

'Exactly,' Bella chimed in again.

'Ah yes. A fast-track for young offenders, I seem to remember. Thirty in a class instead of thirty-five. Earth-shattering. The rich and powerful must be trembling in their beds with their blankets over their heads.'

'Ah well,' Bella extracted a bone delicately from her salmon, holding it like a tiny sword as if it might serve as some kind of defence against Caitlin's fork attack. 'It's easy to sit on the sidelines and moan. It's easy to posit revolution-ary solutions when you haven't got a hope in hell of seeing them implemented. We're an easy target . . .'

'Yes you are,' Caitlin interrupted.

'. . . For those who can afford the luxury of always being in the right but don't have to get on with actually trying to change things. It's easy to criticise and not to have a positive agenda . . .'

'But I have got a positive agenda. Obviously, I'm not expecting them to nationalise the top two hundred monopo-lies but there are a few things I would like them to do . . . I won't bore you with the details, you probably find things like efficient public transport, giving pensioners a decent standard of living, legal rights for unions and affordable social housing incredibly old-fashioned.'

'Hey,' Karl was obviously worried by the harsh tone of the conversation. 'Come on, guys, it's my birthday. Champagne? Brandies? But, please, no politics.'

'Oh get lost,' said Bella startlingly. 'I'm perfectly happy talking to . . . what's your name again?'

'Caitlin.'

'Caitlin, OK. We're having a conversation, right. You can't just sweep politics away.'

'Oh, sorry,' Caitlin returned to the fray, 'I thought that was exactly the objective of New Labour. What is it again? The Third Way. A term also used by fascists over the years . . .'

'So now we're fascists as well . . .'

They settled down to continue their argument and Karl shrugged good-naturedly at Nick and turned back to his own conversation.

'It's all just talk, just words,' said the guy opposite Nick. 'Nothing that gets said in here makes any difference to real people.'

'I'm not sure I agree with you there,' Nick replied. 'It might in the long run make quite a big difference. And I'm not sure what a real person is anyway.'

The man opposite seemed slightly surprised that Nick had ventured an opinion but he fielded it by ignoring it completely and turning instead to the subject of a new bar which was being opened by a Brit-popstar, a Brit-artist and a rising young Brit-actor.

'It might surprise you to know this but they're in fact really lovely, excellent geezers.'

'Yeah?' Nick knew now that he was a dealer because it was a common trait of dealers to tell you about famous people they knew and then add how excellent they were. Nick was getting bored and wanted to talk to Will about Friday. 'That is surprising. Excuse me, I've got to go to the toilet.'

'Oh I'll go with you,' the guy winked at him knowingly and Nick flushed slightly at a few exchanged glances around the table as they made for the toilets together. As they entered, the guy opened the cubicle door and held it open for Nick, but Nick smiled and shook his head and made for the urinal instead.

They took a taxi out of Soho back to the flat, resisting the invitation to carry on at another club. The coke had started to fly around and Nick couldn't be bothered. He had stopped taking cocaine when he had started liking it just a little too much. He had trained himself to find it and its subsequent effects more boring than the boring situations he was using it to add sparkle to. Caitlin leaned her head against his shoulder.

'That wasn't too bad,' she yawned. 'My food was delicious.'

'I need some kind of garlic de-tox programme.'

'Parsley's meant to work. But you'll need a whole field. By the way, speaking of de-tox, you didn't do any charlie when you went to the bogs with that guy?'

'Of course not. I wouldn't do that and not tell you.'

'Wouldn't you?'

'No.'

Back in the house, Nick turned the TV on and curled on a cushion while Caitlin lay in the bath. He grinned as he heard her start singing *I'll be your San Antone Rose* as she splashed about. She always sang in the bath. He flicked channels finally selecting a programme about the first mission to find the wreck of the *Titanic* in the wake of the fin-de-siècle obsession with the ship. The special submarine could descend – as the doomed ship had done – the two and a half miles to the ocean floor where long tubular fish moved with unconcerned languor, resisting the tons of pressure which could so easily crumple the crab-imitating vessel clawing at the scattered artefacts from the wreckage.

Ping, ping, ping.

Back on the deck at the project ship, amid a babble of mixed languages, overexcited crew-members (or grave-robbers, depending on your point of view) sifted through the objects, much of it the hopeful property of the emigres. There were porcelain plates, decaying suitcases, a jar of green olives the size of small eggs. It was simply too much to imagine, the sheer scale of it – everything smashing about in the chaos of the descent through the depths, away from the light, away from the impervious stars which had glittered above its final, floundering agony.

Caitlin came into the room, drying her hair off with a towel.

'Ah, the floating class-system. Or rather, the sinking class-system.'

'You're obsessed with class,' Nick said. 'Millionaires did drown as well.'

'Yeah and they had names, unlike the ones locked down below and threatened with guns. Like Benjamin Guggenheim whose family made their money out of the copper mines of Latin America and weren't averse to something which involved the death of a few striking miners. Still, that's OK because he died like a gentleman and his daughter had a great art collection. You're right. I am obsessed with class. Because it's the fundamental division in society and everything else is secondary.'

'What about the fact that the people travelling in steer-age were Irish. Sometimes, nationality is as important as class. You're Irish, you should understand that.'

'Actually – and I'm going to ignore the patronising ending to your statement – there were Irish, Poles, French, Lebanese and Italians. Probably some Scousers, Cockneys and Geordies as well. Whatever they had in common it wasn't their nationality.'

'I'm not sure . . .'

'People are frightened of class . . .' Caitlin rubbed vigorously at her hair. 'Like the way you used the word "obsessed" as if I were some kind of mad conspiracy theorist. Some people would prefer not to talk about it at all. Or if they do, it's always with that stupid English hang-up about accents or *Guardian*-reading or whether you went to university or have read a book.'

'Yeah, well, thanks for the sociology lecture.'

Caitlin kicked him. 'I guess you would rather I was like that New Labour sap, we could have dinner parties and discuss constitutional reform.'

'I thought you were getting on all right in the end.'

She shrugged. 'I was being civil. She'll have to do better than that though if she wants to be included in the five-a-side games.'

Caitlin resumed her hair-drying and Nick watched the yellow submarine in the ghostly waters of the Atlantic. He remembered a flight to the States during which he had entered the strange dream-trance of travel, causing him to hallucinate that his own spirit was dancing and keening among the dark waves thousands of feet below them. The sensation was so strange that he had suddenly jolted back to full consciousness. When he realised that he was in fact in the no-space and no-time of transatlantic flight, that below them the black waves were shifting and moving to their own immense logic and rhythm, he was gripped with terror. The suitcases in the hold, the duty-free, the in-flight magazines, the trays of food, the passengers themselves – all of these would scatter like confetti across the ocean should something puncture the fragility of their craft. Down, down, down, down – through the freezing air to the nowhere nightwater.

And maybe humans would come in the daytime as the *Carpathia* had come looking for the *Titanic*; they would come with their worker ant-like instinct to clear the debris, to hunt for miraculous survivors and find what they could of their lost ones, the lives which would never be realised, the connections which would never be made. With the night-terror gone, beneath a pale sun on a freezing, millpond sea, they would come to a place which really existed only as a set of coordinates; they would come to trawl for the porcelain plates or the jar of egg-sized green olives, the gift which would never be received.

Still, most ships do not sink; most jets do not rip apart. The roar of the human-designed Rolls Royce engines on Nick's plane did not fail; there was no human-placed bomb in the hold; he did not spin down like some fallen angel to the icy ocean; he arrived safely at JFK with a bottle of Glenfiddich and 200 Silk Cut in a duty-free bag.

'Turn the light off when you come to bed.' Caitlin wrapped the towel around herself and stood up yawning. 'I've got to get some sleep 'cause I've got a big appeal case in the morning. Don't be long.'

Nick closed his eyes. The programme had given him the strangest sensation of unrepeatable points in history, of moments in time which could never return. He remembered

watching his sister doing handstands and turning cartwheels
in their garden as the sun dropped over the woods behind
the house. He remembered when he used to row in the
mornings at college, the bare spiky trees on the bank, the
freezing water dripping form his blade, the cyclist following
and calling instructions. And he remembered a song he had
learned from his childhood:

> *Oh they built the ship* Titanic
> *To sail the ocean blue*
> *And they thought they had a ship*
> *That the water would never get through.*
> *But the Lord's Almighty Hand,*
> *Knew that ship would never stand,*
> *It was sad when that great ship went down.*

It might have been sad, Nick thought, but it had nothing to
do with the Lord and what he did or didn't know. How
could it? The band played 'Nearer my God to thee'; drown-
ing men and women called for him as suffering humans have
always clamoured for some evidence of his almighty hand:
from sinking ships, from cattle trucks, from the torture
chamber and, as usual, the almighty hand proved itself to be
spectacularly absent. Its track record in such matters was
pathetic and it would really be better to believe in the
ineffective or the lazy rather than the almighty hand under
the circumstances, otherwise God might be considered far
more culpable than, say, poor old Captain E.J. Smith who
even looked a bit like the popular image of the Creator with
his Birds-Eye beard, and who did not want to make the
journey anyway.

My God, my God, why hast thou forsaken me? The plea was
as heart-rending as the answer was cruelly simple. There

were ships and planes, there were engineers and naviga-
tors, there were nation-states defending their borders and
multi-national companies defending their profits. There
was Thomas Andrew who knew at once that his fabulous
creation was fatally wounded – *they would sink* – *it was a
mathematical certainty!* And there was Bruce Ismay sneaking
in a cowardly but understandable way onto a life-boat.
There was the jet-engine with its bright blue-flamed power,
mathematical certainties converted into the fierce burning
heat that could carry people from continent to continent or
send a fighter swooping down on a defenceless village.

And there was Nick Jordan, Caitlin Brady, George
Lamidi, DM, even the cleaner at his work – selfish genes,
soft bodies and subtle imaginations. Other ships would set
sail with their bow-doors wide open and it was a matter of
chance whether you were on board or not but not necessarily whether you drowned. Men who believed their country
had been stolen would toss a lifeless corpse to the runway,
another man in an alleyway would try and shield his head
from the blows raining down on him. You could get on to the
wrong tube carriage on an otherwise normal day and somebody might stab you in the head because they didn't like the
way you were whistling. But it was no good blaming some
Almighty Hand for it all. This didn't, as far as Nick was
concerned, make it any the less sad.

the golden fleece

'I'll have a Big Mac meal with a Sprite. What do you want, Will?'

The girl serving them was called Daniela and had three stars on her badge. Little kiss curls sneaked from under her hat to tickle her ears.

'It's a Spicy Beanburger or a Fillet o' Fish. Erm . . . Fillet o' Fish.'

'And a Fillet o' Fish meal, please.'

They had driven from Will's flat in Wapping out through East London, along the East India Dock Road and up over the Canning Town flyover on their way to Sublime. The symbols of supposed regeneration – Canary Wharf and the shell of the Millennium Dome – were superimposed on the bleak landscape of outer East London which had been unaffected by the little flurries of property speculation in the more traditional parts of the East End. Alongside them for a while was the Thames, gradually liberating itself from the city, shrugging away the bridges with their loops of golden light. No pleasure boats would follow the black river any further into the darkness of the wintry countryside on its journey through marshlands and night-spiked trees into the estuary and out to the sea.

Nick and Will were both hungry and early so they stopped in a McDonalds. It was a Drive Thru' with a mock timbered interior, trying to give the impression of a large country house. But it was Friday night in the suburbs and queues of youth stood impatiently, twisting their necks to check out the little clusters of girls giggling over milkshakes, nudging each other and looking back at them from under their hair. At least the design of the place meant that there were different "rooms" so they could find a bit of seclusion.

'No, I don't want fucking ketchup with the McNuggets, I want barbecue sauce, man.'

Nick heard the familiar whingeing indignation of the man at the counter, the tone which suggested that a major crime had been perpetrated, a crime against humanity which fully entitled the aggrieved party to haul the offending underpaid worker across the counter by her hair and smash her face in. It was the voice of young males facing the protective screens of post offices, housing offices, dole offices. It was the voice which would pin down a physical defect in the person who was not immediately giving them exactly what they wanted, and then proceed to announce it to the watching public.

'Hurry up with my order. I've been waiting nearly half an hour. Fat pus-faced bitch.'

The complainant was a man of mixed race with shaved head wearing a tracksuit. Nick suddenly felt the terrible, familiar tug of the urge to say the most outrageous, perverse, unpleasant and dangerous thing possible. The worse the consequences of the speech and the greater the shame, the more he felt the urge to say it. Sometimes, the words were in his head pounding away and he would become terrified that it might actually happen, he might open his mouth to say something and other grotesque, offensive phrases would just slip out. It was like a hidden, lurking Tourette's syndrome, it was Poe's imp of the perverse – the shame, the humiliation, the repercussions.

The girl serving the complainant scurried away to try and find the precious McNuggets that were the source of the fury. She was unnerved by the man's aggression and in her hurry she bumped into a girl carrying two large drinks, one of which was knocked to the floor. The manager scowled at them both.

'Come on, hurry it up, stop messing about, come on, let's get these customers served.'

The girl looked as if she were about to burst into tears. She had no stars on her tunic. Nick remembered a time in one of these restaurants with Caitlin. It was near Christmas and while they had been waiting in the queue, the manager had been bawling non-stop at his staff. Finally, Caitlin had calmly walked to the front of the queue, beckoned the manager over and told him that she was quite happy to wait for her food but would prefer not to hear him screaming at his staff while she did so. Everybody stared at her, although not everybody's eyes contained the same hatred as those of the manager.

Nick bit into his Big Mac. He liked nothing about it but the burger sauce they put on it. Fragments of weakly-green lettuce began to drop into the polystyrene carton and on to the table.

'What we'll do, we'll have a chat with Richard Irvine first,' Will said as he picked chips delicately from his red carton. 'I'll just tell him that you're going to be doing a little piece on the club scene in the East. We'll say that maybe you'll want to speak to a few staff – that'll give you the opportunity to talk to this barman you know there. This Richard Irvine loves talking and he loves publicity. He was well pleased about the little mention he got in our programme so he shouldn't give you any problems.'

'I'll be vague about whether it's TV or an article.'

'Yeah, he won't mind, although he loves talking to cameras. He's got no reason to suspect you. Why should someone be sniffing around about a murder that was wrapped up a few years ago. He came out of it looking good anyway. Our security are well-trained and courteous. We won't tolerate that kind of thing, full cooperation with the police etc. I still think you might be on a hiding to nothing with this one.'

'Maybe. That's what I'm going to find out. As regards the police, I've found out who the investigating officer was. It was his first case. I'm interviewing him next week.'

'We'll go carefully with him if it was his first case. You can get all matey with coppers, as you know, but fall out with them and they'll treat you like a right cunt. And dump the press officer as soon as you can.'

'I SAID I DIDN'T WANT KETCHUP. WHAT IS THE MATTER WITH YOU? NO FUCKING KETCHUP. CLEAR AS DAYLIGHT. IF YOU CAN'T SPEAK ENGLISH YOU SHOULDN'T BE HERE. GET BACK TO ROMANIA AND GET ME THE FUCKING MANAGER.'

Nick brought his fist down slowly on his hamburger carton, feeling the rubbery plastic crushing out of shape and wishing that it was the man's head.

'Let's go,' he murmured.

The streets were lightly greased with rain as they walked to the club. Nick did not even realise that they were approaching until Will suddenly said, 'Here we are.'

Two neon dancers were entwined on the sign above the club, a neon girl's skirt flying as she was jitterbugged by a neon boy. The word SUBLIME was looped below in purple neon letters. It was smaller than Nick had expected, and the entrance-doors were still closed. This was not surprising as they had come early to speak to Richard Irvine. They climbed the half a dozen steps to the entrance and Will rapped sharply. There was no answer and then he knocked again. Nick glanced around and noticed the alley which ran down the side and around the back of the club. Was that where Chris had/had not stomped his victim to an early death?

'We're not open yet,' the bouncer growled as he opened the door. *Argos* was stitched in gold joined-up letters on to his black jacket above a miniature golden galleon.

'I know,' Will replied. 'We're here to see Richard Irvine. He's expecting us.'

The bouncer regarded them suspiciously and then pushed open the door. They stood in the reception area while the bouncer called up to the manager. The till had not yet been turned on but a black-haired girl with a bob was sitting behind it blowing steam from a coffee and watching them with mild curiosity. Further down, another leather-trousered girl with curly hair and eyes that were too close together was arranging coat-hangers and books of raffle-tickets for the cloakroom. There were stairs heading up which were cordoned off and stairs heading down to what was obviously the dance floor — sudden bursts of music pounded up and then stopped just as abruptly.

The reception area extended through the club to a bar which was situated at the back. Busy bar-staff came and went stocking up fridges with beer and soft drinks in preparation for the night ahead. There was something pleasing about the preparation, the familiar drills being enacted. It was like a semi-deserted Soho on a cold, bright morning, watching it open up, the people on their way to all their different tasks and jobs.

'Go through and wait in the bar,' the bouncer announced. 'I'll get somebody to bring you a drink. What do you want?'

'Vodka and tonic, please,' Nick replied.

'Lager. Budweiser, Becks, whatever,' Will shrugged.

The bouncer nodded and they made their way through to the bar which was equipped with big leather sofas. Nick sank down on one gratefully and lit a cigarette.

'It's a tardis,' Nick said to Will as they settled down. 'It looks like nothing from the outside, but it's pretty big.'

'Yeah, we'll go downstairs after we've spoken to Richard Irvine, check out the dance floor. It's all right you know, they've done a nice job here. I have to admit, I can't take all that chaos and shenanigans crap any more.'

'That's why I hardly ever go to clubs. I prefer bars.'

'So everybody keeps saying. But you can't dance in a bar.'

'Yeah, I think that's part of its appeal . . . thank you,' one of the bar staff had brought them their drinks. Nick sipped at his vodka and tonic hoping that it would remove the taste of hurriedly-eaten Big Mac in the back of his throat. It now seemed like the most revolting idea in the world.

'Here's our man,' said Will nodding towards a youngish, gleaming-eyed, expensively-suited character who was walking towards them. He was already holding out his hand in greeting but then his mobile phone went off. He flipped it open, held up his hand in half-apology and stood by the barn in earnest conversation. Nick remembered DM and the ear-tumour remark. There was no sign of DM at all; Nick imagined that he was probably downstairs preparing the main bar.

'So, Will,' Richard Irvine shook their hands as they sat down, 'how's it all going?'

'Can't complain.'

'Can't you? I fucking can. I've had two DJs not show up in the last few weeks. Overpaid primadonnas.'

'Yeah,' Nick chipped in, 'you wouldn't think that it was a job which just involved putting a few records on.'

Both men regarded him silently and Nick realised that this was a *faux pas*. Even Will took DJs pretty seriously, muttering away about who could mix and who could not – an art which Nick regarded as greatly overrated. Will still found it interesting to read books and articles about how 1988 was a more important year than 1917 or 1945 in the history of the world and still kept up with all the new branches on the family tree of dance music.

'Well, we've got a couple of DJs tonight who do a bit more than just changing records. I hope you'll hang about for a bit, it should be a top night.'

Nick nodded politely and allowed Will to explain the purpose of their visit. This was interrupted a couple of times by Irvine's mobile which played a funny little tune when it rang. He snapped it open and listened with rapt attention like a child with a conch shell straining for the sound of breaking waves. Then he flicked it shut again with a grin.

'No problem. No problem at all. There's just one thing. I've seen some of those programmes with hidden cameras and stuff. Now, I'm not going to lie and say nobody in this club takes drugs . . .'

'Don't worry,' said Nick. 'I'm not interested in all of that. I know you can't stop people coming in here with drugs if they're determined. Besides, there's a lot of hypocrisy there. Plenty of journalists making those programmes probably hoover up the charlie at their dinner parties.'

Richard Irvine beamed. He had an appealing face, rather like a cheerful little terrier. Nick felt that if he took a ball out of his pocket and tossed it across the bar, Richard Irvine would bounce off the sofa and go tearing after it.

'Exactly. I've just got to be a little careful with all of that.

We do our best; the bouncers keep a good eye on things. And broadly we're on top of it. It's been a problem around here as I'm sure you know. But we won't just let people get away with flaunting it in our faces. Not any more.'

'As I say,' Nick smiled back at him, 'that's not my agenda at all. It's been done to death, anyway. I'm interested in looking at London's new cultural status. But looking at what's going on as a whole, you know? This will be quite a small item probably, part of an overall package.'

Nick was rather impressed with his own ability to say nothing at all and make it sound convincing. Perhaps he had caught the on-message millennium bug after all. Richard Irvine nodded sagely.

'Well, anything you need just let me know. Now if you'll excuse me.' He gestured to the barman who nodded and smiled at Nick and Will. 'Get yourself another drink and have a look around. You've got a little time before the mob arrives. I'll speak to you later.' His mobile trilled out its little electric melody and he flicked it open and moved away.

'He was nice enough,' Nick sipped at his drink.

'He's a businessman,' Will shrugged. 'He's hard as nails. But he's not stupid. He understands the value of good manners, a lesson which some idiots find very hard to learn.'

'It's OK here though. Even the bouncers aren't that rude. It's quite hard to imagine somebody getting murdered . . .'

'Ah but remember, it was a little while ago. Scratch the surface of anything and you'll find there's more than meets the eye. Eggs get broken in the preparation of omelettes.' Will wagged his finger at Nick in mock-seriousness.

'Slaves die building pyramids,' responded Nick, thinking of his earlier conversation with Caitlin.

'So, the two critical questions are: a) does it matter? And

b) is there a programme to be made about it?'

'Yeah, but who decides whether something matters?'

'We do of course. And so does the public to a degree. You can make as many programmes about miscarriages of justice as you like, Nick. If nobody gives a fuck, nothing happens. Everything just rolls on. Oh what a shame. Who would have thought it could happen here?'

This was a worry to Nick. What if nobody thought it was important enough to bother about? It was one thing to say that there was somebody in prison who probably shouldn't be. Everybody knew that there were scores of people in prison who did not deserve to be there and they were hardly refusing to pay their taxes or staging demonstrations outside parliament about it. In the USA, they had established an execution assembly line and it was blindingly clear that some innocent people – predominantly poor, disproportionately black – must be having poison jabbed into their veins under the mean Texan eyes of bullnecked wardens to the backdrop of self-satisfied shrieks of glee from the bloodlusting mob of inadequates with their cheap epithets of vengeance at the prison gates. *You'll fry like a prawn on a barbecue.* The world just shrugged and said Big Deal.

'Shall we go downstairs?' Will asked, noticing that his friend was lost in thought.

There was another set of stairs at the back of the bar. They picked up their drinks and went down. Nick noticed a fire door on the landing which must lead out to some area at the back of the club. Was *that* where Chris had/had not brought his foot down on somebody's chest and head?

It was empty downstairs, apart from the staff preparing the bar. Again, there was no sign of DM. There was carpeting on the floor and, in each of the four corners, a stairway led down onto the large dance floor. Golden lights sparkled on the edges of the carpet and surrounding the dance floor was a solid-looking dark wooden balustrade which looked like part of the great stairway from some country mansion.

When they returned upstairs, the first people had started arriving. Nick felt edgy. This wasn't his crowd at all: he had no idea of the codes, the hierarchies, who the alpha-males were. He also felt both old and underdressed and wondered whether he had remembered to apply deodorant before coming out. The Prada and Versace were on display, scent drifted intrusively after the women as they brushed past him, the eyes of slim, baby-faced boys slanted at their departing backs over bottles of lager. Anecdotes were being exchanged; raucous laughter followed whispered comments; there seemed to be a constant process of appraisal going on. The atmosphere was not particularly aggressive but Nick still did not feel relaxed.

He was leaning against the bar drinking a bottle of beer while Will went to the toilet, when a girl in a short red dress and elegant knee-high boots drew his attention. Nick felt something catch in his throat as he watched her approach and yet could not say that there was anything so special about her. She was neither small nor tall, her face was delicate but not striking. Perhaps that was her appeal – he had once seen a programme where a computer had produced a woman's face which supposedly represented the ideal beauty. It appeared at the time to be stunningly banal – the ideal of some symmetry-fascist. And yet this girl with her utterly regular features, her straight, healthy, tinted hair, her absolutely neat and well-proportioned figure, her expensive and intensely flattering clothes made him almost want to turn away because he could not bear to look at her.

'Your eyes will pop out, Mr Journalist.'

Nick turned, startled, to see DM standing next to him, almost imitating the way that he was leaning on the bar.

'That's Miss Joanne Sullivan. I think I may have mentioned her name to you.'

'Ah,' Nick glanced at her with renewed interest. As he did so, she turned and their eyes met. She smiled and Nick could not understand why, until he realised that it was DM she was smiling at. He felt awkward but she did not appear to notice him, raising her hand to DM who saluted amicably in response.

'I've cleared my presence with your boss,' Nick said to DM. 'I'm sort of here officially now.'

'Ah,' DM responded, 'then I'll introduce you to the Golden Fleece. You'll be OK with her as long as you remember that when she's sweet as pie she's at her most deadly.' He beckoned to Joanne Sullivan who approached them smiling. Her perfectly made-up skin dimpled as she did so.

'This is Nick,' said DM. 'He's doing a TV programme on the club.'

'Well, it might not be a TV programme. It's just research at the moment.'

Nick felt extremely self-conscious as he spoke, as if his head might start wobbling. He was irritated with himself for his self-consciousness and also irritated with himself for using the word "research" in front of DM, who allowed a faintly sarcastic smile to briefly illuminate his face. DM missed nothing, and Nick was behaving like some weak-kneed teenager in the face of this plastic beauty.

'A journalist? That must be an interesting profession.'

There was a faint twang in Joanne's high voice and, once again, Nick was worried that he might be about to blush. He nodded.

'Most of the time it is, yeah.'

'Where's Mr James tonight?' DM asked.

'He's got a bit of business. He'll be up later to check that I'm behaving myself.'

'And drink me out of champagne at the bar.'

Joanne laughed. 'What can we do, Trevor? Maybe we should elope together. Do you think we could pull it off?'

'Not me, star. I'm too nice for you.'

'Ah but I like nice boys really. Take Nick here, I'm sure he's nice. Have you got a girlfriend, Nick?'

'Yeah.'

'I knew you would have. All the nice boys have got nice girlfriends. I just get left with the . . .'

'Villains,' DM said grinning and she aimed a mock punch at him.

'Careful. Or I'll tell him you said that.'

'You wouldn't grass me up.'

'No. Not unless I had to.'

Will came back from the toilets and Joanne sauntered away blowing a kiss to DM as she left. DM sighed and returned downstairs, leaving Will and Nick alone.

'Who's she? She's a bit of a shag.' Will remarked watching her departing back.

'Not really my type. She's the girlfriend of the guy who runs security here. He sounds a bit of a heavy character but he's not here tonight.'

'Ah, so she's Gangster Spice,' Will narrowed his eyes. 'There had to be one. You know what she looks like? She looks like she's been spoiled all her life. She was Daddy's little darling, never had to get on public transport, always had new clothes, whatever she wanted, never had to get a Saturday job like her mates. Now she's outgrown Daddy so she has to find another one, someone else who will worship her and give her things and tell her she is the fairest of them all.'

'That's a pretty comprehensive assessment given that you didn't actually speak to her.'

'I've met her type. And I got her vibe. I bet she can be a right hard little bitch that one.'

'Maybe,' Nick was still struggling with his hormonal reaction to Joanne Sullivan. It was quite absurd, the strength of the feeling he had. It wasn't even an explicit I-want-to-fuck-you feeling. There was almost something too neat and pretty and ordered about her, too well-proportioned, an excess of delicacy. And yet he had stared at her, had hardly been able to take his eyes from her. He hoped that it hadn't been too obvious but suspected that it had. He also suspected that Joanne was used to it.

Nick and Will went down and danced for a while to the house and garage being spun by Richard Irvine's overpaid primadonna. The dance floor was completely different now – light splintering through the darkness, bodies suddenly frozen by the light, expressions of abandonment illuminated like planes caught in searchlights. After the drinks he had consumed, Nick had lost his edge; he suddenly felt a familiar urge but quickly banished it. He could sense the power of the end of the working week – banks shuttered, offices patrolled by security guards and cleaners, all of it exchanged for this frenzy of motion, as the music powered out through the sound-system.

Nick was disappointed that he had not had the opportunity to check out Terry James but all in all it had not been a bad evening. He had cleared his presence with Richard Irvine, he had met Joanne Sullivan who had known Chris, he had touched base with DM again. He had even had a good time, had enjoyed dancing for the first time in ages. If there was nothing in all of this, then he had also done his duty to George Lamidi.

As they were preparing to leave, Nick went to the toilet. A couple of the cubicles were occupied by whispering couples and Nick grinned as he remembered Richard Irvine's earnest protestations about drugs. There was a sign in the toilets saying that anyone caught taking them would be banned and the police would be called. As Nick came out of the toilets, two of the club staff were clearing up a broken glass from a spilled drink. Nick was astounded to see that one of them was the Uruguayan from his office. The man recognised him as well.

'I know you,' Nick murmured, 'you're . . .'

The cleaner nodded.

'What are you doing here?' Nick asked and immediately felt the stupidity of the question as the man half-smiled and gestured at his broom.

'That's so weird. What a strange coincidence.'

He felt immediately worried as if the man would blow his cover. But he had no cover: he had announced that he was a journalist anyway. This cleaner had no idea why he was down here. The younger man with the cleaner said something to him in Spanish and the older man nodded. The younger man departed, black bag in hand.

'Are you having a good evening?' the cleaner asked Nick politely.

'Well, yes I am, it's partly work actually. I never knew you worked here.'

'Sometimes. Just some evenings. Not like at the office.'

'I'll have to have a chat with you,' Nick said. 'Are you working Monday?'

The cleaner nodded again.

'I'll see you then,' and Nick left him leaning on his broom.

They were getting their coats from the cloakroom when a small entourage swept in through the front door headed by a short, slim man in a black cashmere coat and a gold chain on his wrist. He had cropped silver hair and a face filled with authority. He nodded to the bouncers and slapped one of them on the back. Nick and Will stood back to let them pass before heading out into the night air to return to Will's car. And as they walked quietly through the gentle rain, Nick knew instinctively that he had just had his first sight of Terry James.

Will dropped him back at his house and, when he got in, he found Caitlin lying in bed dipping into a box of Ritz crackers, her book abandoned by her side as she watched TV.

'What did you do in the end tonight?' Nick asked as he undressed.

'Oh, I went swimming after work with Tony from the office. Then we went out for a drink.'

Nick told her about the evening at Sublime. When he arrived at the part about Joanne Sullivan, Caitlin looked at him without any particular expression and asked:

'Did you fancy her?'

'No,' Nick replied, 'not at all . . . she's not really my type.'

Caitlin nodded and switched the light off. 'Liar,' she said before turning her back on him.

proletarian internationalism

'So who was the *rubio* at the club the other night?' Pancho asks me as we make our way to Clapham Common on a bright, chilly Sunday morning.

Pancho has become especially hostile to blond men since Sophie – who is now Dr Sophie after sailing through her PhD oral examination – has been seen bidding a fond blonde farewell to a fair-headed university lecturer in the mornings. This has actually been seen by the jet-haired Pancho himself who has taken to spying on the house that he used to share with her. Dr Sophie is fully aware of Pancho's morning stakeouts since his surveillance techniques are no more sophisticated than hiding behind a tree. She has told Pancho that, if he does not stop stalking her, she will take out an injunction against him and have him prosecuted for Grievous Bodily Harm.

'He's a journalist from the TV company.' I answer. 'He thinks Peñarol are from Paraguay.'

Pancho nods at this piece of information which helps to reinforce his increased contempt for Gringos. We are on our way to a knockout tournament to celebrate May Day for the various ethnic communities of London. In reality, this turns out to mean the Latin American teams who play every Sunday on Clapham Common, plus different factions of Turks and Kurds, and one British team. The Peruvians – Sporting Peru – also appear to have conferred instant Peruvian nationality upon large numbers of extremely tall Nigerians.

Meat is spitting and dripping on barbecues, salsa voices soar out from portable cassette players – the hard-done-by whingeing of men bemoaning yet more harsh treatment at the hands of vicious uncaring women. *Me has matado, mujer traidora.* Women stand with hand on hip watching the juices squeeze from the cooking meat; kids chase each other in elaborately violent games; a few teenaged boys sit taking furtive draws on tightly-rolled reefers.

Pancho – in his new virulently nationalist mood – develops the theme that part of Latin American superiority rests on the greater emphasis given to the family. I am growing bored of his jealousy-fuelled conservatism so I remind him that valuing the family unit did not stop the removal of babies and children from young parents and their subsequent placement with military and business families.

'Although, many of those children had quite a good upbringing,' muses Pancho. '*They* weren't treated badly. If they never found out . . .'

What difference would it make? Would it matter if they never saw the black-and-white photograph of the smiling young couple who were their real parents? If they never knew the last agonised moments of that couple whose earlier passion brought them into existence. Because the *empleada* is clearing away the breakfast things and there's mama waving them off to school in the morning, satchels swinging jauntily, pet dog barking at the patio fence.

So would it benefit the children to know that the labour pangs which accompanied their birth took place in some naval school inhabited by hooded teenagers in leg-irons and not some sunny hospital ward with papa anxiously pacing outside before the triumphal cigar? Or would that just be raking over the past, a refusal to let the scars heal and accept reconciliation rather than retribution. Except, that the young couple cheek to cheek in the photo were real people. They were born, grew up, went to college, fell in love, had a child. To Pancho, they are just a photograph carried by women in scarves. He can simply shrug his shoulders in acknowledgement – *son los desaparecidos*. Why go on about it? It was twenty years ago; it's just too boring and obsessive to keep insisting on it. And Pancho can take this attitude about thousands and thousands of young people precisely because he does not acknowledge anything real about them – they are just a category from the past, photographs pinned on scarves; they are flat; they are black and white.

But for some people, time alters nothing; time is an irrelevance; there can be no closure and no settling of accounts.

'Here, people don't stay with their families. There is no loyalty. As soon as they get to eighteen they move out.' Pancho continues eulogoising the Latin tradition.

'Good,' I say. 'So much the better. All you are really talking about are financial and social pressures which force young people to sneak around in parks until they are so bored that they get married. And mothers who have to wait not only on their husbands but on their slobs of sons as well.'

Pancho flushes because before his doomed relationship with Dr Sophie, that was obviously exactly what he was doing, lying around in his flat in Pocitos waited on by mother and maid. Then Sophie provided another flat where he could stay with impunity, only returning home from time to time because Sophie wouldn't make his breakfast or do his washing. It was when two flats became one in London that everything started to go horribly wrong.

'You're different, though, Orlando, you had all that free love stuff in the Tupas didn't you?'

I laugh at the contempt with which he refers to "all that

127

free love stuff". The young patronising the old for having had the audacity to think more adventurously than them.

'Not exactly,' I reply.

'Good in theory,' Pancho deserves philosophically, 'but it could never work in practice. Like communism. You're up against human nature.'

Ah yes, human nature.

I remember a hot day after we had just arrived in Argentina when my wife and I were taking our small children to the theme park to play on the *super-aviones*. My wife and I were arguing – she was planning to take the children to Mexico – and the children were misbehaving. At one point, my wife's patience snapped and she hit my daughter Sara across the back of her legs. There was real fury in the slap. A chorus of outrage arose from a bus which had stopped at the traffic lights. *Hey what are you hitting la nena for? Don't hit the kid.* The sudden outburst of sympathy caused Sara to howl even louder and I could see that my wife was tempted to slap her again. Later, I took a photo of my kids in their mock jet plane. The photo still stands in my living room – Sara and Claudio are smiling and waving, delighted by this imitation of flight.

Dagmar Hagelin was also little more than a child when she made the mistake of visiting a friend with connections to the Montonero guerrillas. She fled in terror when challenged by armed men, so Alfredo Astiz – later captured by British troops during the Malvinas war – went down on one knee and shot her. He was a good shot and also – according to his British captors – capable of courtesy, a real gentleman, perhaps capable of joining in the protests of a child-loving nation at a mother slapping her child in the street. The shot crippled Dagmar and, although it became clear to her captors that she had no political involvement, she was held in a torture house, confined to a wheelchair for the very banal reason that it was too embarrassing to own up and return her. One ex-torturer remembers the girl in the garden of the house politely asking him if he could help her to shift the wheel of her chair which had become stuck in the earth. Before the World Cup – which Argentina won – many detainees were killed so that they could not be visible to the large numbers of foreigners pouring into the country. It is assumed that Dagmar Hagelin was one of these, since she never reappeared in public.

Human nature. It trips easily off the tongue. It means nothing. Alfredo Astiz was – still is – a murderer, rapist, torturer, traitor and spy. I do not share his nature; I want no reconciliation; I want retribution so much that I ache with my desire for it. I have no doubt that I could and would shoot him were it in my power to do so, but this establishes no parallel between us. The end of his worthless, despicable life would make the world a much better place and I would raise a glass to toast his departure. The fact that he still walks around smiling and laughing, strutting his impunity, is an insult to those whose hearts have been permanently scarred by his depravities. And while I may have a few more doubts now about the NEW MAN, I do not believe in any defeatist, quasi-religious philosophy about HUMAN NATURE with the tiresome refrain that in every one of us there lurks a Mengele or an Astiz. Most of the people that I knew who were prepared to kill were suffering from an excess of imaginative compassion and not its absolute absence.

A fight breaks out on the pitch between one of the Turkish and one of the Kurdish teams. It looks as if it is going to turn into an all-out war until one of the Nigerian-Peruvians has the bright idea of shouting "Immigration!"

which brings everything to a halt and sends various illegals flying away in different directions. It is not unknown for the authorities to come down and pick people up from the pitches. During the lull, the officious Bolivian referee sends off a player from each side and announces that both teams will be fined £50 for violating the spirit of Proletarian Internationalism. This nearly causes another riot and the sole British team watches in comic amazement. Their link with the tournament is not completely clear – the team captain appears to know one of the organisers but the rest appear baffled and are making faces at each other as the importance of not brawling on Workers Day is rammed home to all the teams.

Pancho and I wander around the pitch, stopping to buy a sandwich from one of the stalls. I keep an eye out for my son who said that he might be coming down. Finally, we sit down by the side of the pitch to watch a Chilean and a Colombian team – neither of whom appear to be imbued with the spirit of proletarian internationalism – to eat our sandwiches, sip slightly warm beer and let the early-spring sun warm our heads.

I wonder idly what Nick, the blond journalist from the TV company was doing at the club the other night. I know that he is working on a programme about a trade-unionist who was accused of stealing money so it can't be anything to do with that. The whole series is about miscarriages of justice, people accused of things that they didn't do. They are neat little episodes of injustice which suggest that, apart from these aberrations, the system works well; they are the sort of programmes which make people happy to live in a liberal democracy.

There are many things that I know about Nick Jordan, while he knows virtually nothing about me. I am even surprised that he recognised me at the club. I hear him in the late afternoons talking to his girlfriend or his friends, making arrangements for the evening. I have heard him arguing with somebody about his young daughter with whom he does not live. I see the confident way that he relates to those around him in the office, especially his young researcher whom he bullies slightly. I have heard another young female member of staff confess to another how much she likes him and how he appears oblivious to her existence. He eats sandwiches at lunchtime and always drops bits around his desk. He crumples pieces of paper and throws them at the bin but they usually miss and he leaves them on the floor. I know that he is ambitious. And I am the person who empties his rubbish bin – invisible but not empty.

My son arrives with a red-headed, freckle-faced, English girl with pale arms. She is pretty with big eyes and a snub nose. Her hair is not the pale ginger of some British people but falls in soft red curls. There is still something slightly repellent, almost unhealthy about her paleness. I offer to buy her a sandwich but she announces that she is a vegetarian. Pancho snorts contemptuously as this is a topic about which he used to fight with the lovely *doctora*. He starts talking about how he will not be happy until he eats a *chivito* again in his favourite bar facing the sea along the *ramblas*. Claudio is subdued and says that he has a headache, that the light is hurting his eyes.

We sit and watch the football for a while. The final of the tournament has begun and the players from eliminated teams sit about in their kit, rubbing their muscles, socks down around their ankles, supporting one or other of the competing teams. It is a good match with a lot of goals and, after a while, everybody becomes a little confused as to the score, including the players on the pitch. Chaos breaks out when they check with the referee with about a minute to go and it turns out that he is not sure either. It is 5–4 or is it 5–5 but there is nothing even approaching a majority view. Spectators begin to spill onto the pitch to air their opinions, producing mini-arguments and jabbed fingers. One of the goalkeepers sits forlornly on his line, arms on his knees, waiting for some kind of resolution. His friends laugh at him from behind the goal, joke about an earlier error, but he does not turn round and just waves a hand, half in acknowledgement, half in dismissal. At least he is playing. Pancho wanders off to buy some more sandwiches and beers, safe in the knowledge that the dispute is going to drag on for some time.

'What's going on?' asks my son's red-headed girlfriend.

'It's fucking typical Latin Americans,' my son replies contemptuously. 'And then they wonder why their countries are in such a mess.'

'At least we're not cold and frigid like the English.' Pancho has returned with the sandwiches and beers, also speaking provocatively in English so that the girl can hear, 'you can tell they hardly ever get any sun.'

The girl – whose name is Emily – giggles nervously. I want to explain to her not to take it personally, that Pancho is not really talking to her but to a blonde-haired expert on the subject of human rights and impunity in Uruguay, the infamous *mujer traidora*, the evil, injunction-threatening Sophie (PhD) who has committed grievous harm to Pobre Pancho's tender heart.

'That's true,' Emily says in a conciliatory way. 'Well, not about being frigid . . .' her giggle becomes slightly more high-pitched '. . . but we could certainly do with a bit more sun although it's difficult for me because I burn really easily; I go out in the sun and zap! I just turn into a tomato or a lobster, although lobsters aren't really red, you know: they're blue until people drop them into boiling water which I think is barbaric especially because they cut the tendons of their claws so that they can't fight back . . .'

I can see my son wriggling in embarrassment, while I find Emily's nervous gabbling quite endearing, almost compensating for her white eyelashes. It turns out that she has been working with a group building a clandestine video-dossier on cruelty in circuses.

'Yes,' says Pancho, looking at me for support. 'Lots of fuss about elephants getting mistreated, but they don't care about the clowns who are exploited.'

But I am not going to allow Pancho to get away with playing the radical to bully Emily just because she is English and a vegetarian. What Pancho knows about the exploitation of clowns is zero and what he cares is even less. The Latin American upper classes are very good at indignation about exploitation carried out by foreigners, they will hold forth about it at dinner tables while Rosita the maid carries the plates away, watched only by the sons of the family, who will also use her at some time to relieve themselves of their virginities.

'I always like it when the tiger that has been reared as a cub turns round one day and bites the trainer's arm off for no particular reason,' I say. 'Just because the tiger gets bored of being whipped and made to jump through hoops and sit on uncomfortable stools.'

Emily flashes me a smile. 'Yes and then they shoot the tiger which is just totally unfair.'

'The world *is* unfair,' mutters my son irritably with his eyes still closed. Claudio would never pretend to care about elephants, clowns, tigers or even beautiful star-spangled trapeze artists – basically, because they cannot be switched on and off, do not have a mouse (of the click-click rather than the elephant-scaring type), and cannot be communicated with by e-mail.

'Well if the world is unfair,' Emily says, 'then I think you should try and change it. Even if you don't succeed, I think just attempting is worth something. You make yourself better by trying. That's what I think.'

She blinks defiantly at Claudio who rubs his eyes and moans slightly.

'I suspect that my son finds your view rather old-fashioned, Emily, but I think you might be right,' I tell her.

'It's not that,' Claudio groans, 'it's my head. I can feel it in my neck now as well. I might not be able to go to work tomorrow.'

Now I know that it is serious. Claudio missing work is tantamount to the hardened alcoholic casually deciding not to have a drink for a few days. I am about to comment on this when the organisers and referee arrive at a solution to the unknown score problem. They will play another half an hour with the golden goal rule applying and then if nobody scores, it will go to penalties.

'It will be a bit unfair if the team who thought they were winning go on to lose,' Emily murmurs.

This is, in fact, exactly what happens. The team who thought they were 5–4 up, and have been the better team throughout the game, concede a goal within ten minutes after a hopeful shot takes a terrible deflection. The victors are ecstatic; the referee has to run for the changing room as the losers bear down on him with a complete lack of internationalist spirit – proletarian or otherwise – in their eyes. At the award ceremony, during which the losers refuse to accept their runners-up award, a special prize for fair play in the spirit of proletarian internationalism is awarded to the sole representatives of an imperialist nation – Britain. They are the only ones who can remotely lay claim to it given that they have been generally ignored and have not tried to kick the opposition off the pitch. It is a pleasing irony which is lost on Pancho but not on Claudio-the-virtual-Gringo who manages to forget his illness for a moment and applauds them vigorously. Their leading scorer, a skinny, spotty sixteen-year-old with a floppy fringe holds the trophy up like the FA cup to a few sarcastic cheers from his teammates, says thank you very much and escapes behind the changing room where an international brigade of Kurds, Turks, British, Chileans, Bolivians, Colombians and Peruvian-Nigerians are creating a thick, sweet fog of marijuana.

Claudio is really suffering now; he cannot concentrate on anything that anybody is saying. It is as if the light is tormenting him. In the end, I am sufficiently worried to decide that he should go to the hospital. He protests weakly but it is obviously that he is also becoming worried. He does not want to stand up and suddenly leans forward and vomits violently.

'Perhaps he's eaten something bad,' murmurs Emily. 'We went out to a restaurant last night. I only had vegetarian moussaka but Claudio ate fish – it was tuna I think . . .'

Claudio groans as he wipes his mouth on a hankie which Pancho has silently offered him. It sounds suspiciously as if he is telling Emily to shut up, but his voice is slurred as if he is half-drugged.

'Help me with him, Pancho,' I say. 'I'm going to take him to the hospital.'

We walk slowly across the Common and it is obvious that every step is causing Claudio acute distress. He vomits again beside a tree and I remember him as a little boy, his inability to travel; even after his flight on the *super-aviones* in

Buenos Aires he went green and was unable to eat his ice cream.

'I'm dying,' he moans. Were anyone else to say this I would consider it melodramatic, but this is Claudio.

We manoeuvre him to the edge of the common, looking out for the orange light of a taxi. When we finally manage to hail one, the driver looks warily at my son.

'He ain't gonna throw up in the back of my cab is he?'

'He's ill,' I say. 'I'm taking him to a hospital.'

'I ain't a fucking ambulance service,' growls the driver tossing his cigarette disparagingly from the window and pulling away.

I feel a wave of Pancho-like hatred for this stupid, ignorant, bald-headed, semiliterate, English anti-samaritan. At least Claudio does not appear to have noticed.

'We should get his number. We should report him,' cries Emily indignantly. 'They can't not take you, you know, if the destination is within a certain radius they're obliged to take you . . .'

'Well, it's a bit late for that now,' I half-snap, flailing my arm at taxis without the welcoming orange glow in the hope that one might have just forgotten to put its lights on.

Finally, a cab comes; we bundle Claudio into the back, promising the driver that he will not vomit, and make our way to the hospital.

In the casualty waiting room there is an electronic sign which informs us that the waiting time is three hours. On the rows of plastic seats, a man is sitting holding his head, another wearing a chef's uniform has stabbed himself in the neck at work, an Asian woman rocks and moans holding her stomach, and a drunk paces around irritating everybody by firing off sudden salvoes of incoherent insults which might or might not have something to do with his pain.

'My son's very ill,' I tell the receptionist.

'Well, the triage nurse will see him in a minute,' she responds without looking at me.

'The what?'

'The nurse will assess him. Take a seat, please.'

We sit down. Claudio is covering his eyes.

'I think it must have been the fish,' Emily says hopefully. 'My mum got really sick on fish once, I told her that's what happens to you if you eat dead animal. She said that fish weren't animals, which is silly: some people even leave the heads on and you can see their eye just staring up at you . . .' Emily cocks her head in a passable imitation of a fish eye staring up from a plate. '. . . I do hope Claudio will be OK,' she concludes wistfully.

'How did you meet?' I ask, wondering what on earth two such incompatible people find to talk about.

'There's a new Cuban bar in town. I went there when it opened and got really drunk. I met Claudio there. We were drinking *mojitos*.' Emily pronounces the *j* properly to my surprise. 'They were miles better when I drank them in Cuba.'

'You've been to Cuba?' I was even more surprised.

'Oh yes. My mum and dad go every year now. It's really cheap and the beaches are beautiful. Also, my parents think it's their duty because they're communists. Claudio told me that you were sort of a communist as well. That's kind of how we got talking.'

'Your parents are communists?' I try not to let my surprise show. I am also wondering quite how Claudio has described me to this girl.

'Mainly my mum. My granny – that's my mum's mum – she was a communist because she used to work as a receptionist in a hospital. The Communist Party had a raffle at

Christmas and the prize was a goose. My granny won the goose and joined the Party. It's sort of a family thing. I always liked that story when I was little . . . before I became a vegetarian of course . . . but it was during the War and food was really short so I suppose it's kind of understandable that they ate the goose.'

We are interrupted by a nurse who has come to check on Claudio. There is something in her attitude, something cursory that I don't like. Claudio also seems to have rallied a little and the nurse betrays impatience.

'There's been a lot of very nasty flu about. This place is really for Accidents and Emergencies, hence the name. It might be best to see your GP if there is no improvement.'

'OK,' says Claudio.

'It's not OK,' I say. 'I've never seen him like this before; it seems like more than flu to me. He should see a doctor. Hence our presence.'

I know that the nurse finds my voice annoying, the slight foreign accent combined with well-spoken English. It is a combination that reminds British people of uppity natives who need to be taken down a peg or two. I know she is thinking "what right have you to tell me my job?".

'Well, he can see a doctor. But he will tell you what I have just told you and you will have a very long wait.'

What she means is that she is putting us to the bottom of the queue. Claudio groans.

'He should lie down at least,' I say.

'If you want him to lie down, I really suggest that you take him home and put him to bed and call your GP if his condition alters. It is very clear to me that he has picked up the virus that is doing the rounds. It's not very pleasant I know, but it tends to work itself out in the end,' snaps the nurse who has dyed orange hair which is unfortunate, because she was naturally ugly enough before committing that particular atrocity. I have started to hate her, especially because she is already beginning to edge away.

'We'll wait,' I say.

She shrugs and disappears.

'Did you hear that, Claudio?' Emily attempts to rally his spirits. 'You've got a virus. It's a shame you're not one of your computers or you could cure yourself.'

There is little point in Pancho waiting with us so I tell him to go. He protests weakly but I know that he is growing anxious to get away.

'See you tomorrow,' he murmurs, patting Claudio awkwardly on the head. Claudio winces.

'My neck is sore,' he whispers.

We sit and we sit and we sit. Emily buys coffee and KitKats. One by one, the various casualties around us are seen. The drunk is escorted out by security, the Asian woman moans her way to a cubicle, the orange-haired nurse vanishes, white-coated young doctors pass by with stethoscopes curled round their necks like sleeping snakes. The red numbers announcing the amount of waiting time do not change.

Finally, when I am actually considering taking Claudio home so that he can at least lie down, Emily's patience snaps. She grabs a passing doctor by the sleeve of his white coat.

'Excuse me, I'm sorry, but this is totally outrageous. This is disgusting. We've been waiting here for hours. At the very least, my . . . erm . . . my friend should have been examined by a doctor, he's in real trouble.'

Emily's pale skin is flushed as the blood of protest rises to her face.

The doctor promises that he will see Claudio in five minutes, which irritates me because I am sure that he would not have done so had Emily's English tones not rung out through the waiting area with such force. We have waited so long that I can hardly believe that Claudio will be called, but finally he is taken away to be examined by the young doctor who smiles at him encouragingly.

It is some time before the doctor re-emerges, and he does so without Claudio. His face is troubled.

'You are Claudio Menoni's father?' he asks.

I nod.

'I am afraid we are having to do some tests on Claudio, Mr Menoni . . .'

'Tests?'

'Yes. As a precaution. Some of the symptoms he is displaying are associated with meningitis. The sore neck, the difficulty with the light . . .'

'But we explained those when we arrived.'

'Yes.' The doctor looks embarrassed. 'Yes. That should have been picked up . . . erm . . . well what we are going to do is take some fluid from Claudio's spine. There are many different types of meningitis,' we have to make sure we know what we are dealing with so we can establish the appropriate treatment; if it is meningitis he'll be on antibiotics . . .'

'Meningitis?' Emily looks astonished. 'But that is really serious. He's going to be OK?'

'Can we see him?' I ask.

'Not at the moment,' the doctor replies. 'He's having some tests done at present. As I say, we still don't know exactly what we are dealing with.'

'He was waiting all this time and he had meningitis?' I stare at the young doctor.

'Well, we don't know for sure . . . until the lumber puncture . . .'

'But it's important to treat it early, surely? And he's been waiting for nearly four hours.'

'It's always difficult with meningitis. The symptoms are very inexact. It can easily appear as a bout of flu. If it is meningitis, then we might have to consider giving you both a vaccination as a precaution, although it might be too late. You are his girlfriend?'

Emily flushes. 'Well, not exactly, I don't think so but we're sort of . . .'

'You've been quite close with him over the last week or so?'

Emily blushes even more. She glances sideways at me.

'Yes, yes. Sort of close, yes.'

'Ah well, it might be sensible to give you the vaccination just in case. What about other close family?'

'They don't live here. It's just me,' I say, suddenly wondering about the best time to phone my ex-wife.

The doctor nods calmly and I remember Emily's unanswered question.

'He's going to be OK?'

'Meningitis is a very tricky illness. We will keep you informed. And as soon as it is possible to see him, we will allow you to do so.'

'Oh that's big of you.' Emily's eyes are suddenly glittering with fury. 'You've kept him waiting here for hours, seeing people who have sprained their ankle while he has a life-threatening illness. If anything happens, we're going to do something; we'll definitely take some action, we'll have to go to court or something . . . we'll definitely do something.'

Life-threatening. Emily has said the words that have been unspoken but have been coiled in the back of my mind waiting to slither out flicking their poisoned tongues. My son might die. This started out as my day off, a bright spring day, a football match, a comic misunderstanding of the score, the British winning the proletarian internationalism award, a belligerent taxi-driver. Now there is a possibility that my son might die. Claudio, who chose to stay when his mother and sister went back to Holland. Claudio, with his young man's seriousness, his disapproval of the waste of my talents and the state of my liver. This is little Claudio who vomited on planes and buses as the trap that our continent had become grew ever tighter, the places to run to ever fewer; this Claudio who waved at me delightedly from his jet plane in a theme park in Buenos Aires; the same Claudio who chased wind-blown newspapers on our roof-patio in Montevideo. This is my son conceived in Punta del Diablo in a hotel with a sandy floor to the timeless crashing of the waves outside. It is Claudio the computer-loving nerd, who counts his alcohol units and plays tennis to keep fit and still has a soft spot for an awkward red-headed girl with communist parents. My son cannot die; he cannot die before me; he cannot die before me.

'So what will happen to him after this test?' I ask the doctor.

'Well, he'll be on a drip and if, as I suspect, it turns out to be meningitis then we'll start immediately on the antibiotics. We'll need to find him a bed as well, that's our first priority, the hospital's very busy at the moment . . .'

'I want to stay with him tonight,' I say. The thought of leaving Claudio here on his own and returning to my empty house is unbearable. I anticipate a row with the doctor about this but he does not appear to think that it will be a problem.

'We'll probably be able to fix you up with a camper bed next to him. It won't be the most comfortable thing in the world . . .'

He shrugs and smiles at me. This is his job, this is what he does; I am thinking about the possibility of my son dying and he is probably thinking about the end of his shift.

When we get to see Claudio, he is feverish and barely coherent.

'Papi, I'm sick, I'm so sick,' he mutters to me. The drip in his arm, the slurred speech distress me and I stroke his hair lightly.

'I'm staying with you tonight,' I murmur. 'I'm not going to leave you.'

I promise Emily that I will call her with any news and almost feel sorry to see her go, this unexpected new girl-friend with her pale skin and red hair, her nervy chatter, her tenacious vegetarianism, her communist grandmother winning the goose in the Christmas raffle. At the same time, I want to be alone with Claudio; I feel that my presence and my presence only can make him better; only my vigil can save him.

How can it be possible that anything can happen to him when I have lived so much closer to danger than he has. From Montevideo to Santiago to Buenos Aires, it could easily have been me hanging from the tree, dumped in the gutter or tumbling down towards the icy water. My son came out to watch a football game on a bright spring morning and ended up in a hospital ward with a virus that could kill or spare him depending on a combination of circumstances impossible to know – the whim of the virus, Claudio's constitution, the skill of the medical staff.

And perhaps his constitution was affected in some way by being dragged about from place to place, the small boy in shorts with his face to the rain-streaked windows of buses and planes, no longer able to chase newspapers on the roof-patio. What sort of childhood did I give him – I, the proud revolutionary and architect of the NEW MAN, believing in the poetry of rebellion, bright slogans about walking among the stars, the whispering spirit of Tupac Amaru – dragging him and his young sister from city to city? Shortly before returning to Holland – our original arrival point in Europe – my wife looked out from the window of our tower-block flat, turned to me and said "Was it all for this, Orlando, was it all for this?" And I hear the words in my head again as I look down at my helpless son, as an incomprehensible virus attacks his body. I think, was it all for this?

Later, they bring a camp bed to the room and I lie there listening to Claudio's breathing and the odd disjointed phrases which he murmurs from time to time. The hospital is quieter now; outside Claudio's room the nurses come and go and often they enter, to look into Claudio's eyes, or check the many tubes and drains coming from his body, as if attempting, with such close attention, to compensate for the hospital's earlier negligence. I watch disease-ravaged old men shuffle down the corridor in their pyjamas and cheap tartan dressing-gowns to smoke the roll-up which has probably reduced them to this emaciated state. I watch a woman in a raincoat passing by dabbing a tear from her eye; from the window I watch the sky turn a strange and awe-inducing blue before darkening into night. I imagine every one of the people in their beds, each history, each set of stories dividing and subdividing as powerfully as any virus within their suffering bodies, and all the people they know and have known – like the red-headed girl with her tale of the communist goose, her painful confession of intimacy with my son in front of two men she had never met before today – all within the walls of this old building, the traffic gently humming outside.

'Papi,' Claudio murmurs from his bed, 'Papi, are you going back? Are you going back?'

'Back where, Claudio? I'm not going anywhere.'

'Are you going back? They'll hurt you,' Claudio repeats anxiously and then subsides again; he cannot hear me.

I know I am not going to sleep. I try to empty my mind, I try to focus almost obsessively on trivia, on football results, on a single image. I think that tomorrow I will have to phone my wife and wonder whether she will come over straight away or wait for news; whether she will bring Sara. I think of a hotel room in Buenos Aires, a window open and a curtain flapping out of it caught by the breeze. I force myself away from that image and think about phoning Claudio's work to let them know that he is ill, and phoning in myself to say that I will not be going in to clean at the TV company. I think of the hotel by the sea where Claudio was conceived at a time when my wife and I still loved each other. I think of my wife naked, I think of . . .

No.

I was held in a cell once when I was the same age as Claudio. They would come and take one of the guys from our cell to be tortured and we would hear his screams from adjoining cells. He screamed and pleaded for his mother: it was incessant; it would not stop. *Mami, mami, por favor, quiero mi mama, mama, ayúdame, ayúdame mama*, probably affording his torturers great amusement. It was unbearable hearing his pleas for his mother, the desperate cries for the woman who had given birth to him, who had at one time appeared capable of the resolution of all pain, of all suffering. It was terrible to think of his mother probably searching for him, imagining him and setting her hope against her imagination, demanding interviews with the bureaucrats of death, men who also had mothers, who would wave her away and reject her petitions of *habeas corpus* because the son who was calling and calling so desperately for her protection was not officially detained.

145

They would bring him back to the cell and we would try and help him. I always remember the way he would lie in the corner of the cell, curled into the foetal position repeating over and over and over again:

Iwanttodie Iwanttodie Iwanttodie Iwanttodie.

Now I lie smelling the canvas of the camp bed, beside my son who has been at my side since I first had to leave my house with its green shutters, high above the harbour, the Río de la Plata, my river of silver with its winds blowing in from the ocean. And my son is ill; he needs my protection but I do not know if I can give it to him although I would gladly lay down my life for this serious-minded boy who prefers computers to revolution, who is more fascinated by Bill Gates than Tupac Amaru. But I stop thinking about the hotel room in Buenos Aires with its flapping curtain, and the broken boy curled in the corner of his cell. I think of the little boy and his sister waving delightedly from their jet plane in a Buenos Aires theme park and I think:

Pleasedon'tdie Pleasedon'tdie Pleasedon'tdie Pleasedon'tdie.

the edit suite

The man in the pub, he said that I should say all that stuff about the dog-leash and the football shirt. I thought it sounded stupid, but he was a punter like . . .

'OK, that's great. The In is 10.07 and the Out is . . . 11.04.'

Nick was in the edit suite going through Mandy's interviews on the Ron Driver case. Mandy was an interviewer's dream. She was good-natured, unfazed by cameras, and came out with little unrehearsed jewels such as 'he was the punter' about the not-such-a-mystery-spook who had succeeded in making the trade-unionist look like a thieving pervert rather than the bore Nick had come to know so well – collector of model cars and fan of all things that involved manufacturing.

Nick glanced down at the typed transcripts of the interviews in his hands.

Then he brought this journalist from one of the tabloids and they was buying my drinks and then we did the interview and by that point I was so pissed I was adding in stuff myself and when the journalist went to the bog the first bloke even says to me to calm down 'cause it sounds bloody stupid like and nobody's going to believe it, do you know what I mean?

Dirty Tricks. Perhaps if all they had done was to suggest that Ron Driver had enjoyed wearing a Birmingham City shirt and a dog-lead, that could have been called a dirty trick. But the vindictiveness towards Ron Driver had gone much further than that, extending to the accusations of

embezzlement of union funds which had landed him in front
of a jury. Poor old Ron found that last accusation easily the
most horrifying – he would have held his hands up to
virtually anything other than stealing from the Brothers.
Now Ron Driver was an irrelevance and his union was no
longer part of that eclectic army that had once constituted
the "enemy within". The new General Secretary was an
arch-moderniser issuing the odd mild reproach to the government it had worked so hard to put into power, and its
Regional Officers would no more sanction irresponsible
strikes than they would give up their air-conditioned Ford
Mondeos.

Nick wandered back to his desk to check his voice-mail.
There was a message from Karl inviting him to the launch
party for a new book on football hooliganism; there was a
message from Marianne reminding him that he was to pick
Rosa up at 5 p.m. Since he had never once forgotten to
collect Rosa, Nick found these reminders annoying. He was
especially unlikely to forget at this time because Rosa was
staying for a couple of days a week since Marianne's mum
was in hospital with breast cancer and Marianne was visiting
her almost every day.

The last message was from George Lamidi saying that he
wanted to arrange a time for Nick to visit Chris in Wandsworth Prison. Nick wondered whether DM had de-briefed
George on his visit to Sublime and concluded that it was
highly likely. He did not particularly want to imagine their
conversation. He opened his lunchtime sandwich and started
to eat it without a great deal of interest, brushing bits of
cress that fell on to his chest to the floor.

Nick's series producer wandered over to his desk.
Penny was a BBC and Thames TV veteran. She was about
fifty years old, elegant, grey-haired and with a deserved

reputation for not suffering fools – gladly or otherwise. More than one person working in the office had felt the lash of her tongue when they demonstrated unacceptable sloppiness. So far, Nick had had no problems with her and he was hopeful that, when the series was recommissioned, then he would have his contract renewed.

'How's it going, Nick?' Penny sat down on the edge of his desk.

'Yeah, the edit's going well. Mandy's a star.'

'And how's Mr Driver? Is he happy with everything?'

'Well, he's never exactly happy about anything. But he needs this badly. He's aching for it so much, he's in no position to cause problems.'

'Good. Good. I just wanted to say, tracking that prostitute down and getting her to talk was pretty impressive. I'm getting some noises about another commission. You might want to start thinking about a few ideas, you know, just give it some thought.'

Penny wandered off and Nick basked in her approval. If he could have the Sublime story ready to run, then he would be at a massive advantage. On the other hand, he was still worried that people would only talk off-camera if at all. The balance of evidence still indicated that the police were hardly operating like brutal racist pigs in charging Chris. There was no dispute that Chris had taken the boy outside, a boy Mark's cuttings trawl had now given a name to. Nathan Clemence was eighteen years old when repeated stamping on his chest and face by a bouncer from the Sublime Club caused his death through a fractured skull and blood inhalation.

Nick took out his note-pad and wrote down names:

D.I. Kinch – this afternoon.
Chris – V/O from GL.

Richard Irvine – ??
Joanne Sullivan – find out more.
Mrs Clemence – Mark to arrange.

Mrs Clemence had appeared in the local papers after Chris
had been sentenced. She was a grey-skinned woman,
dumbed down by a life of nicotine, tranquilisers and generally being ignored by those around her. She had stated
bullishly that she hoped that Chris would rot in hell, that her
great regret was that capital punishment had been abolished,
and that Nathan had been a smashing son and a gentle boy
who loved fishing. The accompanying picture and criminal
biography of Nathan suggested that his juvenile love of
fishing had been superseded by others and that the neigh-
bours' description of him as 'no angel' and, even more
uncharitably, 'white trash' might not prove to be entirely
inaccurate. Still, angel or not, somebody had seen fit to drag
him into an alley and kill him in an appallingly brutal way.
And perhaps that person was sitting right now in Wandsworth Prison, waiting for the journalist/saviour promised to
him by his friend George Lamidi.

Although Nick was anxious to interview Chris as
quickly as possible, the thought of entering a prison again
filled him with dismay. Several times during his career, he
had stood waiting with his Visiting Order to talk to a man
who was neither being brutalised by wardens nor gang-
raped in his cell, but who was instead going crazy with
boredom, with the incessant drab tedium of life inside, the
proximity of excrement, and the daily currencies of tobacco
and Class A drugs. The smack which had policed the places
where the men had come from, dutifully did the same when
they were inside. Nick came out of prisons or young offenders' institutions with the same after-visit feeling he had had

when his grandmother was slowly dying and he had left her behind in the suburban hospital while he walked to the station, down a long busy road on a greyish afternoon as kids were just coming out of schools.

Mark came bouncing into the office looking cheerful. He had apologised to Emma which had gone down well, but then invited her for a drink which had not. His lack of success on the sexual conquest front meant that he was forced back to the one topic that never failed him, that he could bring out at any opportunity, not only easily accessible but seemingly inexhaustible.

'See Rudy Gullit on the TV last night?' Mark flopped down on his chair. 'Say what you like about Vialli, we can't really complain about what he's done since he took over from Rudy . . .'

'Yeah, erm, Mark I need you to do me a favour. This woman, the mum in the cuttings you dug out. I want to interview her. Can you sort something out for me as soon as possible?'

'No worries. What's her name again? Mrs Clemence. Sounds a bit Tottenham to me, know what I mean? Did you see Ray when his son got sent off. I mean the boy shouldn't have got sent off really just for diving but you've gotta have a laugh at the yiddoes . . .'

'Just try and shut up for one minute about football, Mark. Please? OK? I just don't want to hear a single football-related word . . .'

'Well nor would I if I was a QPR supporter . . . ha ha . . . no only joking Nick . . . only joking . . . erm . . . right . . . right.'

Nick tried not to laugh as Mark subsided into silence.

'OK, now, Mark, try and answer a question without any reference whatsoever to football. Have you seen the cleaner recently?'

'What cleaner?'

'The one with whom you sometimes talk about football. I know that doesn't narrow it down much but I mean the Latin American guy, greying hair, speaks pretty good English, slightly posh accent, supports some team with which you are familiar . . .'

'Oh yeah. I thought he supported Peñarol 'cause we used to talk about the time they won the Copa de Libertadores but in fact he's a Nacional supporter – Peñarol's big rivals, well their only rivals really . . .'

'Mark, I'm not interested in what football team he supports. Have you seen him?'

'No, man. Why should I have seen him?'

'No particular reason. I just want to talk to him about something important and I haven't seen him for a few days.'

'Maybe he's sick; maybe he's on holiday; maybe he's left for another job. There's a pretty fast turnover you know. I think he's the supervisor anyway. For this floor at least. He only cleans when there's staff missing. Ask one of the others. What do you want to talk to him about? Looking for a job when your contract's up here?'

'Yes, that's quite hilarious. Try and find out for me, yeah? I've gotta go out for the afternoon. Ask the cleaners when they turn up. You can get me on my mobile if anything else urgent comes up.'

Nick picked up his mobile, his pad, his cigarettes and his car keys. He whisked his jacket from the back of the chair and slung it all into the pocket. When he turned back at the office door, Mark was giving surly mock Nazi salutes to his back. He stopped immediately like a naughty schoolkid and bent over his desk, obviously hoping that he hadn't been noticed. Nick laughed and took the stairs instead of the lift.

As he drove across London, his mobile rang. It was Will.

'I'm gonna do you a big favour,' Will said. The mobile was breaking up a little, it sounded as though Will were trying not to sob which was unlikely as Will was not given to spontaneous outbursts of emotion. Nick noticed that the middle-aged woman in the car next to him was pointing and frowning as if there was something wrong with his car. Then he realised that she was telling him not to use his mobile when he was driving. She was gesturing and frowning ever more urgently, which Nick found annoying since they were only able to travel at about five miles an hour as they approached a busy roundabout – it was hardly a major risk.

'Hold on a moment, Will.' Nick took his other hand off the wheel, stuck two fingers up at the woman and mouthed *fuck off* at her. The woman frowned and wagged her finger and shook her head even more urgently. She consequently failed to notice that the car in front of her had halted and shunted into it hard enough to break its tail-lights. Nick's use of the mobile had indeed caused an accident as the woman had predicted. Fortunately for Nick, they were just at the roundabout so his lane was able to continue unimpeded while behind he began to hear the blaring of horns.

'Sorry, Will, you were saying?'

'Yeah, I've got a mate who's doing this piece for one of the Sundays. It's just a jokey little piece on club toilets, you know a bit like they do on football stadia – who's got the best bogs, the worst pies, the stupidest mascot, that kind of bullshit. Get a little quote from Richard Irvine and he'll stick it in. Irvine'll fucking love that, man.'

'That's excellent. I'm in traffic now. I'll call you later.'

'Yeah, hold on, did Karl ring you about the hooligan book launch? There's going to be loads of babes apparently.'

'No hooligans?'

'Fuck that. They can't come to their own book launch.

Well, maybe the geezer that wrote it will be wheeled out. It's probably all made up anyway. Nah, it's all babes and journalists . . .'

'Yeah, maybe, I'll get back to you. To be honest I'm getting fed up of all that shit. I've gotta go and see a copper . . .'

'Lucky you. Well let me know if you can make it . . .'

The police station smelt most strangely and powerfully of cloves. The pungent smell reminded Nick of fireworks night when he was a child, standing in the garden eating treacle toffee and being given sips of mulled wine by his mum, as his dad moved like a shadow, bending to the ground, about to light up the dark sky.

The source of the clove smell turned out to be an exasperated woman whose car had been stolen while she was shopping. In her urgency to report the crime, she had dropped a designer bottle of olive oil with a red chili, some peppercorns and various cloves inside like two-headed sheep trapped in formaldehyde. The smell of spices was annoying the coppers on the front desk who were holding their noses ostentatiously and glaring at the woman. While overpowering, Nick found it rather agreeable.

Caitlin and Nick always argued about the police since Caitlin claimed that it was impossible to be indifferent to them. As far as she was concerned, hating the police was an imperative of citizenship: if you did not hate the police you had been badly brought up, absurdly over-protected or you were simply a fascist or a freemason. But in his work, Nick had met many police officers and, although a few had been corrupt and several had been deeply unpleasant individuals, he did not hold a generalised prejudice against them. He had also met quite a few who appeared to genuinely believe that it was their task to protect society from murderers, rapists and paedophiles and performed this task with some dedication and honesty.

Unfortunately for Nick, his lack of generalised contempt for the forces of law and order did not appear to win him any favours with DI Kinch, who clearly held a generalised contempt for Nick's profession with the sole exception of those who worked for *Crimewatch UK*. Journalists appeared to occupy a place only marginally higher than murderers, rapists and paedophiles in Kinch's league table of undesirables.

DI Kinch was in his early forties, a blandly handsome man with silvering hair and slip-on shoes. He made it clear that he had a moral code but that he doubted whether Nick would have any access to it. Villains were villains and if, occasionally, they had to go down for something they had not done, this should not over-concern society since the seesaw of justice meant that there was almost certainly something that they *had* done which they had got away with. This kind of justice might be rough but it was still justice of sorts because the constituency from which DI Kinch came, which he represented and defended with quiet fervour, had struck a blow against scum.

'So,' Nick blew on the cup of tea which Marjorie the PR girl had brought him in an institutional pea-green cup and saucer before thankfully disappearing. 'What I'm interested in is violence in clubs. I understand that you had a case of a boy who was kicked to death outside a club . . .'

'And you're going to tell me that the evidence is all wrong, that the boy who went down is a victim of racism . . .'

Kinch had a bit of trouble with his Rs so that he pronounced it *wacism*. Nick's imp of the perverse hopped monkey-like on to his shoulder, giggled and whispered *wound the wagged wocks the wagged wascal wan. Ask him if he can say it*?

Perhaps Kinch saw just the flicker of suppressed smile because his eyebrows knitted and he flicked his foot.

'Oh no,' Nick replied quickly. 'This isn't really anything to do with *Reason to Doubt*. It's an idea for a programme on clubs. The way in which bouncers operate is just one of the angles we're covering.'

'It was a totally straightforward case with Christopher Gayle. He was seen taking the boy outside. He had the boy's blood on his shoes; he was only stopped by other bouncers who gave evidence against him.'

'He had the boy's blood on his shoes?'

'Yes.'

'What about the other bouncers?'

'What about them?'

'Did they have blood on their shoes? 'Cause you would think there would be a lot of blood about, right? So if they pulled him off, then you would expect them to have blood on their shoes as well.'

Kinch frowned at Nick.

'I thought you were just looking at it from the issue of clubs . . .'

There was an uneasy silence. Nick stared straight back at Kinch. Since he had got in this far, he might as well continue and try and get the most that he could from him. He shrugged.

'It's an interesting story. The way the club was transformed from the sort of place where somebody was getting kicked to death outside to what it is now. What about him by the way? The boy who died?'

'Nathan Clemence? What about him?'

'What was he like? And why did Chris have such a hatred for him that he wanted to kill him.'

'Maybe he didn't want to kill him. He was a bouncer.

Too much testosterone, maybe . . .' Kinch shrugged and sipped at his tea.

'But, you know, what was the story? I mean, had he provoked Chris Gayle in some way? What reason was given for taking him outside in the first place?'

'Off the record?'

'Of course.'

'Nathan Clemence was scum. He was a piece of shit. Nobody wept when they turned his life-support off apart from his old dear. He was a known dealer . . .'

'So Chris Gayle took him outside for dealing drugs?'

Kinch laughed drily. 'No. It was over some girl. She complained to Chris that Nathan Clemence had been giving her grief. The story is that Chris had a bit of a thing for this girl. So he took Nathan outside and the rest – like Nathan Clemence – is history.'

'Who was the girl?'

'Does it matter?'

'Not really.'

'It was cut and dry. Motive, witnesses . . . the jury was back in before you could blink.'

'OK, well that's great, that's really informative . . .'

Nick gathered his papers and prepared to leave. Colombo-like, he had reserved his most sensitive question for last, presenting it almost as an afterthought.

'Oh there's just one thing . . . erm . . . just a detail. Chris Gayle worked for Argos Security?'

'That's right.'

'You've never had any other trouble with them?'

'No, they're a reputable local firm as they say. I'm sure no security firm is without its . . .'

'And the owner is a Mr Terry James. Do you know him?'

Kinch's eyes flickered, his voice became metallic.

'Not personally.'

'But like his company, he has a clean reputation? Which means that Chris Gayle was just the black sheep of the firm – as you were about to say before I interrupted you.'

'I might not have used that phrase. You have to be careful with that sort of language now . . .' Kinch half-smiled, half-grimaced.

'But Terry James?'

'Yes . . . a reputation . . . yes certainly.'

Nick knew that he had not received an answer but he could press the point no further without putting Kinch's back up and setting more alarm bells ringing. It was time to turn on the charm, even if it would do nothing to melt the policeman's hostility. DI Kinch would be courteous to this journalist he loathed and detested because those were the rules of the game.

'I really want to thank you for giving up your time to see me. You've been incredibly helpful . . .'

'No problem, Mr Jordan. Just give me a ring if there's anything else I can help on.'

Kinch's eyes were pale and unflinching. His handshake was hard.

'I shall certainly do that. Please thank Marjorie for arranging the interview.'

Kinch nodded and watched Nick depart without returning the false smile that Nick threw at him before closing the door.

Nick drove straight from the police station to East Ham to pick up Rosa from Marianne's. He sat in the car for a moment staring at the front door of the terraced house. The tree outside was covered in white blossom – *see what I can do*. The air was sweet with the smell of spring. Nick looked at his watch, and then got out and walked up the path to knock briskly at the front door.

'Hello, Nick.' Marianne was wearing a short denim pinafore and trainers, she had had her hair done.

'Hi, Marianne. Your hair looks nice.'

She smiled and held the door open for him to enter. Rosa was sitting in the living room with Marianne's sister Jo. Nick felt a wave of relief at the sight of Jo. He had always got on quite well with her, and Marianne was unlikely to cause a scene with Jo there. Jo was like Marianne without her defects but perhaps this was just idealising Jo or demonising Marianne; perhaps they weren't so different after all, the two sisters sitting having tea together.

'Daddy, Daddy.' The little girl ran into his arms; he picked her up and swung her and she giggled delightedly. 'We're getting a cat; we're getting a pussy cat; Mummy says we can get a cat.'

'That's nice of Mummy. What are you going to call it?' Nick brushed a curl from his daughter's face.

'Porridge,' shouted Rosa. 'It's going to be called Porridge.'

'An excellent name.'

'She wanted to call it Rosa,' Jo said. 'We've fought quite a battle on that one. How's everything, Nick? Work going well?'

'Oh well, you know . . . how's your mum?'

The two sisters glanced at each other and said nothing for an instant.

'Not too well,' Jo said quietly so that Rosa could not hear.

'Are we going in the car? Can we play music?' Rosa interrupted. 'Can we play the Spice Girls?'

'I'm afraid I'm don't have . . .'

159

'Ah but Rosa does . . .' Marianne grinned wickedly. 'Darling, go and get your tape. Daddy won't mind if you play the Spice Girls in his car.'

Nick laughed. 'Done up like a kipper. No of course Daddy won't mind. When are you getting Porridge?'

'Next week. Lucy's cat had babies and we're having one of them.'

'Lucy's cat had *kittens*,' Marianne said bending down to adjust her daughter's hairband. 'People have babies. Cats have kittens. What do dogs have?'

'Kittens,' replied Rosa hopefully.

'No. Don't be silly. Dogs have puppies.'

Driving back across London, Rosa sang along to her Spice Girls tape, in particular 'Spice Up Your Life', which even had Nick tapping his finger on the steering wheel.

'Who's your favourite Spice Girl?' Nick asked Rosa.

'Girl Power!' shouted Rosa. She obviously wasn't in the mood to answer any more questions about kittens, puppies or favourite Spice Girls.

'I've got to go to my office,' Nick said. 'I've got to pick up some papers. Will you help me?'

Rosa nodded emphatically.

The office was empty by the time Nick arrived apart from the cleaners. He swung Rosa up on to the desk and gave her some giant coloured paper clips while he looked quickly through some interview transcripts with the man who had been Deputy General Secretary of Ron Driver's union at the time of his trial.

'*Hola, linda*, what's your name?'

Nick turned to face the Uruguayan cleaner he had seen at the Sublime club, grinning at Rosa. She feigned extreme shyness and buried her head behind Nick's arm.

'Her name's Rosa. I'm sorry I don't know your . . .'

'I'm Orlando,' said the cleaner. 'I like your hairband,' he said to Rosa. 'It's very pretty.'

'I haven't seen you for a while.' Nick gathered his papers together. 'I was going to talk to you about the Sublime Club.'

The cleaner nodded. 'My son has been ill, I've been off work for a few days.'

'Oh dear. He's better now though?'

'Yes, he's getting better. He had meningitis. Let me just take your bin.'

Nick glanced down at the floor where bits of his lunch-time sandwich still lay.

'I suppose I should try and use it a bit more . . .'

The cleaner shrugged and smiled.

'It's a strange coincidence you working in both places . . .'

'I have worked in a lot of places.'

'It must be tiring, having two jobs?'

'Yes, but I don't have to work there every night. The money is good; it's better anyway than some of the other places. I might give it up soon though. It's too far away. I only started doing it to cover for a friend.'

The cleaner emptied Nick's bin into a black plastic bag and replaced it by his desk.

'What are the people like at the club. Do they get a lot of fights down there?'

'Fights? No. Well, sometimes of course. But it stops very quickly. The bouncers . . . you would not want to have a fight with them.'

'Yeah, I've seen them. What about drugs?'

'Are you making a programme about drugs?'

'No. I'm not making a programme about anything yet. I'm just trying to get a picture of what it's like down there.'

'I think it is normal. There are a few fights but not many.

There are drugs, but that is also quite normal.'

'Do the bouncers control the sale of the drugs?'

'I'm not sure about that. But I don't think a complete stranger could just walk in there and start selling drugs.'

'The people selling drugs, they do it openly?'

The cleaner shrugged again.

'It depends what you mean by openly. Not so openly. But you get to know their faces. Some of them are girls now. And if I know their faces, then I think the bouncers do as well.'

'What are the bouncers like?'

'They are like bouncers. I do not have anything to do with them. They don't talk to us really.'

'Have you ever heard them talking about a murder? About a bouncer who went to prison for beating somebody to death?'

The cleaner frowned and leaned on the end of the desk. Rosa lay on her back and started rolling towards the edge of the desk. She was getting bored. Nick put out a hand to stop her falling off the edge.

'It was a long time ago. Before I started working there. I haven't been there so long.'

'Do you know what it was about? It was about a girl, I think.'

'I don't know. I haven't heard anything about a girl.'

'You know Terry James?'

'I know enough to keep out of his way. I am just a cleaner, you know. We don't have much to do with any of these people. More with the bar staff . . .'

'The bar staff? There's the bar manager, Trevor Hooper. You know him?'

'I know him.'

'What do you think of him?'

The cleaner sighed. 'He is a clever man. He is frustrated. Sometimes that combination makes him cruel to people – some of his staff. He can be a bully.'

Nick was surprised. He could imagine DM humiliating somebody, but had not particularly felt that he had that much edge about him. He had seen his barbed tongue as more laconic and amused than vicious. Still, he did not have to work with him and he could certainly believe that DM would be impatient with slackers and intolerant of clumsiness, especially since he appeared to do everything with authority and precision. The cleaner must have seen his surprise.

'He treats his staff well also. He creates loyalty.'

'Daddy I'm hungry,' Rosa whined.

Nick glanced at his daughter rolling on the desk. She had knocked all the coloured paperclips to the floor.

'I have to take my daughter home now,' he said to the cleaner. 'But I would like to have a chat with you again. Are you in next week?'

'Every day except Thursday. That's my day off.'

'Well, I'll talk to you in the week. I'm sorry . . . you told me your name I know.'

'My name is Orlando.'

'Right, well, I'm Nick.'

The cleaner smiled and patted Rosa on the head. 'I know. *Ciao, mi amor.*'

'We're getting a cat,' Rosa said from behind Nick's arm. 'Called Porridge.'

Orlando chuckled good-naturedly. 'That's a nice name. A good name for a cat.'

He waved half-ironically at Nick and walked away. Nick watched him go. He wondered about the cleaner. He seemed to have a degree of self-possession about him which Nick found curious. His English was superior to most of the other cleaners Nick had come across but perhaps that was due to the fact that Nick had never really spoken to any of them at anything other than the most cursory of levels. But it wasn't just the language – he appeared to have something almost cultured about him; he was dignified, obviously an educated man. In a sense, this was perhaps not so surprising – within a twilight world populated by emigres and exiles you were bound to find people with interesting backgrounds if you took the trouble to look hard enough. Nick began to wonder idly about the documentary possibilities of this world; there might be something in it, especially if it could be tied into the whole issue of asylum-seekers and refugees which was still a live topic with the new government and its supposed ethical stance on such issues. But this Uruguayan was not a new arrival; he was no wide-eyed victim of ethnic-cleansing in ex-Yugoslavia struggling to earn a few pounds in order to feed his young family.

'Can we go now, Daddy?'

Nick swung his daughter up by the waist and threw her above his head. She cackled with laughter. Out of the corner of his eye, he saw the cleaner in the doorway pause and watch him.

They drove to the flat where Caitlin was waiting for them. She tickled Rosa who squealed with laughter.

'Look what I've got,' shouted the child showing her the tape.

'And who's your favourite Spice Girl?'

'Porridge,' Rosa replied.

'Right,' Caitlin looked puzzled. 'I'm not sure which one is Porridge Spice.'

'I'll tell you about it later,' Nick said putting some fish fingers under the grill and opening a can of spaghetti hoops.

Caitlin brought him a glass of wine.

'Get this down you,' she said. 'You look knackered.'

Later in the evening, with Rosa asleep and Caitlin on the phone to a friend from work, Nick sat half-watching the news. The curious thing was that there was no news and there appeared to have been no news for some considerable time. Somebody else was trying to break the world record by going around the world in a balloon; the government had announced that it would connect every school to the Internet; a plane had careered off the runway at Manchester airport and somebody had sprained their ankle sliding down the escape chute; some girls had screamed at Prince William in Canada. Even things which were of potentially terrible significance such as the rain-forest fires darkening Third World skies, the collapse of the Asian financial system, or far-right nationalists fighting in the Russian parliament, seemed oddly drab and uninvolving.

It was only nine thirty and Nick was suddenly filled with a sharp – almost painful – feeling of dissatisfaction. It was Friday evening in early spring and he was sprawled in his living room watching TV. He felt it like a sudden longing; it was unspecified desire; it was as if his blood was being pulled like a tide by some mysterious moon, each tiny red cell raising a small cry, the collective clamour making him almost dizzy. Outside in the city, things were going on: there was action and noise and movement. A siren wailed; car engines throbbed; laughter broke out into the mild air of early May. He remembered the honey-sweet air that afternoon when he had stopped to pick up Rosa. The night was just beginning for some people, while he was contemplating whether he could be bothered to wash up the plates with half-eaten fish fingers and a pan stained with the tomato sauce of spaghetti hoops.

Nick glanced at Caitlin – she seemed completely relaxed and at ease with the situation so why wasn't he? And he felt it like a sudden twist, a yearning to be back in the club he had visited during the previous week, to exchange ironic banter with DM, to hear the beat of music signalling week-end pleasure, and perhaps to see a girl with flying hair and short red dress frozen for an instant by the lights on the dance floor.

He rose from his seat and wandered into the spare bedroom where Rosa was sleeping, clutching a battered old floppy-eared dog that he had bought for her when she was born. Her looked down at his sleeping daughter and won-dered – as he supposed parents had done through the ages – with a mixture of trepidation and excitement at what lay in store for her, what the future held for this sleeping child whose dreams now probably revolved around nothing more complex than the cat she had been promised. *Cats have kittens, People have babies.*

Nick had been a child like Rosa; he never would be again. He had also slept watched by his mother or his father as they too looked back on their own lives and felt the bewilderment of their passing years, as even their youth began to recede, as events and institutions and ways of thinking that they had depended upon began to crumble and fragment. Nick remembered his father sending rockets fizz-ing into the winter sky of their garden, the smell of the smoke in the air as they tumbled invisibly back to earth, hunting with his friends the next day for the charred remains in the damp morning grass. He remembered his mother crying when her own father died – the first time he had seen one of his parents weep; he remembered singing 'Big Rock Candy Mountain' in the back of the car with his brother and sister, the bobbles on the plane trees outside his bedroom window. And cutting across these memories of a middle-class childhood in North London, there was an image of an as yet unknown man staring at the ceiling of his prison cell and a girl tied by an invisible golden halter to a grey-haired gangster.

Oh the buzzin' of the bees in the cigarette trees,
The soda water fountain . . .

Nick tried to subdue his restlessness. He thought about Caitlin sitting in the next room talking on the phone amidst her papers for work, a clever, attractive witty girl who was not dissatisfied. She went swimming during the day to stay fit; her skin smelled of chlorine; she read voraciously; she had strong opinions. She believed in things in a way that Nick did not. He was, of course, opposed to social ills such as poverty, injustice, torture, corruption – a consequence of his liberal education and bookish upbringing. But he had no concept of change; no belief in fundamental restructuring; no faith that these concepts which he opposed might one day be vanquished. That was what they were for him – concepts. Disliking the status quo, he could envision no alternative to the status quo.

Equally, the world in which he moved amused, irritated and disgusted him to varying degrees at different times. It had its fair share of charlatans, backstabbers, and arselickers, all busy with their social networking and mutual favour-swapping. Petty jealousies, lazy gossip, snobbish ignorance, playground rivalries – it was all undeniably there. And yet it was *his* world: this was the world he had been made for just as Joanne Sullivan had been destined for her world by virtue of . . . by virtue of what? He knew what Caitlin's one-syllable response would be – *people are frightened of it;*

everything else is secondary – and perhaps she was right. He had gone roller-skating with George Lamidi while they were at school but then he had changed to a private school for the Sixth Form and then to Oxford University and then to a journalism course and then to a job on the local paper and then into television.

Caitlin despised this world, although she was happy to dip her toe into it every now and again. She accepted Nick in spite of it and, Nick also suspected, because she had to have proximity to it in order to manifest her distaste. Caitlin could be more sure of herself and what she was by virtue of the fact that she had this panorama available from which she could turn with amused disdain, allowing Nick to pick his way through it with as much delicacy as was compatible with their dignity as a couple. Because Nick knew that Caitlin was often pleased with the picture they presented as a partnership; she liked stepping out with him, found their contradictions amusing rather than unsettling. This did not mean that Caitlin was false, that she denied what she secretly admired. Caitlin's loathing for Nick's world and most of the people who inhabited it was genuinely and passionately felt. She particularly detested the way in which the mediocre or inept were still granted access and allowed a voice because of their background and upbringing. She would arch one eyebrow when Nick saw somebody from the television or in the papers with whom he had been at school or university. *It's no coincidence* was one of Caitlin's favourite expressions; it was no coincidence – obviously – that Bella the Blairite was the daughter of a Hampstead Marxist, had attended a prominent North London school for girls (her mother still appeared in the papers claiming that her children had been educated at the local comprehensive), had moved up to New College, Oxford, had worked for a while

campaigning for an end to Third World debt before marry-
ing a brilliant Labour Party moderniser (already the subject
of several profiles in broadsheet newspapers – one written
by a good friend of Bella's from university) and entering her
current position advising the government on how best to
reform the welfare state. *What the fuck would she know?* This
was another of Caitlin's favourite refrains.

Rosa sighed and threw her arm above her head, lying on
her back like a sleeping lion cub. Nick bent down and kissed
his daughter gently on the forehead before leaving the room
and pulling the door half-closed behind him to re-enter the
living room where Caitlin was still on the phone. She was
giggling softly at something the person on the line had said
and just for a second it seemed unpleasantly to Nick that she
had taken advantage of his departure from the room to
subtly change the tone of the conversation, to snatch a
moment of intimacy for which his absence had been crucial.
She looked up at Nick and smiled at him over the receiver
and Nick smiled back.

'Who was that?' Nick asked as she replaced the receiver.

'Oh, it was only Tony from work. You know we go
swimming sometimes at lunchtime.'

Nick had met Tony a couple of times at Caitlin's work
events. He was in his late thirties, a pleasant-faced, stocky
black man with Chinese eyes who always appeared to be
vaguely grinning. Nick dimly remembered the hazy afternoon of a work barbecue in Brixton Hill, a squat CD player
balancing precariously on a chair playing Massive Attack,
scorched corn-on-the-cob like giant buttered wasps in silver
foil, a pale, neurotic girlfriend who kept starting rather
trivial arguments about missing corkscrews and kitchen
towels. They were housing officers and social workers and
welfare rights advisers. They liked the fact that they lived in

Brixton (Hill) and they had also established a network of urban domesticity with their talk of childminders and nurseries and holidays in Ireland. All of them had been slightly obsessive about Caitlin: she had that enviable easy mastery that made her presence important, that made people compete for her attention.

'Is Rosa OK?' Caitlin asked.

'She's sleeping.'

'How's your case going?'

'Oh, I should get back to the club again, I need to go and visit this guy in Wandsworth . . .'

Caitlin frowned. 'I meant Ron Driver.'

'Yeah, we're editing at the moment . . .'

'You may not like Ron Driver much,' Caitlin said, 'but his case *is* important. This is a really important story. I mean, I'm glad you've followed up on this other thing but a murder in a club hardly compares with the framing of a major trade-unionist.'

'You're talking rubbish. I've worked really hard on the Ron Driver programme.'

'I didn't say you hadn't worked hard. I said his case was important. In the wider sense.'

'Oh get off my back. I'm not in the mood.'

The telephone rang. They looked at each other for a moment and then Nick picked it up. It was George Lamidi.

'Trevor tells me that you went down the club.'

'Yeah, that's right. I've spoken to the officer who investigated the case as well. It was quite interesting.'

Caitlin got up and left the room.

'Well, I've got you a Visiting Order to see Chris. There's just one thing.'

'What's that?'

'Don't be . . . like . . . don't be put off by Chris. He's kind of always been a bit weird, do you know what I'm sayin'? And he's kind of weird about all of this; he didn't wanna see you at first. I don't know what he'll tell you.'

'Great. Does he want to spend the next fifteen years in prison?'

'Maybe he doesn't want to spend the next few years in prison thinking that he might get out only to be disappointed. But that's not really it. He's weird, man. You'll see what I mean.'

'George, you remember what I said to you at the beginning. I'm just nosing about. There are no guarantees that this will make a programme or even an article regardless of whether you or I think that he's innocent.'

'Just as long as you're trying. I appreciate what you've done so far. Now talk to Chris.'

Nick replaced the receiver and rested his head back staring at the ceiling. A sudden image of Caitlin and Tony alone in a swimming pool filled his head with a searing almost pornographic intensity. It was pathetic; it was juvenile, this voyeuristic jealousy, the perverse enjoyment at the idea of her being desired, of her ability to gift what was desired, of her giving in to her own desire. But it was in his head now like an unwanted nagging tune from the radio, a feeling not dissimilar to the twist of frustration he had felt earlier, his sense of leaden wings on the mild Spring evening which called for flight.

He stood up rubbing his eyes. He drank the dregs of the wine from the glass and switched off the light.

the devil's little horse

Claudio lives in a flat by the river where it makes a basin. The flat is like a child's toy: red blue and silver; all sharp angles and repetitive symmetries. At weekends, children canoe in the river basin, people stroll along the bank to have Sunday lunch. Claudio tells me that they used to hang pirates in chains near here until three tides had washed over their bodies. There is something utterly contrived about the housing complex, something that suits a well-paid computer expert.

At present, the well-paid computer expert is gracelessly recuperating from his brush with bacterial meningitis which did not kill him as I had feared so intensely but has left him impatiently convalescing in his designer riverside flat. He clicks furiously on his computer, sending off and receiving virtual sackloads of e-mail. He visits meningitis websites. I doubt whether he is too concerned about human visits but he receives them anyway from myself and from Emily, a person of whom I have grown very fond and who appears to have simply attached herself to Claudio as if it were the most natural thing in the world, as if she were a new but interesting computer peripheral. She makes him falafels and spicy chick peas and tofu provençale, and Claudio smiles weakly and begs me when she is not there to bring him meat: a roast, a hamburger, a bacon sandwich, a sausage roll – anything which contains something that once roamed about on four legs.

Sometimes, Emily and I sit in the living room chatting

173

and I wonder how I could ever have found anything repellent about her; her white skin appears now as an endearing idiosyncrasy. She has a lightness of touch and a sense of humour which is not arch or dry but rather gentle and pleasingly direct. '*Che* Orlando!' she always greets me after I explain to her that *che* is an expression common to those from the great ports of the River Plate and hence the reason the Cubans gave it to Guevara as a nickname. '*Che* Emily,' I reply.

She has a gift for talking to me as if I am Orlando Menoni, a fellow human-being, and not Orlando Menoni, father of her boyfriend. She is also fascinated by stories of our pre-exile life and the history of the Tupamaros. I teach her Tupamaro songs, much to Claudio's irritation – *Tupamaros! Compañeros! Haciendo el camino a seguir* . . . I hear her singing to herself as she chops organic aubergine and courgettes for a ratatouille. *Prenda de los Tupamaros, flor de la banda oriental*, she trills as she stuffs mushrooms with vegetarian cheese.

I tell her about the advisor to the brutal President Pacheco who had the misfortune to be kidnapped twice. First by a Tupamaro Commando in 1968, when he was released a few days later, but then again in 1971 when he was not so lucky, being consigned to a 'people's prison' for over a year.

'That's bad luck,' Emily giggles. 'He must have felt terrible the second time when he realised that it was the same people again. I bet he keeps looking over his shoulder even today.'

I tell her about the early years: the assaults on banks, the shootings of police torturers; the kidnapping of the British Ambassador Geoffrey Jackson; the prison escapes including the legendary mass departure from Punta Carretas; the seizure and execution of the CIA agent Dan Mitrione; the bloody attempt to take over the city of Pando. I tell her about the 'redistribution' of food in poor areas like the *cerro* above the city with its huge meat-chilling plant (which I now believe serves as offices for the municipality) and the old fortress looking down upon the harbour.

The conversion of the meat-chilling plant into municipal offices is not the strangest transformation to have taken place in Uruguay. The prison of Punta Carretas, where many political prisoners were housed and tortured, from which over a hundred escaped through the guts of the city and into the *Guinness Book of Records*, is now a shopping centre. But if you walk around it, past the shops selling kitchen implements, the supermarkets, the CD emporia; if you look up to the high roof of this commercial cathedral, you are able to see the narrow barred windows, the landings on which the guards used to patrol with rifles and machine guns. Violence is the midwife of consumption – forget the torture, forget the corpses, forget memory; just don't fall behind on your monthly repayments.

I tell her how everything changed in 1972, especially with the capture of our leader Raúl Sendic. That was the beginning of the end, the flight to Chile and then from one country to another with the feeling that the trap was growing ever tighter, that there was no escape, just as when Hitler's armies began to spread across Europe and recapture those who had fled Germany in the 1930s. Once, when I was working cleaning the offices of a big newspaper, I struck up a friendship with one of their critics who would give me the free copies of books sent to the newspaper for review. One book about Nazi operations against Jews in Poland described dawn raids against Silesian villages which contained German Jews banished from Frankfurt and

Hamburg. Their terror at the reappearance of their tormen-tors, men who had previously shared the same nationality, was a terror I understood all too well.

It is strange this idea of fellow-citizens torturing each other to death. I never agreed with the tendency of the nationalists within our movement to blame everything on the Americans. This is partly because I have never been tortured by an American, while a man from my home-city – a man who has listened to tango, eaten *chivitos* and walked the *ramblas* with his family – has beaten me while I swung upside down from a bar watching my blood making small red islands on the floor.

Emily asks me whether I feel responsible for some of the things that happened; whether I feel that I had a share in the descent into barbarism.

'I mean, if you shoot policemen and kidnap industrialists you create the climate where the things that happened to you were made possible.'

It is a brave question because I know people who would have thrown her out of the house just for asking it. I have heard it before many times, especially from liberals. We opened the door to the terror; we broke up their so-called democratic institutions; we created a culture of violence. The torture was bad but we brought it on ourselves and others more innocent.

'I don't feel responsible in the way you mean. We may have been naive in our belief that we could change the country through slogans and guns. But we were not the same; we were not in the same moral universe as the people we were fighting.'

Ladies and Gentlemen of the jury, I offer in evidence Alfredo Astiz going down on one knee and shooting the fleeing, terrified teenager Dagmar Hagelin. Did we devise increasingly cruel forms of torture? Did we take babies from their murdered mothers and turn them into currency? Did we lie about what we did? They called us terrorists and we were often repudiated in the same breath as those who condemned the methods of the dictatorship. But when it came to terror we were poor pupils and they had so much to teach us! In terms of remorse, I do not feel anything for the torturers we shot, nor the industrialists who had to pass a year of their time in the 'people's prison'. I save my remorse for something different, something inside me as corrosive as acid. It is similar to the remorse that survivors sometimes feel, a tremendous pain for those who became images on photographs, for those cut down with the slogans still on their lips – *the revolution is not a game, comrade.*

I teach Emily a new song:

> *Vamos a hacer que la sangre*
> *Do los muertos no sea en vano,*
> *Vamos a hacer de esa sangre,*
> *Semilla de Tupamaros.*

> *Con palabras compañeros,*
> *Con el puño desarmado,*
> *Ningún pueblo prisionero*
> *Del yugo se ha liberado.*

'Claudio hates the fact that you still clean offices,' Emily presses me on another topic. 'He says he would rather give you the money you earn.'

'Claudio is stupid. I don't want his money and I want to work. I want to be among people. Once, I might have said 'the people'. Now, it is just people. I like being with people, I don't want to sit at home.'

'You used to be a journalist though.'

'I used to work for a magazine. Before I went into exile. It was closed down anyway. I have had many jobs. Even here, I haven't always cleaned offices.'

Emily nods. 'Claudio says that you are trying to make up for the fact that the Tupamaros were all middle-class or students . . .'

I laugh at this oft-repeated criticism.

'Oh yes, and the fact that I went to a Jesuit school means that I just substituted one religion for another of course.'

Emily grins provocatively.

'Maybe it's true.'

'I certainly owe the Jesuits a great deal. They allowed me to develop sufficiently to reject the absurdity of Catholicism. I may be more sceptical now about some of my previous political beliefs but I do not question the central premise. Religion for me was mainly a matter of aesthetics; I never truly believed anyway.'

'Don't you miss working on something like journalism?'

The fact that I work as a cleaner does not mean that my mind has gone to sleep – the implicit assumption behind this by now familiar interrogation.

'But I could not be a journalist now anyway. I have worked with a lot of people whose qualifications are not recognised here.'

'Your English is very good.'

'You know that is not the point. Anyway, this business of being middle-class, it is a stupid concept. In my day, I would even have called it unscientific. But it is still a useless, a meaningless concept. What do your parents do?'

'My mum is a midwife. My dad works for British Telecom.'

'And what does that make you?'

178

'Boring, I suppose.'

'No, you're not boring.'

When Emily blushes, it is as if her head is transparent and the blood raises to the roots of her copper hair.

'My parents don't care about animal rights,' Emily says reproachfully.

'Nor do I,' I reply.

'Everything is linked,' Emily says. 'The people who ignore cruelty to animals will ignore cruelty to humans as well.'

'I don't believe that animals have rights. Strangely enough, I don't really believe in human rights either. What does it mean?'

'It means people can't take you off the streets and torture you. Put you in prison without a proper trial.'

'But that's the point. They always can if they want to. It really doesn't matter what your so-called rights are. A pig can have all the natural rights in the world and still end up roasted with an apple stuffed in its mouth. A person can have constitutional rights and they can just suspend the constitution. If they want to do something they will, if they need to do something they will.'

'Rubbish!' roars Claudio from the bedroom where he has been pretending to be asleep. 'Dinosaur! Conspiracy Theorist! You're always going on about "they". You sound like one of those militiamen in Montana. Of course there are human rights. Wake up and smell the coffee, Papi. This is Britain in the 1990s not Latin America in the 1970s. Don't tell me there's no difference.'

'I think he's on the road to recovery,' Emily says.

'I never said there was *no* difference,' I shout back. 'Get back to your computers, you nerd. Send yourself an e-mail.'

'You're still a dogmatic old bastard. You *should* have been a priest.'

'It's a career which would have at least saved me from one major inconvenience,' I retort.

There is silence. I can tell Claudio is trying to work that one out.

Emily smiles and picks up an aubergine which she is about to stuff with hazel nuts and ricotta cheese.

'Isn't it lovely,' she says stroking its dark-purple skin as if it were alive. 'Look how smooth it is, look at its colour. What do you call these in Spanish?'

'*Berenjena,*' I reply. The light from outside reflects on its dark skin, the cries of children in their canoes filter through the open window.

'*Berenjena,*' repeats Emily softly. 'Look how lovely it is.'

'And you are going to roast it, *asesina,*' I joke and then regret my flippancy.

'Tell me about Argentina,' she says to me. 'You came here from Argentina didn't you?'

I came here from the city of Buenos Aires, a city of wide avenues; a city where the sleep-patterns of the residents are a mystery; a city where people drink coffee and eat ice cream at midnight accompanied by their children. It is also a port lying at the opening to the Atlantic. One of its major football teams takes its name from the English version of Río de la Plata. The other is from the proletarian port of la Boca. River Plate vs. Boca Juniors – white-skinned money vs. dark-skinned migrants – sums up many of the conflicts of this city pulsing with life and all of its contradictions.

Argentina in 1976 was also a country where few people

cared when the military took power. The government of
Isabel Perón was almost as pathetic and inept as the Bordaberry puppet government in Uruguay. Unlike Chile, the
Argentinians were quite used to the military taking power,
hence the day of the coup had nothing in common with the
blitzkrieg which had descended on Santiago three years
earlier. They flew Isabelita out of the Casa Rosada in a
helicopter, then they packed her on to a plane to a remote
region of the country and that was that.

But not for us.

It wasn't so long ago. Can you remember what you were
doing, can you remember who you were in the late 1970s?
Were the summers hot? Were the winters cold? When I see
a horrible crime reported on the news, I always think now:
what was I doing at precisely the moment that it was taking
place? Was I drinking wine and laughing? Was I chatting to
Pancho after a shift in the Sublime Club? Was I asleep? Was
I in the bath? During the last terrifying seconds of somebody's life, was I shivering against the wind and cursing the
non-arrival of a bus? Or was I staring from a plane window
almost dumb with grief?

The repression in Argentina was different in scale from
Brazil, Uruguay, and even Chile. It was incessant; it was
psychotic; it had aspects of Nazism although there was no
Führer, not even a Pinochet. Men in Ford Falcons arrived
at houses to smash down doors and snatch young people.
Nobody was immune. The novelist Haroldo Conti vanished
as did two of Uruguay's well-known politicians in exile.
The Senator Zelmar Michelini and the former chairman of
the House of Representatives Hector Gutierrez were taken
and murdered. Buenos Aires became a holiday resort for
secret police from across the continent — there were DINA
agents from Chile, OCOA agents from Uruguay; there

were emissaries from Brazil, while Stroessner's hirelings hunted down Paraguayans.

We went to the United Nations High Commission for Refugees. They managed to get my wife and children quickly to Mexico where they would wait and then join me in whichever country would accept me. Meanwhile, I was offered a place in a UN hotel while they worked on my case which was complicated by the fact that I was wanted in my own country. Silvia was living with a friend from Montevideo who did not have any particular political affiliations. She had been to see Senator Michelini in the week before he was murdered – he had known her parents vaguely. The old social and class connections counted for nothing, however, in that whirlwind of violence. Michelini helped fellow-Uruguayans but in the end he could not help himself.

We were very scared. On the surface, things were almost normal and few of the papers made any reference to the purges taking place. It was no war – it was a hunting party. We were as defenceless as wild birds with the rifles cracking and dogs barking below. We could come tumbling down at any moment. Our persecutors gave each other nicknames; they drank Chivas Regal; they set up their hunting lodges. It was easy for them, they could indulge their every impulse.

One afternoon, Silvia came to my hotel room. We undressed each other slowly for the first time kneeling on the bed. It was a beautiful spring day and the cheap curtain of the hotel room flapped softly in the breeze. We made love on a creaking bed in a room of paper-thin walls and it was as much an act of desperation as an act of passion. She had grown thin, and as we lay naked afterwards I felt her heart beating under her ribs. A dragonfly came into the room and we watched it for a while as it bumped against the walls and the curtain, its subtle transparencies reduced to clumsiness by its entrapment. Finally, Silvia got up and guided it gently towards the window with the newspaper. Strange names for strange creatures: in Spanish, a dragonfly is called *Caballito del Diablo* – the Devil's little horse.

We lay and talked for hours until we were both cold and hungry. We walked the great avenues of Buenos Aires until our feet were sore, talking until we were exhausted, a frenzy of conversation to compensate for our separation. She showed me some of her poems which were typical of the poems written by thousands of young people of the time. Many were filled with starry rhetoric and slogans, messages of hope some of which I now know to be incontrovertibly false – *the people never tire of the struggle, truth and justice are coming, there will be a country for all or a country for none*; they spoke of her belief in love, in the future, in the country, in the struggle, in the NEW MAN, in an end to misery and suffering, in a future which would – if necessary – be paid for with the blood. But there was also a gentle poem to the child kicked out of her stomach in Chile's National Stadium. After she had read me her poems, she put them back in the leather handbag which she always carried with her and with which she had already travelled from Montevideo to Santiago to Stockholm and back to this city just across the water from the country of our birth.

'I had a cousin,' she told me once when we were sitting in a park drinking *mate*. 'He was a daredevil; he was always in trouble; always the first to accept a challenge. He was my first great love. I was six; I worshipped him. He drowned when I was still very young. He swept out to sea. Our two families were on holiday together. My uncle walked up and down the beach, looking out for his favourite son, looking far out to sea. There was even a photograph of my uncle in the paper looking out towards the horizon.'

'Did they ever find the body?'

She shook her head slowly. 'I'll never forget my uncle looking out to sea.'

'Where did it happen?'

'In Punta del Diablo,' she said.

That night was so hot and I held her in my arms just watching her sleeping, listening to her little sighs, watching her eyelids flicker as she escaped into dreams. And all across the city there were young people lying together while other men checked names and gave instructions.

One morning, I had to go to UNCHR as there was a possibility of obtaining a safe-conduct to travel to Holland. I wanted to go to Britain because even then my English was almost fluent while I could not speak a word of Dutch. When I returned to the hotel, there was an enormous commotion of shouts and screams and curses. The men in Ford Falcons had raided the hotel and taken several people away. The door of my room had been smashed down; half the contents of a brown leather bag were strewn around it; there was a slight smear of blood on the wall; a cheap curtain flapped in the breeze. Silvia had come to visit me at the moment the hunting-party arrived and they had taken her. I pleaded with people to tell me what they had seen; what they had heard; anything that might give a clue as to what had happened. But people were too caught up in their own terror to give any coherent answers. Silvia had been bundled out of the hotel with several others, both Uruguayan and Argentinian, a rough hand forced her head down as she was pushed into the back of a waiting vehicle. It was by now a familiar story.

I tell Emily all of this, give or take a few details, on a warm spring day in the flat overlooking the river.

'Did you ever find out what happened to her?' Emily asks.

'We hoped that she might have been returned to Uruguay. Some people survived that. But she was apparently seen. In the Naval Mechanics School. Hardly anybody who went there got out alive.'

'If you had been at the hotel at the time, they would have taken you both there and I would not be sitting talking to you now,' Emily murmurs.

'If she had not come to see me that day, maybe she would not have suffered what she did; she would have been safe in the house of her friend,' I reply.

'You can't think like that. It's pointless. Life is not like that,' Emily says almost harshly.

And as she speaks, a surprising coincidence takes place. A dragonfly flits into the room, the devil's little horse with its invisible rider, out of the early summer light, its wings as fragile and delicate as the most intricate spun-glass, whirring at the warm air, this little shimmering miracle of flight, an image from some early aviator's dream. It has come from the river; it has blundered into this room; it begins to bump painfully up against the window.

I am not superstitious and have no concept that this dragonfly is or even represents Silvia in any way. I do not believe in spirits, not that the warm air is filled with the soft murmurings of our lost loved ones. My dreams and memories are sufficiently complex, sufficiently unsettling to make unnecessary any appeal to the supernatural, to the persuasive poetry of whispered voices from beyond the grave. What I do think is how much the coincidence would have amused her, that if she *could* have arranged this tiny surprising incident then it would have given her great pleasure; she would have enjoyed the timing of it; she would have smiled her generous and expressive smile. She was a woman who noticed things and I think that she also taught me to pay attention to things more carefully.

'Isn't it amazing,' says Emily, 'how they never seem to be able to find the space to fly out, even though it is right next to them. They'll be there for hours if you don't . . .' she picks up one of Claudio's computer magazines and steers the little creature towards its liberty, back towards the river '. . . help them.'

That night I stay in Claudio's spare room and I lie in bed thinking of the day's conversation. I think about Rosa Luxemburg and how her beaten body was tossed carelessly into a freezing canal. Splash! A warm-blooded person of fierce intellect reduced to a floating object by a corporal's rifle-butt. I think about the hotel room in Buenos Aires with the cheap flapping curtain that I will never see again. I think about the ultra-cruelty of disappearance – the intensely deliberate way in which maximum psychological damage is inflicted on survivors who can only imagine the fate of the person so deeply loved and missed. That Silvia suffered pain, humiliation and terror is certain. But I do not know how exactly she suffered it, and hideous images present themselves to me – images which are probably not exaggerated.

The testimony placing her in the Naval Mechanics School was trustworthy. It came from somebody who spent a few minutes with her and to whom she whispered her name and nationality. *My name is Silvia Ortiz. I am Uruguayan.* She was broken, said this witness; she was already broken. She was *hecho pedazos*. And when I heard those terribly exact and appropriate words, something also broke inside me – the clatter of horses straining for each corner of a dusty square – and I knew it would never mend again.

No Harald Edelstams were allowed to stalk the Naval

Mechanics School castigating the torturers, there was not even a Major Lavandero on whose conscience as a human being such a person could operate. The preferred method of disposing of people at this establishment – after sessions of brutal torture conducted for gratification rather than information – was to fly out over the estuary at night and throw them into the sea. Often they were still conscious and fingermarks around the plane doors testified to their desperate struggle for life, their fight not to be cast out flailing their useless heavy human limbs in that horrible drop, that terrifying darkness.

So my son can call me naive and old-fashioned and they can turn the Punta Carretas prison into a shopping centre. People can ignore the barred windows and the walkways for the guards as they make their purchases; they can talk about reconciliation and letting scars heal. Generals can become Senators-for-Life and only a few lunatics will howl with rage. But I don't care if people no longer want to hear about it, if it saddens them too much, tires them out, makes them a little depressed, or if they've heard it all before. *What's the point in going on about it? Yeah, yeah, change the record.* The shopping centre was a prison. The silver river is filled with corpses. The child swinging its satchel was stolen from its real parents and sold. And out on the streets – talking, laughing, unrepentant – are the men who did this, the men of the blows and the *picana*, the men who took a half-drugged, torture-broken young woman and threw her hooded body from a doorless plane into the sea. She was not just a photograph, she was Silvia Ortiz; she was Uruguayan. I watched her sleeping, I touched the curve of her back, I listened to stories from her childhood. She will never return to me but she makes me what I am.

I get out of bed and pad through to the kitchen to find a

glass of water. As I walk quietly through the flat, I hear the
sound of Emily and Claudio whispering and laughing. I hear
Emily giggle and say "shhh, what about your dad.' And I
hear Claudio say, 'he wouldn't care even if he heard. He's
probably thinking up new songs to teach you. I think he
fancies you.' And Emily laughs and says 'Don't be horrible.
His stories are really interesting.' Then I hear the sound of
movement and breathing and the first faint murmurs of
pleasure and I move quickly into the kitchen and pull the
door behind me so that I cannot hear.

I know I shouldn't hold this conversation against them,
they don't mean me any harm, but I feel a sick sense of
belittlement, of betrayal. In a sense I find Emily's reply more
disturbing although I am sure that it was not intentional –
she did not mean to imply that I was just an old man with
some surprisingly interesting stories, it is just her way of
expressing herself. I have also been guilty of such clumsiness, of shortcuts in conversations which do not express
what I really mean. Still, I am hurt. I take my glass of water
and stand by the kitchen window watching the lights from
the buildings breaking and reforming on the dark river basin
outside where the canoeists once splashed and yelled. And I
know that for all my passionate desire for revenge, my
outpourings of anger, I am just a tired, ageing and powerless
man staring at my greying reflection, mocked by my dreams
and my memories. History marches ruthlessly on; the dead
are dead, and young people lie in each other's arms laughing
at those they imagine to be sleeping.

visiting order

Nick woke up worrying how to get to Wandsworth Prison. He hated waking up in this way, with whatever was going to dominate his day already at the forefront of his mind at the moment of opening his eyes. Usually, money worries did this to him, especially when he heard the post in the morning and knew for certain that a thin bank letter or a fat bill was lying on the mat. Even worse was some oversight on the TV programme, something he had forgotten to check or verify. It would nag away at him, filling him with a deep impatience, a need to resolve it as quickly as possible.

Caitlin stirred in her sleep. Since their sharp exchange about the Ron Driver case, there had been a slight chilliness between them. Nick was still irritated by her intervention and her suggestion that he was not taking it seriously enough.

'What time is it?' Caitlin murmured.

'It's seven. I'm going to see if Rosa's awake. She'll need her breakfast.'

Over breakfast, Nick tried to work out the best way of getting to the prison since he was leaving Caitlin the car for the day as she was taking Rosa to her nursery on the way to work. He was forced to conclude that there was no best way from Kentish Town and was almost tempted to splash out on a taxi to get the whole thing over with as quickly as possible.

'Listen Nick,' Caitlin spoke briskly but in fairly neutral tones: 'this party in Shoreditch tonight, I might skip it. I could really do with a night just watching TV and sorting out some papers. You go though.'

Rosa was returning to Marianne's that evening after nursery and Nick had been looking forward to going out. Will had invited them to a party in Shoreditch which he had promised Nick would be good. It was in a massive loft; there wouldn't be many people; it would just be really chilled. Nick wanted to speak to Will and he certainly did not want to spend another night in the house feeling the frustration that he had experienced the night before.

'It won't be mental or anything,' Nick replied. 'It's just a few people, we could just go and have a drink. Anyway, you stayed in last night just watching TV and sorting out some papers. In fact, we've been doing that for the whole week.'

He half-expected Caitlin to snap at him but she appeared determined to remain calm, especially in front of Rosa who was playing with the milk from her cereal with her spoon, dripping it back into the bowl so that most of it splashed back out on to the table.

'Stop it . . .' Nick said to her sharply. Caitlin wiped up the milk and ruffled Rosa's hair. Rosa stared belligerently at her father.

'I just really don't feel like going out at the moment to that sort of thing. You go though. You know what I'm like. I get these moods, I'd rather just stay in and read or whatever.'

Rosa threw her spoon deliberately on to the floor. 'I want to play with Babe,' she said. 'I want my piggy.' After Rosa had become obsessed with the film *Babe*, Caitlin had bought her a battery-powered pink furry porker which shuffled noisily along the floor, jerking its little trotters, stopping to wrinkle its nose and make piggish noises. It had annoyed the hell out of Marianne who complained that the noise drove her crazy, something which Nick could understand. Marianne also said that it was vulgar and non-educational, which was really just because she knew that Caitlin had bought it. Marianne's attempts to break, hide and lose the pig had prompted such hysteria from Rosa that, in the end, the compromise was exile and it had had to come and live with Nick and Caitlin. Caitlin always laughed uproariously at Marianne's stupidity in allowing the pig to get to her and in not understanding that everything that drove her crazy about it was what made it so entertaining to a small child.

'You can play with your pig another time,' said Nick. 'Just eat your breakfast. Come on, Caitlin, it's good to get out. Maybe you'll feel differently tonight.'

'No. I'm just going to go swimming after work tonight.'

'With Tony?'

'Maybe,' Caitlin glanced up at Nick over her toast. 'So what?'

Nick shrugged. 'So nothing . . .' but he couldn't resist continuing, jealousy prodded him into foolishness. 'He's getting very into swimming all of a sudden. I don't remember him having such a compulsion to swim.'

Caitlin stood up and put her hand on her hip.

'And what do you remember about him, Nick? Given that you hardly directed two words to him the one time you met him and described the people at the party as a bunch of losers.'

Nick had forgotten about the aftermath of the Brixton Hill barbecue. He had been slightly drunk and had thoughtlessly given his judgement, causing Caitlin considerable outrage. Nick had had to spend the whole of the return journey attempting to retract or at least modify a statement which was hardly susceptible to a variety of interpretations. *You don't even have the courage of your convictions* Caitlin had pronounced contemptuously as he wriggled around trying to avoid the disapproval that he had foolishly brought down upon himself.

'I remember he was pretty boring and he had a horrible girlfriend,' Nick said now provocatively.

'Well, I suppose it's lucky that you don't have to have anything to do with him then.'

Nick knew that a strange rational calm and extreme anger often walked hand in hand with Caitlin. He knew that he was treading on very thin ice.

'I want my piggy!' wailed Rosa.

'I told you to eat your breakfast! Eat your breakfast and not another word. Do you hear me?'

Rosa began to cry. Caitlin gave Nick a look of contempt and scooped her out of the chair.

'Let's go and find piggy,' she said. 'But you mustn't sit on him or you'll break his legs. He's only got small legs like you've only got small legs. What would happen if I sat on you? Eh?'

Rosa started to giggle and Nick was left alone in the kitchen. He began to clear up irritably as he heard the pig begin its noisy shuffle around the living room and Rosa squeal with laughter. Caitlin came back in and glanced at Nick.

'I'll be off soon,' she said coldly, 'so you had better say goodbye to Rosa.'

'You're definitely not coming tonight then?'

'No. I think it would be good for you to have some time on your own.'

'That's very thoughtful of you. Maybe you're right.'

Nick stomped out of the kitchen, his temper hot inside him.

'I mean next season it's going to be between three or four teams really. Chelsea will be there, of course, but I can't see any more teams being in with a shout . . . hi, Nick. Can't see poor old QPR getting back into the Premiership.'

Nick nodded brusquely at Mark as he threw his jacket behind his chair. He resisted his impulse to have a go at Mark for jabbering away about football. Nick hated coming to work with an unresolved argument and would often phone Caitlin during the day, not because he was genuinely contrite but because he found it hard to concentrate when he was fuming and conducting silent debates with an invisible adversary.

'Mrs Clemence has agreed to an interview,' Mark said. 'She's a bit of a horror. Wanted to know how much you were going to pay her. But she can do it next week. She lives in Manor Park. You just have to ring and confirm.'

'That's good, Mark. Well done.'

Nick glanced down at his interview transcripts.

They talked about the enemy within and it was really like they had declared war on us. I have no doubt that Ron Driver was the victim of an elaborate setup because he had supported the miners and because he continued to support industrial action by his members. Everybody knew that Ron Driver wasn't corrupt. People have forgotten what it was like in the 1980s: there were some very shady goings-on, a lot of people working in the shadows . . .

Nick picked up the papers and headed for the edit suite.

The journey to the prison that afternoon was as bad as Nick had feared. Wandsworth was a terrible borough, Nick decided, with its right-wing council, its most depressing of prisons and its virtually non-existent public transport. Even the name sounded depressing. The day was miserably over-cast and drizzly as well; people stood hunched by the bus stops as if oppressed by the city and the thick grey-white canopy of cloud hanging over head.

In the end, Nick chose to walk a long way rather than stand waiting for a bus. He remembered to stop and buy cigarettes from a small newsagent's with pornography stacked so tightly on the top shelf that it was beginning to slide off and which smelt of papers and stale sweets. Nick normally smoked Silk Cut but decided to buy Bensons.

A familiar sense of foreboding clawed at him as he saw the long wall of the Victorian prison, the barred windows. He remembered a time when he had been working in Manchester during the Strangeways riot. He had driven past the prison and seen the shadows of men on the roof and it had filled him with a strange terror. It had been the surreal anarchy of it, those shadows moving about where they were not supposed to be, the coldness of the night and imagining what mayhem was taking place inside the prison before the inevitable reimposition of order by the authorities.

Nick waited in the queue with the other visitors, watching the dogs with their tongues lolling listlessly, enduring the tedium of the search until he finally passed through into the section where the prisoners were waiting in their uniform of sweatshirts and trainers, the chairs in front of them gradually filling up with wives, girlfriends and children, nodding and smiling as the first eye-contact was made. The room smelled of washed floors and even the screws looked bored.

He chose a screw who bore an uncanny resemblance to Mr Barraclough in *Porridge* to ask for Chris Gayle and was pointed towards a tall man, lounging on his plastic chair and staring around casually. He was a handsome, lean, long-legged man, golden-skinned with shoulder-length locks and a faint goatee. Nick noticed that he had very large feet.

'Chris Gayle?' Nick held out his hand. The man blinked slowly and took it rather limply.

'George sent you,' he started.

'That's right,' Nick sat down. He offered Chris a cigarette but it was waved contemptuously away.

'I don't pollute my body or my mind with poison,' Chris said.

'Right,' Nick said, already getting an uneasy feeling about the prisoner.

'Tobacco is for fools. They used to send us off to wars. The battle of the Somme – we died in our millions. Now they kill us with those,' Chris continued sternly.

OK so you don't smoke, you self-righteous fucker. Do you think I care? Nick hated evangelists of any type.

'So, erm, I just wondered if we could start with what happened the night of the murder,' He began.

'You're presuming it was murder.'

Nick stared at Chris. He was beginning to get impatient. Chris stared back at him. There were golden flecks in his eyes. They were like the eyes of a large cat.

'Well, he didn't stamp on himself,' Nick half-snapped. 'Somebody did it.'

'It depends on your definition of murder. What this society calls murder might be something different altogether. You have to work with your own definitions. What *you* might think is murder might be something quite different in my book.'

Prison had obviously brought out the philosopher in Chris. Nick was worried that they were going to spend the whole hour arguing about whether jail was a metaphor for the human condition, and whether stone walls and iron bars were necessary for prisons and cages. He became even more worried when Chris began to expand on the presence of a protecting angel in which he trusted completely and which controlled his destiny whatever Nick did or didn't do under George's instigation.

'Why do you think George is so keen for me to help you?' Nick asked when he could get a word in edgeways.

'George thinks I saved his life once. But I was just an agent. We used to work together. He thinks he owes me his life. You can ignore your angel but it's always there.'

Nick made a mental note to ask George about this since he was more likely to get a straight answer from him. He was desperate to bring Chris back to the topic of the murder and away from angelic bodyguards.

'Do you know Joanne Sullivan?' he asked.

This at least had the effect of giving Chris a jolt. He stared at Nick with near-hostility as if Nick had no right to be using her name.

'Yeah I know her.'

'Was the fight with Nathan Clemence to do with her? Were you arguing about her?'

Chris glared ferociously at Nick and kissed his teeth.

'Arguing about her . . . with him? With that pussy? No man, you're miles off course; you've lost your navigator; you're all out at sea; you're shipwrecked. I'll tell you something now: I ain't going to mention her name again. And I'm going to ask you politely not to mention her name either. I took that boy outside because somebody made a complaint about him. So I took him outside and I give him a few licks, I bust his nose which is why I have the blood on my shoes that the coppers make such a fuss about. Then the people come out and tell me to stop, that's enough. So I stop and I go back inside. But when I leave him, he still standing and cussing me holding his big ugly nose. No way my man dead when I leave him.'

'Was it Joanne Sullivan who made a complaint about him?'

Chris kissed his teeth again and rolled his head away ostentatiously.

'OK, you don't want to talk about her. What about Terry James?'

'My executioner walk behind me. Do you know what I'm sayin'?'

'Not really.'

'In China or somewhere, when they sentence someone to death, their executioner walk behind them with a sword. They never know when it going to happen. Might be hours, might be days, might be weeks. Suddenly, boom, chop off his head. But he never know when it going to happen and that drive him crazy. But I ain't gonna go crazy 'cause my angel is watching over me.'

Nick sighed inwardly. He was probably going to have to put up with a lot of this gobbledegook to get the smallest nugget of information. Still, at least he had heard first-hand now the basics of what had happened. Chris had admitted that he had taken the boy outside and given him some slaps. Now the question was whether he was telling the truth about the condition in which he left him.

'If you didn't kill Nathan Clemence then who did?'

'I'm in this prison because somebody name me. They say I did it when they know that the most I do is bust his nose, something everybody had been wanting to do for some time. But if I start naming people, then what am I? I'm as bad as them. I've got inner peace and they ain't when the judgement

197

day come. Do you read the Koran?'

'Not recently, no. When you left Nathan in the alley, did all the bouncers go back in with you.'

Chris nodded. 'It weren't me that killed him but it weren't them neither, you know what I'm sayin'? They all come back in with me. Hey, maybe it was the police. You thought of that? Won't be the first time they do something and frame up an innocent black man. Then you'll have found your Rodney King and you can become a celebrity and clear my name.'

Chris began to laugh. Nick decided to ignore him.

'The other bouncers say they saw you continue beating him. That it took four of them to get you off him and that by the time they had managed to do so, Nathan Clemence was already unconscious.'

'Well, dat is a wicked lie. And they will suffer damnation and brimstone . . .' Chris actually broke into giggles at his mock patois as if there were a sane Chris somewhere inside him and it was all an elaborate joke.

'When did you first know that Nathan was in a coma?'

'When the police came in. Half an hour maybe after I got back in.'

'They arrested you straight away?'

'Yeah, somebody had already told them.'

'Why do you think they lied?'

'Man is a feeble instrument.' Mad Chris was struggling to reassert himself after two straight answers from Sane Chris. He wanted to launch himself back into the kind of safe, vague reassuring gibberish sometimes found on the back of album covers or in interviews with musicians: lazy profundities about Creators and Masterplans that curiously invited respect rather than ridicule. Mad Chris was up and running again now. 'But I have greater knowledge now, I have dedicated myself to the pursuit of wisdom . . .'

'Chris! Why did they lie about you? What reason would they have?'

'They didn't have a choice. I don't hold it against them. You can only truly blame somebody when they choose to do you wrong.'

'Why didn't they have a choice?'

Chris laughed. 'I think you'll be able to work that one out for yourself. Say hello to my man the Nigerian when you see him. Tell him my angel still looking after me. Tell him, so far so good. Tell him to find Chick.'

'Who's Chick?'

'He's an ugly Glaswegian motherfucker. Tell him Chick knows.'

Visiting time was over.

'Stupid mad fuck,' George Lamidi said when Nick had got back to the office and called him on his mobile.

'Well, it wasn't a complete waste of time. At least I got a reasonably coherent story about what was involved that night. He says he saved your life once by the way. Is that true?'

'Yeah, he did. He ain't always been like that you know. All that stuff about angels and shit. He ain't stupid.'

Nick decided not to point out that that was exactly how George had described him just two seconds earlier. George clearly felt the kind of right normally reserved for families to say what they like about each other, while fiercely denying an outsider the right to do likewise.

'How did he save your life?'

'Some geezer was going to shoot me. We had thrown him out of this club and he come back with a shooter. Chris ran at him and got it off him. Nearly got shot himself. But Chris can handle himself, man. When he goes, he's something else.'

'Some people clearly think that he was "something else" with Nathan Clemence.'

Nick was aware that he sounded slightly priggish and self-righteous. There was silence for a moment from George.

'It weren't him,' George said. 'I was hoping you would know that by now.'

'I believe you,' Nick replied seriously. 'But it doesn't matter what I do or don't believe. What matters is whether other people can be persuaded to believe it. And at the moment, frankly, there's nothing that I can see that will make them believe that.'

'So why are you going on with it?'

'I don't know,' Nick replied. He put the phone down and stared at an interview transcript on his desk.

They kept saying that if I confessed then I might not go to prison, just a suspended sentence or something. But I could never admit to that. I've given my whole life to the movement and they were saying that I'd been stealing money; I couldn't believe it. I thought well soon everybody's going to realise that this is just a joke. Even my members who didn't like me much, they were coming up to me and saying it was a joke. But then I was in the dock and the jury came in and said "guilty" and I wasn't laughing . . . I wasn't laughing then.

Nick sighed and ran his hands through his hair. Caitlin was wrong. Just because "they" were slightly less clearcut in Chris Gayle's case, it didn't make the story any less interesting. He had a feeling that it would make a better article than a TV programme, but he was hooked now and wanted at least to come to some resolution on what had really happened. He wanted to go back to Sublime.

Scoreditch

Will was at the party and so was Karl. Nick took the industrial caged lift to the top floor and found them drinking vodka and doing lines of coke from a massive table that ran widthways across the space of the loft. Karl was with a new girl although she looked more or less like Katie from the roof-garden party where Nick had first met George and where he had heard about Chris Gayle. It was startling sometimes how time passed and experience accumulated, how he had visited Chris in prison that day. Karl's new girlfriend was called Bobbie. 'Like in *The Railway Children*,' she said archly. Bobbie was pretty and petite with a squeaky voice. She worked in publishing, which explained Karl's previous invitation to the hooligans book launch. She had a writer in tow but he was not a hooligan or even a writer about hooliganism; he had just written a short novel called *Crack*.

'What's it about then?' Nick asked unkindly.

The writer was wearing Dolce and Gabanna glasses and a polo-neck sweater. He glowered at Nick and did not answer him.

'It's about a couple who completely fuck up their lives on crack,' Bobbie squeaked. 'She has to become a prostitute in Kings Cross to finance their habit. Then he does an armed robbery.'

'Wild,' said Nick.

'Where's Caitlin?' Will asked.

Nick was feeling strangely light-headed, almost hyper.

He hadn't eaten anything that day and the alcohol was going straight to his head.

'She's being a moody snob. She thinks this sort of party is full of wankers.' He looked around. 'Can't think why. Who cares anyway?'

'Do you want a line?' Karl asked him. Nick glanced down at it on the table. It didn't look unpleasant or threatening.

'Go on,' he said. 'I'm knackered. It'll just be a pick-me-up. I deserve it after today.'

Will raised his eyebrows. He looked like he wanted to say something to Nick but then just shrugged and smiled almost sadly.

The party was to celebrate the birthday of a girl Nick did not know. She had worked on a controversial video involving the lesbian dwarf and the schoolgirl about which Karl had been so delighted. The loft was vast, with speakers fixed high in the rafters and there was a set of decks in one corner of the room. There were bottles of black-label vodka and tequila placed strategically around the huge space; there were great bunches of sweet-smelling flowers, some of which were strewn loosely across the table. Nick felt the cocaine dropping down the back of his throat and nearly retched. He already regretted his lapse and reached for some tequila and orange juice. Somebody was walking around with plates of baked pears in a raspberry sauce. Nick waved his away. He was leaning on something that proved unstable; when he looked down he found it was an antique rocking horse from some long-ago nursery, a few strands of rough black hair all that was left of its mane.

'How's it going?' Will offered him the tequila bottle.

'Not bad. Will, do you fancy coming with me to that club again?'

'What, tonight?'

'Yeah, I want to check a few things out. Talk to that guy Irvine again.'

'But tonight? How the fuck are you going to get there?'

'Cab it. It's not so much. I can stick it on expenses. Come on, what are you going to do, stay here all night just get nutted?'

'Well, I had thought about that as quite an attractive option actually.'

'Look around. How bored are you going to get?'

They took in the party-scene. People were dancing or sitting in little groups chatting and laughing. It all looked pretty harmless. Will turned back to Nick.

'What are you getting so wound up about? These people aren't your enemy. Look around yourself. They're just young kids getting off their arse and making some money. Most of them don't come from super-privileged backgrounds. They're enjoying themselves. I never knew you had a Puritan streak, Nick.'

'It's not that . . . it's . . . there's just something missing. Don't you find there's something missing.'

Nick was already drunk. He had been gulping back tequila and he could feel an inability to communicate coupled with a reluctance to give up trying to do so – a combination which nearly always produced a stream of nonsense.

'What's missing?'

'It's all surface; there's no depth.' Nick thought of Caitlin gliding effortlessly through the water; her well-practised lengths; the somersault and kick-off at the end of the pool; drops of water clinging to her bare shoulder. He thought of Tony watching her, Tony pulling the straps of her costume away from her shoulders, and quickly banished those thoughts.

'Well you know, Nick, it's just a party. You can hardly expect them to be sitting around talking about whether New Labour are selling out the unions or the spiritual void as we approach the Millennium. Are you trying to make up for the fact that Caitlin's not here?'

Nick sighed. He knew that the note that he was striking was clumsy and self-important. He knew that the question implicit in Will's response was: *What right do you have to criticise? What do you do that makes you so different?* And Will was right on all counts – Nick usually played this game to the full and these were just people enjoying themselves; he did not even know them, had no real idea about what they did or did not think, how they constructed the foundations of their lives. And yet . . . and yet. Nick did not particularly like Ron Driver but there were poignant phrases from the transcript that niggled away at him. *I gave my whole life to the movement . . . I wasn't laughing then.* Chris Gayle was a lunatic but he was sitting in prison because a careless judicial system had probably opted for plausibility rather than reasonable doubt. The most important item on the news was a businessman – *trust me, trust me, trust me* – attempting to get around the world in a balloon. It was as if there was a kind of ruthlessly quiet apartheid, a grinning segregation dividing those whose stories counted and whose opinions mattered from those who were to be ignored. And Nick, who was making a programme about Ron Driver and might do something with Chris Gayle's story; Nick felt suddenly as if he had sticky wings, as if none of it mattered in the larger scheme of things.

'Take no notice of me, I'm just tired, you're right. But come with me down this club. I hate going to places like that on my own. And we can talk to Richard Irvine about this article your mate's doing. We had a laugh last time didn't we?'

Will laughed. 'OK, but I want a cab back as well. And I'm not going yet.'

'No of course not.'

Bobbie wandered back over with her writer in tow.

'Got any Salvador?' the writer asked with a surly contempt.

'What?' Nick snapped irritably although he knew what he was being asked. There was a kind of overarching vulgarity about this person which extended to his ridiculously fake accent.

'Salvador Dali, Charlie,' Bobbie chirruped.

'Oh . . . erm . . . no . . . sorry, mate. Have you got any crack? We could all pipe up.'

'I don't do crack any more,' the writer glared at Nick.

'Well I think that's very sensible. It might have been "My Crack Hell" for you. You might have ended up selling your arse in Kings Cross or having to stage an armed robbery instead of writing novels.'

'It's a great buzz though, one of the best, I have to admit,' Bobbie said. 'You need plenty of downers for the come-down. Valium, Rohipnol . . .'

'I didn't think Rohipnol had any purpose other than for date-rape,' Karl said.

'So what's the hilarious rhyming slang for Rohipnol?' Nick asked. 'Helmut Kohl? Grassy Knoll? For whom the bell tolls?'

'It tolls for you, mate,' scowled the writer.

'You're probably right,' Nick answered and turned away from the barbed tedium which he had helped to initiate. 'Just give me a shout when you're ready, Will.'

Coming out of the toilet, he saw a strange sight. In the

narrow street beneath the window, a fat man with a tracksuit holding a briefcase was being punched hard in the face by another man. He wasn't fighting back, he wasn't even protesting or attempting to shield himself from the blows. There was a third man with a suit who was acting as lookout and intimidating anybody who passed and turned to watch. Finally, the man doing the punching stopped and took a handkerchief out of his pocket and passed it solicitously, almost tenderly, to his victim in the tracksuit. The man held the handkerchief to his bleeding face and was then led away – again without offering any resistance – both men holding an arm but as if steadying rather than detaining him. What was going on? What was in the briefcase? Nick felt dizzy and unsettled by the scene. Already edgy from the line of coke, he wanted to get away.

Will got bored of the party rather more quickly than he had thought and they made their way across London in a cab driven by a figure who gabbled so incessantly and drove so erratically that Nick suspected him of similar consumption patterns to the people in the party they had just come from. They had to stop several times to consult his giant *A-Z* with torn pages falling out of it but finally ended up beneath the neon sign of the jitterbugging couple.

Richard Irvine was in expansive mood when they were escorted up the cordoned-off stairs and shown into his office. He insisted on refunding them the money that they had paid to get in and had bottles of beer brought up for them. Will was correct in thinking that he would be delighted by the chance to offer another quote. As he was in full flow, however, the door to his office opened and the man that Nick had assumed to be Terry James swept in. He was wearing an expensive cashmere coat and was followed by Joanne Sullivan plus another bouncer who looked as if he had the words Canning Town running all the way through him like a stick of rock.

'These are a couple of boys doing a piece on good practice in clubs and the scene out East,' Irvine explained to the silver-haired man with blue eyes like stained glass. 'This is Terry who deals with our security.'

Nick tried not to look at Joanne Sullivan, who sat on a chair at the back of the room with crossed legs, folded arms and a distant, amused smile on her face. She was wearing a light dress with thin straps over the shoulders and black high-heeled sandals with a single buckle.

'I met you before,' she said. 'You was talking to Trevor.'

'That's right,' Nick said.

'Trevor who?' Terry James asked.

'Trevor the bar manager?' Richard Irvine asked.

'That's right,' Nick nodded again.

Terry James pulled out a small plastic bag filled with cocaine and scooped some out on to the table with a gold credit card. Irvine glanced nervously at Nick but Nick made a small gesture to show that he was unruffled by this. Terry James did it without blinking, without even thinking of seeking Irvine's permission or approval and certainly without caring that Nick and Will were a pair of journalists. He looked up at them with a small hand motion to the powder on the table, asking them if they wanted some. Nick glanced at Will and they both nodded. He cut out five large lines. Since there were six people in the room, Nick wondered who was excluded. It turned out to be the bouncer, who hadn't uttered a word. Terry James rolled a fifty-pound note and handed it first to Joanne Sullivan.

'Bet you haven't had charlie like that in a while,' Terry James said when they had done their lines.

'No, that's fucking great stuff,' Will said.

'Nobody plays hopscotch over this gear,' boasted James.

Nick couldn't say anything, which was fortunate because his imp of self-destruction was instructing him to tell James that his coke was rubbish, that it had been morris danced on, and that he could shove it up his gangster arse. But the line was too big and the coke was too uncut to permit any speech at all. Nick was terrified that he was going to retch; his throat was numb and he wanted to gag. He took a long pull on the cold beer in front of him and lit a cigarette without daring to inhale for a few seconds. He took his mind off it by making a quick mental note about Terry James. Although he gave an appearance of utter authority and control, he was still showy enough to put on this little exhibition and to partake himself.

As if he felt that some kind of press conference were taking place and that his contribution was called for, Terry James took the floor from Richard Irvine. He kept fingering his tie.

'Order. That's what we've brought to this club. Without order you're fucked. There used to be all sorts going on here. Look at it now: people come here to have a good time; they don't have to worry about nutters or people trying to kick off 'cause somebody nudged them. We won't have that and people know it. What they do outside the club is their business but not in here. It's comfortable; it's pleasant . . .' Terry James paused as if the last word were a delicacy to be savoured, as if 'pleasant' were the highest accolade possible, the Oscar, the Nobel Prize of adjectives. 'Yes, pleasant. Nice sofas, friendly barstaff, good clean toilets. It's not really my sort of music but it's uplifting; people come here and they relax. That's what it's all about.'

Will and Nick nodded vigorously. There was something rather hypnotic about James and his emphatic voice which was both curiously soft and vehement at the same time. He reminded Nick of the head of year at the school he had attended with George Lamidi. Mr McLean never shouted; when he was called to an unruly classroom his voice dropped almost to a whisper. He instilled total terror. But there was also something beguiling about the way James pronounced the place comfortable and pleasant – even Richard Irvine was nodding his head benignly as if he had just had it pointed out to him. Only Joanne Sullivan sat at the back with a sceptical, almost contemptuous expression on her face. She was staring at Nick and Nick wondered whether she was doing it to unsettle him. He tried looking back at her but she met his gaze fully until he became so embarrassed that he had to look away.

'People stopped wanting to come here a few years ago,' Terry James continued his oration. 'The Old Bill was coming in most weekends . . .'

'What's your relationship like with them now?' Nick asked.

Terry James paused just long enough to show that he had noted that this was an interruption as well as a question. He flicked his wrist so that his thin chain shook free and stared at it for a moment.

'They're good as gold,' he said. 'Because we've brought order to the place. That's important to them as well.'

I bet it is, thought Nick. And it starts with a neat resolution to a murder so that they don't have any headaches.

'Will you do me another little line, babe?' Joanne Sullivan asked.

Terry James held up the palm of his hand to demonstrate that everything would be done in his own time. Nick was growing restless and he knew that Will was as well. He could also sense that Richard Irvine was pleased that it had all passed off OK but that he would rather winds things up now. Nick glanced at Will.

'Well, that's great . . .'

'What's this all for?' Terry James asked suddenly.

'Oh, it's just one of the Sundays – you know that supplement *City Life*. It's a feature on different clubs. You know, what are the toilets like, are the bouncers friendly . . .'

Everybody turned to look at the bouncer still standing beside the door. Terry James laughed.

'You're friendly ain't you Roger? You're a pussycat. Your boat's no fucking picnic but you can't help your genes I suppose. We've taught him how to say "goodnight, safe journey home". It was an uphill struggle to make him sound like he meant it but we got there in the end. One thing that's important to me is good manners. All my staff here have to have good manners, don't matter if they're on the door or the bar or the cloakroom. That's essential. That makes people feel comfortable.'

The bouncer grinned. Joanne Sullivan rolled her eyes. All *my* staff? Freudian slip there, Terry, Nick thought. Well, there was nothing particularly Freudian about it, but it illustrated something that DM had pointed out, that Terry James was the *de facto* owner of Sublime. He had waltzed into Irvine's office without knocking, chopped out cocaine on his desk, and taken over his interview.

'Go on, babe, just another little line,' Joanne Sullivan dimpled and whined simultaneously. It was clear that she had to play up the little girl factor when James was around. James got his bag of coke out and began the procedure again. Nick and Will stood up.

'Well, thanks for everything . . . I won't have another one thanks —'

'Course you will.' James made a long snake of coke on the desk and then swiftly and skilfully segmented it into five more enormous lines – if this were Joanne Sullivan's idea of little then Nick would hate to see what a binge was like. Terry James handed Nick the note.

'One for the road. Go on . . . that's right . . . ah you lightweight . . . have another shot at it . . . that's it . . . wipe your nose, boy . . . see your mate's had more practice.'

Nick felt the top of his scalp start to prickle and tingle. He had to get out of this office, talk to Will, dance, anything. Little fragments of the coke had fountained out over his shirt-front. He picked them off with his fingertip and rubbed them on his gums feeling stupid.

'Well, I've got a few errands to run,' Terry James said standing up also. 'I'll be in a bit later, Richard. Come on, Roger.'

He crossed the room to Joanne Sullivan and put his hands on her shoulders, began murmuring gently in her ear. She held out her hand and he deposited the bag of coke in it. Nick and Will nodded at Richard Irvine and escaped out of the office and back down the stairs towards the music.

'Back again, Mr J. Anybody would think you were starting to enjoy yourself here.'

Nick turned his back from the bar to find DM grinning at him.

'Vodka and tonic?' DM asked.

'Oh . . . erm . . . no . . . I'm drinking beer.' Nick held up his nearly full bottle. He stared at the fridges stacked with beer and wine, the upside-down spirits, the neon signs and mirrors. It was like the gingerbread house in the forest, all colour and glimmering and liquid promises. Bottles and bottles and bottles – golden whiskies, treacly rum, pale vodka, straw-coloured wines. At the end of the bar, he saw Joanne Sullivan and she saw him. She looked at him for a second as if she only half-recognised him and then she looked away.

Nick had to guard against blurting out to DM how attractive he found her and then explaining at great length exactly why he found this strange because she wasn't really his type. Not like Caitlin who definitely was his type. But Caitlin wasn't there. She was at home lying on the sofa watching TV or reading a book about the Soviet space programme – Laika the space-dog, Yuri Gagarin the cosmonaut, the Mir space station which appeared to be tied together with string. He mustn't start babbling to DM; he must keep his control. There were parts of his brain that drugs unlocked which should really remain barred and triple-bolted because some of his sexual obsessions would come charging out like rodeo cattle and by the time he had lassoed them it was usually far too late. This was why he had stopped taking anything and he could not understand why he had succumbed so rapidly and without a struggle tonight at the party in Shoreditch which now seemed like a couple of centuries ago.

'How's your research going?' DM asked.

'I've found out a couple of things. Spoken to a few people. Have you seen George at all?'

'George and I are acquaintances more than friends. I don't see him that often . . . Wipe your nose, Mr J. And remember that drugs are better left to gangsters and losers. Here, have another beer.'

DM handed him a beer and returned to his bar duties. Will went to dance downstairs. Nick was smoking another cigarette when Joanne Sullivan arrived at his side.

'So are you comfortable, Nick?' she asked.

'I'm OK, yeah. A bit wired.'

'Enjoy your little lecture upstairs?'

'Well, he certainly seems to know his business.'

Joanne nodded and smiled. She had clearly been continuing to ingest copious amounts of James' drug supply.

'Come and sit down with me, Nick.' She took his arm and led him towards the leather sofas. Nick saw DM watching them go.

'Where's your minder?' Nick asked.

'Roger? He's not a very good minder. Easily distracted. He's got other fish to fry.'

'Oh yeah? Chasing girls all night?'

'No. He refills people's pockets when they're empty. Not quite with the same quality as we've just had, but it's not rubbish either.'

'They hold it so that the dealers don't have to keep that much in their pockets?' Nick wondered how Joanne could be so indiscreet with somebody she barely knew but then he concluded that she probably felt that she had little to fear. Nor was she exactly sober. Joanne shrugged.

'Run the door, control the floor.'

So Terry James was not just franchising the dealers, he was also supplying them with their drugs. Nick had to make sure that he remembered everything in the colander that his brain had become throughout the evening.

'Tell me about your girlfriend.' Joanne moved back into flirtatious mode. 'I remember you said you had one.'

'There's not much to tell,' Nick said uneasily.

'Is she pretty?'

'Yes.'

'Prettier than me?'

'Different.'

'Tactful. Is she clever?'

'Very.'

'Do you think I'm stupid?'

Nick stared at Joanne. She was asking him almost urgently and the mocking tone had dropped out of her voice.

'Well, stupid people don't often ask that sort of question,' Nick said.

'Boredom can make you stupid . . . I did English at school. And drama. I wanted to do drama for a while. My mum and dad put me down for a drama school. But I never went.'

'Didn't you?'

'No. But I studied *The Merchant of Venice* at school. Do you know that?'

'Not very well.'

'Gold, silver, or lead.'

'Yes, I remember that bit.'

' "Ornament is but the guiled shore to a most dangerous sea." See, I can remember it. I can remember whole lines. I loved that play. English was my favourite subject.'

'Right,' Nick looked around. 'Do you ever get any trouble down here?'

Joanne looked surprised at the abrupt change of subject.

'Why, is somebody staring you out? Don't worry, Roger will kill them for you. He'll probably torture them as well if you want.'

'No, nobody's staring me out. It's just that it used to have a bit of a reputation this club, didn't it. Isn't that what your . . . what Terry was saying?'

'Oh it used to be terrible a while back.'

'Wasn't there even a murder down here? Somebody got killed.'

Joanne looked down at her feet, letting her hair drop in front of her face. She clasped her hands in her lap.

'That was a while ago.'

'What happened?'

'One of the bouncers . . . he went a bit crazy . . . he attacked some kid outside the club.'

She shrugged and stared inside her glass as if the scene were replaying itself in miniature inside.

'Did you know him?'

'The kid? Not really. Apparently, there was a bit of a queue for the privilege of switching his life-support machine off.'

'What about the bouncer?'

Joanne was quiet for a moment. It was a telling pause.

'I knew him a bit.'

'What was his name?' As soon as he had asked this question, Nick knew that it was a mistake. Joanne stared at him.

'What do you want to know that for?'

It was Nick's turn to shrug.

'I don't really. I'm interested in bouncers I suppose because they're such an important part of the club. And there's a lot of attention on them at the moment. Registration schemes and all that.'

'His name was Chris. It was sad 'cause he was . . . he was OK really. I heard he's gone a bit mad inside . . . thinks somebody's just waiting to have him knocked off.'

'Why did he attack this kid?'

'Actually, the kid was hassling me.'

'You?'

'Yeah, he was always hassling some girl. Anyway, he tried it on with me, wouldn't give it up, so I told Chris. I never thought he was going to kill him. I just wanted him to throw him out. But he took him outside and he . . . he went a bit over the top.'

'You didn't see what happened though.'

''Course not. I wasn't going to follow him outside was I?'

'I suppose not. Do you think he did it? I mean you knew him. Why would he have got so angry about some boy hassling you? It must happen a lot.'

Joanne arched an eyebrow.

'Not to me. People aren't that stupid.'

'So why was Nathan that stupid?'

'How do you know he was called Nathan?' Joanne retorted sharply.

Nick could have cut his tongue out. Joanne was staring at him.

'OK, I'll level with you. I know a little about the case because we did some background research on the club. Obviously, that's what you do when you're doing a piece like this. I was interested in how things had changed, how one minute there was some psycho stamping on a kid's face outside the club and then everyone was going on about what a turnaround there had been.'

'Chris wasn't a psycho.'

'So you don't think he did it?'

There was silence. Then Joanne said utterly unconvincingly:

'I don't know. It's not for me to say is it? A jury certainly thought he did.'

'Juries get things wrong.'

Again there was a long pause. Nick did not want to pressurise her too much. He knew that he was skating on paper-thin ice. But he also knew that Joanne Sullivan had knowledge that she was not disclosing. There had been something between her and Chris, he was certain of it. Perhaps the banal truth was that Nathan Clemence had been hassling Joanne and that this had angered Chris so much that he had taken Nathan outside and kicked him to death. Except nobody working in the club – from DM to Joanne – gave the impression that they really believed that Chris had done it. Joanne shrugged again.

'It's boring. It was a long time ago. Anyway, let's change the subject. Where was you brought up?'

'Well, I lived in Suffolk when I was younger. Then we moved to London.'

'What part of London?'

'Chalk Farm. What about you?'

'We lived in Dagenham. My dad worked at the Ford plant. He's dead now. We moved to Brentwood. How old are you?'

'I'm thirty-one.'

'I'm twenty-two. I bet you're a Pisces. Pisceans are creative.'

'I'm a Cancer.'

'Well, it's still a water sign so I was nearly right. I'm water as well, I'm a Scorpio.' She made her hands into two mock-claws and giggled.

'I'm afraid I don't really believe in all of that. We're not really into superstition, us Cancerians.'

'Oh, it's not superstition. Especially if it's done properly. You've got a posh voice haven't you. I don't know anybody who speaks like you.'

'It's not really posh,' Nick said, remembering the writer from the party and his sad attempt to sound like a geezer. Caitlin always said that one of the reasons she liked Nick was because he never assumed a false accent. Assumed accents were a mark of insecurity; she liked Nick's indifference.

'Yes it is. I love it when people speak like you; all I ever hear is fucking this and cunt that. I like it when people speak like you do.'

'You haven't heard me on a bad day. I'm not always this polite. You've got a nice voice as well.'

'Thanks. But it could never be like yours. Anyway, I need another little line. Do you want one?'

Nick glanced around. 'I should get my friend . . .'

Joanne smiled. 'I'm not inviting your friend. I'm inviting you. Your friend's dancing downstairs.'

Nick felt sure that he was blushing.

'Where shall . . .'

'We'll go upstairs,' Joanne finished his sentence for him. She stood up and smiled down at him. 'Come on.'

Nick started moving towards the front entrance and the stairs to Irvine's office but she detained him with her hand, shaking her head slightly.

'Not that way, we'd better not disturb Richard again. Follow me.'

Nick walked behind Joanne as she made her way to the other end of the bar and the stairs down to the dancefloor. But instead of going down, she unhooked the rope that cordoned off the stairs heading up and beckoned him to follow. Nick felt extremely apprehensive; he knew that what he was doing was foolish. He couldn't stop himself though; it was as if she were leading him by some invisible chain; he had to see what happened. He watched the shape of her legs under her dress and felt his throat tighten. It certainly wasn't the danger or the risk that was attracting him, quite the reverse; when he thought about the risk he nearly did a 180-degree turn and started walking back down the stairs again.

They passed through a narrow corridor in which some coats and jackets were hung on hooks. Mops, black bags and other cleaning materials were stacked against the white-brick wall and a fluorescent light flickered. At the end of the corridor was a small room like a kitchen with a couple of chairs, a table and a sink. There were paintbrushes in the sink and a kettle on the side.

'We'd better go in there,' she said. 'There's no proper surface here.'

'OK.' Nick was finding it hard to speak.

Joanne wiped the table and began to spill coke care-lessly on it.

'That's quite a lot,' Nick said. She ignored him.

'Do you want to hear a joke?' she asked as she chopped out two huge lines.

'Go on then.'

'How does an Essex girl seduce a journalist?'

'How?'

'She invites him upstairs for a line of coke.'

Nick said nothing. Joanne took her line and stood up. He bent down to take his and his hand was shaking. He felt her hand cool on the back of his neck. He stood up and they faced each other.

'I knew,' Joanne said 'that you fancied me the first time I saw you.'

'That's embarrassing. Did you mind?'

'What do you think? I'm just sorry that Richard's still in his office.'

She moved forward and kissed him lightly. She had a soft fluttering kiss. He could smell an unknown shampoo. He put his hand on her breast and then down to her hips. Her body was new and strange; he felt how fragile she was. She pushed his hand further down until it was touching the bare leg at the hem of her dress. She sat him down on one of the chairs while she stood in front of him and he put his hand on each hip and lifted her dress up until she took it from him, holding it around her waist, scrunched handfuls in clenched fists like somebody fording a river.

There were certainly voices in Nick's head: there were tiny recriminations; there were dim warnings of conse- quences and guilt and unwanted changes. It was all useless – conscience and better judgement lay stunned and powerless under a far more powerful onslaught. Far better not to think at all, to turn the sound right down, to press the Mute button. Perhaps if she turned and walked out he would feel relief; it would be as if a strange enchantment had been broken. But his hand was moving; it was cupped as if to receive a gift; it began to subtle navigations, giving and receiving simulta- neously, and her eyes flickered as if no longer seeing him, the veils came down. He pulled her towards him and on to his lap and she put her arms around his neck.

'You're very beautiful,' he whispered, but she shook her head slightly as if she had no time for irrelevancies, for platitudes she had heard on countless occasions. She ran his hands down the curve of her back and lifted her easily. She opened her eyes suddenly and then closed them again.

There were footsteps on the stairs.

Somebody was coming up the stairs.

Nick wasn't sure who heard it first, how they were shaken into reality, back to the present. But they froze. She took her arms from around his neck.

'Who the fuck is that?' Nick whispered and she half- snarled silently at him to shut up. She got off him quietly and pulled her dress down. She brushed a strand of hair from her face and listened at the door. The footsteps came down the corridor and stopped.

'Jo, are you up here?'

It was DM. Joanne sighed with relief.

'Trevor? What the fuck do you want? I'm just doing a line.'

'I thought you might want to know that I heard a whisper that Mr James will be arriving very shortly. I thought you might want to meet him downstairs when he arrives.

Joanne was silent for a moment.

'Thanks, Trevor. You go down. I'll be there in a second.'

'OK.'

There was the sound of footsteps retreating.

'I didn't realise it was so late,' Joanne muttered. 'You go down first, I'll follow you. Just go straight down and find your mate.'

'Are you OK?' Nick asked. She stared at him as if he had just said the dumbest thing she had ever heard.

'Hurry, yeah? Just act normal. Go on. Now.'

Nick opened the door and peered out as if there might be an ambush outside. The corridor was empty and so he walked purposefully along the corridor and down the stairs. Nobody seemed to notice as he emerged into the club. DM was back behind the bar. He looked at Nick without expression, certainly without any obvious recrimination. Nick decided he had to front it out and pushed his way through to the bar.

'Trevor . . .'

'Your mate's looking for you. He's a bit vexed. I told him you would be down in a minute, that you had just gone off for a bit of a nose-up.'

Nick felt stranger than he had done in a considerable time. He couldn't believe what he had just done; he couldn't believe the whole evening. He had started out that morning at work; he had gone to visit a man in prison; he had been in a party in Shoreditch; he had fallen off his wagon with a crash which must have been heard across the whole of the city; he had gone to a strange room in a club with a girl he barely knew and been caught in the act by the bar manager. Which was still better, infinitely better, than being caught by her gangster boyfriend.

Joanne Sullivan walked casually across the bar. She seemed utterly calm now and smiled at Nick as if nothing had happened. It was obvious that her only concern was the possibility of detection. Once she had established that Terry James was not there, she had reverted back to her normal self.

'Hello,' another voice to his side said before he could speak to her, establish the reassuring contact that he craved. Nick turned and saw that it was Orlando the cleaner. He felt utterly disorientated.

'Hi,' Nick muttered thickly.

'How's your little girl? Rosa? She's got her cat now?'

Joanne overheard this and arched an eyebrow.

'Ahhh . . . that's sweet. Have you got a little girl then?'

'Yeah but . . .'

'Where the fuck have you been, Nick?' Will was more than a little irritated as he pushed his way impatiently through to them. 'You bring me here and then just vanish. I thought you might have just gone and left me here. I've been looking everywhere for you.'

'Nick's just been telling us about his little girl.' Joanne's eyes were gleaming with amusement. 'How old is she, Nick?'

'She's four . . .'

'I think we should make a move, Nick. There are cabs outside.'

Nick glanced towards the entrance and saw Terry James come in, followed by a small entourage.

'Well, I hope I'll see you both again,' Joanne said. 'Nick, thanks for looking after me, you were the perfect gentleman. I've got to go and look after His Lordship. See you.'

She waved blithely at Terry James who raised his hand in salute.

'Come on!' Will said impatiently. Nick turned to the cleaner.

'Sorry, I have to go now. I'll talk to you in the office.'

'Of course,' the cleaner replied. 'It's late.'

'Yes,' Nick looked at him and felt a sudden moment of intense envy for this dignified grey-haired man who was only here because he was doing his shift, who could go home at the end of it and put it all out of his mind. He imagined him returning to his family, drinking a beer and eating a sandwich prepared by his devoted wife. Orlando's life was not turned upside-down in the way that Nick felt that his was all of a sudden; it would have its sustaining daily rituals. 'Yes,' Nick repeated. 'It's very late.'

Neither Nick nor Will spoke much in the cab back across London. It seemed to take a century. They had to drop Will off first and then Nick travelled from Wapping to Finsbury Park alone. The journey would have been worse if he hadn't had so much to think about. Images of Joanne Sullivan still teased him, standing before him with her dress held in her hands, her fluttering kisses, the expression in her eyes as he touched her. He did not feel particularly guilty: his desire had been too intense, too separate from everything else; it had nothing to do with Caitlin. He felt profoundly unsettled and strange, but he felt more guilt about the cocaine he had consumed than about the curious scene with Joanne. He would have to start from scratch again, start counting the weeks again: tomorrow would only be Day One.

Caitlin was in bed when he got home. She was asleep, her book on Soviet space exploration by her side.

'You've been a long time,' she said as he got into bed, 'and you're coked off your face. You woke me up with all that sniffing coming up the stairs.'

'I had a lapse,' Nick said plaintively.

'You're an idiot,' she said, but she was too drowsy to argue. 'People say that it was cruel,' she murmured.

'What?'

'Laika. But Laika was a fortunate dog. How many dogs get to see the earth from a space rocket? How many dogs will have their name remembered forever? Not Strelka and Belka, and they came back.'

She sighed, turned over, and her breathing deepened into sleep again. Nick put his hand gently on her forehead and then lay awake with his mind racing and his eyes open, staring at the ceiling.

the beach

I have a deep longing for the ocean. When I am watching a film late at night, images of coastlines fill me with an aching nostalgia. Beach houses where people take coffee in the mornings on a white-fenced verandah, the grass on sand dunes blowing in a light breeze, foaming surf breaking on a long, sandy shore, the distant view out to the hazy horizon – it fills me with yearning. But proximity and access to beaches have always been an explicit function of money – the best are reserved for the wealthy. One of the few pleasures of great riches for me would be the ability to retire to my house by the ocean, just sitting with a glass of whisky and ice watching the waves and hearing them at night beating ceaselessly on the shore.

When I talk to Emily about this, she says that she will drive us down to Brighton. I do not have the heart to tell her that I was thinking of something a little more dramatic than the grey English Channel, fish and chips, and seagulls wheeling over a pier. Emily seems very keen on the idea, however, and even Claudio is agreeable – it is as if they have some plan – so at the weekend we decide to head for the coast. Emily's car is old – it would even be considered an antique in Montevideo – and has a sticker in the back window which says *Stop the bloody whaling!* When it comes to the day of our trip, however, the car acts its age and refuses to start so we have to get the train from Victoria instead.

'I saw something strange and funny the other night,' I tell them as we sit waiting for the train to leave the station, our bags on the fourth seat so that nobody will come and sit with us.

'What was that?' Emily asks. She is still scowling at Claudio because she caught him wolfing down a Bacon Double Cheeseburger when she returned from browsing the magazines in John Menzies. She had wrapped houmus and tomato sandwiches in silver foil for the journey and has brought a flask of coffee.

'Well, there is a journalist where I work. At the offices in Kentish Town. And by coincidence he also turned up at the club. He's looking into something down there but I'm not entirely sure what. Anyway, the other night I see him wandering about but he hardly notices me. He is following this girl about. She is very pretty but she is the girlfriend of the man who organises the bouncers. This man, he is not the sort of person you should mess about with.'

'But the journalist fancies his girlfriend?' Emily looks up from her magazine.

'Well, this surprised me because I have heard him talking to his own girlfriend all the time on the phone at work. They have always seemed really close. I would never have thought that he would go to a club and start running about after somebody. Although she is very pretty this girl.'

'I don't find that surprising at all,' Emily says. 'Men are like that.'

'Not all men,' Claudio rolls his eyes and returns to his magazine – glossy images of laptops opened up and fetish-ised for the lusting eyes of men like Claudio who are never satisfied with what they have got but are always itching for the latest model.

'Anyway,' I continue, 'I'm cleaning up and I see them go upstairs together to where we keep our cleaning stuff.'

'No!' Emily puts her hand to her mouth. 'The dirty dog.'

Emily knows how to respond to a story. Claudio is looking out of the window and tutting at the slightly late departure of the train, pretending not to be interested.

'They are up there for about twenty minutes and then the bar manager goes up and he tells them they have to come down. And two minutes later, the journalist appears and then one minute later the girlfriend.'

'But nobody else found out? They didn't get caught by the man. Where was he while all of this was going on anyway?'

'Oh, he's only ever there at the beginning of the evening and at the end. He's out doing his business, whatever that is.'

'So they didn't get caught?'

'No. Only by the bar manager.'

'And by you.'

'Oh well I don't matter really. I was just observing. I think the bar manager was warning them actually, because twenty minutes later the man walks into the club.'

'Romantic or sordid,' Emily cups her chin in her hand in mock-thinker pose. 'Which shall we go for?'

'Perhaps a bit of both,' I say, 'like most things.'

'I think it's disgusting,' Claudio says suddenly. 'That sort of behaviour is so juvenile and exhibitionist.'

'Ah, but you're a prig,' Emily remarks jovially as if she were pointing out that his shoelaces were undone. 'I don't know where you get it from because your dad isn't like that at all. That's the question we have to solve on this journey: how did Claudio get so anal?'

To my great surprise, Claudio starts to laugh and aims a mock kick in her direction. He certainly appears to have become better-natured since the arrival of Emily and even to have developed a degree of self-mockery, deliberately setting himself up for teasing, exaggerating his short-tempered self-righteousness in order to allow people to laugh at him. This is an unusual but welcome development.

We go a rather roundabout way from the station down to the seafront and I feel suddenly light-hearted and happy. The sun is shining on the tall white façades and there is a warm breeze. I realise that it is a considerable time since I have been out of London and it is a welcome feeling, especially with the sea air in my nostrils. The only downside when we do arrive on to the seafront is the pebble beach. In spite of the pleasing hiss of the waves on the shingles, a beach without sand is something I have always considered a travesty, a particularly English horror. Claudio picks up stones and tries to skim them but they sink instantly.

'The idea is to pick flat ones,' Emily says. She kneels down and scrabbles around, before finally selecting her stone and flipping it across the water. It bounces four or five times in great leaps before entering its decline, making ever smaller skips and then finally sinking. Claudio tries again and his stone manages one jump but he still looks extremely pleased with himself. Emily puts a hat on to protect her pale skin from the sun.

'It's even worse when its slightly windy,' she says, her hand on the hat to stop it blowing away, 'because then you don't notice that you're burning.'

We sit down by the sea watching the waves and a few children and dogs playing in the lightly-breaking surf.

'We've got something to tell you,' Claudio says suddenly. 'We're going to live together. And we think we might get married as well. I know you've still got all those stupid 1960s prejudices and think that marriage is a bourgeois institution but I happen to think that commitment is important . . .'

'Shut up, Claudio. It's not an argument . . .' Emily snaps.

'I'm just clearing the air,' Claudio says.

'Well for what it's worth,' I say, 'I'm delighted and surprised. Throughout your life, Claudio you have rarely given many indications of good taste. I haven't known Emily for long but I will be very happy that she is my daughter-in-law.'

Emily blushes ferociously and looks away.

'Well,' she says staring out to sea, 'there's this other thing. We're thinking of going to Uruguay for our honeymoon. I would love to see it after hearing so much about it. And it's time Claudio went back to see where he came from.'

'Ah . . .' I say.

'Yes, Claudio says you are always talking about this place. Punta del Diablo. We want to go to Montevideo and also to Punta del Diablo.'

'I see,' I murmur and also look out to sea because my eyes are brimming with tears.

'The thing is, we were wondering . . . we thought that it would be nice to be there for a while with . . . you know . . . with somebody who knew the country . . .'

'I can't go with you on your honeymoon.'

'No, but what we thought was that we might go off for a week on our own. Then you could come out. I know you've been back but Claudio has never . . .'

I went back once during the 1980s when a plebiscite was being held to decide whether the military would be granted impunity for their crimes. The vote was in favour. Let the process of reconciliation begin!

'It's very nice of you to ask . . .' I watch a boat out on the horizon, far away perched on the point of mystery where the sky dips into the sea. The boat hardly appears to be moving as it makes its way across the liquid skin of the earth.

'Really, I'm grateful to you but I don't think it's a very good idea,' I conclude. 'And I couldn't afford it.'

Claudio stands up. He picks up a stone and looks at it in the palm of his hand, rubbing it with his finger as if giving it a quick polish.

'You know, Papi . . .' he says, '. . . when I was a kid there was a point when I didn't know where we were going to be next, what bus or plane we were going to be leaving on. And when you were in Argentina and we left for Mexico, I thought you were dead and that I was never going to see you again. You may have had a hard time being the great hero but mum was having to cope with us crying for our dad and trying to make us sleep at night. I don't take anybody's side but I don't think you've ever questioned properly where some of her anger towards you comes from. And then we arrived in Holland and I stayed there for six months but you decided that Britain would be better so we came here. I did my best to settle down, but I got picked on at school for not speaking English and where the fuck were you then? Where the fuck were the fucking Tupamaros and all the songs and stupid slogans when I was getting my face rubbed in the dirt? And I made some friends in my computer club and I got into computers and now I make my living from it. Which doesn't stop you from laughing at it whenever you can. So, if I want you to be there when I go back to Uruguay, which is something I actually want to do, I think you should be there. And if I offer to pay for your ticket, then I think you should show me a little respect and some good manners, swallow your stupid pride and accept gracefully. Because – and I've never said this to you before – you fucking owe me.'

Claudio throws the stone in a long, looping arc. It splashes into the sea and disappears. He strides angrily off down the beach. Emily looks out to where the stone landed.

'I think he has a point,' she says.

'When he was little,' I say, 'he used to chase papers on

the roof of our patio. He used to laugh and laugh chasing the papers around. He was a happy kid.'

'He doesn't have many friends,' Emily says. 'But he's still happy in his own way. He really wants you to come out. And you shouldn't use the money thing as an excuse. That's cheap.'

I cannot say anything; I am too overwhelmed by what Claudio has said. Has my whole life been lived without caring for others? Was I just selfishly playing at revolutionaries while my wife put the children to bed and dried their tears? Was it real passion that motivated me or just a need for a cause, a vague anger against the establishment that found fertile ground during the 1960s in futile posturing? Have I wasted my life in elaborate poses, avoiding the daily transactions, the careful, quiet negotiations which allow people to carry on as social beings?

'He'll be back soon,' Emily says calmly. 'He's thought a lot about you coming with us. He got quite excited. I think he's just disappointed by your reaction.'

'I never wanted to hurt anybody,' I say. 'It's true what he said though. He got dragged about all over the place. At the time though . . . it's difficult to explain . . . it didn't seem to me as if there was any other option. I didn't mean to be careless.'

'He's told me quite a bit about getting bullied at school.' Emily is throwing a stone from hand to hand. 'Didn't you know?'

'No,' I say miserably.

'Why did your wife go back to Holland?'

'She didn't like Britain. And our relationship had been over from years before.'

'Why did she not go back to Uruguay?'

'Lots of people leave Uruguay. Not just for political

reasons. She was happier in Holland. My daughter is happy there. She was able to study. Claudio was just sick of moving around though . . .'

'And he didn't want to leave you on your own,' Emily says. 'He loves you and he admires you. Come on, let's go and find him. I'm hungry.'

We walk down the beach and find Claudio sitting disconsolately staring at the small waves breaking on the shore. Emily pats his head and wanders off down to the shore where she begins paddling, holding her skirt up and letting the waves slap against her bare legs, making little jumps with each wave. I sit down next to Claudio.

'I'm sorry.'

'It's OK.'

'For everything,' I add. 'You were right.'

'I wasn't right about everything,' he says. 'I respect what you did. It was doomed to failure but at least you tried. You can't not do what you believe in because of your children.'

'Not everyone would agree with that,' I reply.

'Oh yes. It's like those politicians who say that they can't make their children suffer for their political beliefs so they send them to private school. I mean, that is the most pathetic argument.'

'It certainly lacks logic,' I say.

He turns and smiles at me. 'It's the logic of the hypocrite,' he says. 'At least you're not a hypocrite.'

'I'm glad you're getting married to Emily,' I say. 'She's a very good person. That sounds patronising but it's true. I'm happy that she'll be my daughter-in-law.'

We watch her for a moment, holding her skirt up around her knees as the wavelets break on her shins. She flashes us a smile.

'And you'll come and see us in Uruguay?'

I nod and there is silence. Emily walks back up from the sea, holding her sandals in front of her like flippers.

'I'm starving,' she says.

'Let's go and get some fish and chips,' Claudio says, 'although the price of being a freak for Emily is that she only gets chips . . .'

'I'm a freak because I don't want to eat flesh?'

'It's natural to eat meat. We're lucky; we're the top of the food chain; we can eat anything we want. Anyway, if we got stuck on a desert island and there was a cow, what would you do?'

'I'd eat you,' Emily says linking her arm in his, 'and save the cow for intelligent conversation.'

I walk behind them as they continue bantering up the streets of this famous English seaside town with the sun warming the streets and parents herding their children. Two gay men walk arm-in-arm, chatting and laughing. I wonder how they would react to this now in Punta del Diablo.

We are tired as we sit in the station waiting for the train for London. Emily is resting her head on Claudio's shoulder. She has a white paper bag full of sticks of rock for her nieces and nephews who are apparently numerous. Just as the train is about to leave, we hear raucous laughter and shouting coming up from the platform and then four men jump onto our carriage. They are all very drunk and have the appearance of off-duty soldiers — a couple with little moustaches and short gelled hair.

Everybody appears to slump down into their seats as the men get on. Their noise does not abate; they scream lewd comments at two girls walking past with rucksacks, inviting them to join them in the carriage. The two girls look as if an invitation to jump into a pit full of cockroaches would be more attractive and hurry away.

As our journey begins, the noise from the men is incessant and intrusive. Ugly laughter and dreary obscenities conducted at a decibel level that makes it impossible to ignore. People close their eyes and pretend to be asleep. The men derive great hilarity from the fact that the man in the seats in front of them is bald. *Oi Kojak, hey boiled egg, baldy you deaf or what?* They intimidate the young boy pushing the sandwich trolley because he does not have the type of beer they want. *No surrender to the IRA*, they scream at a kid of about ten who is wearing an Ireland football shirt. Any other type of conversation becomes impossible. We exchange a few words but the pushing, bullying noise, the screamed laughter, the endless vulgarity makes it impossible.

'*Qué son asquerosos los ingleses a veces,*' Claudio murmurs to me quietly. It is true. The English who are capable of such good manners and easy elegance are also able to take pointless violence and loutishness to a different level and nor is this particularly a function of social class – it might just as well be the medical school rugby club sitting at the end of the carriage.

In Latin America – a continent of considerable poverty, cruelty and violence – somebody might take your money and stab you for good measure but their main objective would be your money. You might sit drinking all night at a christening and end up fighting with somebody you barely knew. But this, this level of degenerate behaviour, so at odds with the families playing by the beach with their kids and their dogs, so alien to the little courtesies, the gentle charm, that make life in this grey country more bearable, this ostentatious baying and shrieking is something utterly English.

'I need to go to the toilet,' Emily whispers to Claudio.

Going to the toilet at the end of the carriage involves passing where the men are sitting.

'Can't you wait?' Claudio asks. Emily shakes her head.

'I'll come with you,' he says, but she shakes her head again.

'I'll be OK.'

She makes her way down the carriage and passes the men who do not have time to notice her because they are howling with laughter at some remembered experience, some joyful anecdote from their day out, something undoubtedly involving humiliation for whichever unfortunate happened to cross their path. I relax a little and look out at the countryside speeding past, the gradients of blue in the sky as the twilight deepens into night.

'Ginger! Oi ginger, come and sit on my lap.' The men have seen Emily returning from the toilet. She smiles awkwardly, painfully, trying to shrug them off.

'Ginger, are your pubes the same colour as your hair? Eh? Have you got ginger pubes? Go on, show us.'

They put their legs out so that she has to try and step over them. The train is jolting so that she stumbles and has to support herself on the seats. The men cheer. Claudio stands up.

I'm just going to help her,' he says quietly.

I feel terrible because I know that Claudio's intervention will only make things far worse; it is exactly what these men want. In a moment, Emily will pass and they will probably stop their taunts or start taunting somebody else. But I know why Claudio cannot leave it.

'Why don't you shut up?' Claudio says as he approaches the men. He holds out his hand for Emily and pulls her past them. One of the men stands up.

'You what?'

I stand up and walk down the train.

'Look, we don't have an argument. Just . . .'

'Shut it, cunt.'

'Go on, Luke, fucking smack the silly cunt,' one of the men sitting down urges his accomplice.

'OK,' Claudio says with a seeming calm which appears to both infuriate and perturb his adversary. 'If you say one more word to my fiancée, I'll kill you. You'll have to knock me down and keep knocking me down and I'll keep getting up again and I'll kill you. It won't be that easy for you. I'll hurt you. Even with your friends.'

Everybody on the train is gazing resolutely in front of them or pretending to be asleep. The man on his feet stares at Claudio and Claudio meets his gaze levelly. Suddenly, the guard comes into the carriage collecting tickets. He is a big man and sees immediately what is going on.

'OK, sit down, come on, I'm not having this. I'll radio through to the next station and have the police waiting for you if you want. It's completely up to you.'

He makes no obvious distinction between us but I know that he is directing his words towards the four men.

'Go on a fucking diet, you fat cunt,' one of the men says, but it is obvious that they are not going to start a fight now.

'Come on,' the conductor says. I notice that he is wearing his union badge on the lapel of his work-blazer and I find this oddly reassuring. 'Come back to your seats. If you boys cause any trouble, I'll have the police waiting for you. Just sit down, enjoy your beer and leave people alone.'

'Fuck off, lard,' says Luke. Suddenly, and most surprisingly, a middle-aged woman with blonde permed hair and thick gold chains rises from her seat.

'You make me sick,' she says. 'You're disgusting. We've had to listen to you all the way from Brighton. I just wish my husband were alive because he would have given you such a seeing to. You're not men, you're little boys.'

'Did your husband die of nagging?' one of the men says but it is clear that the balance of forces has swung against them decisively.

We return to our seats and the conductor sits down at the end of the carriage. The men keep up a barrage of insults and lame puns revolving around Emily's red hair – *I bet she uses Duracell batteries in her vibrator*, the conductor's weight – *we've got the fucking fifth Teletubby in our carriage*, and about the woman's dead husband – *maybe he died 'cause he put his glasses on and saw her face*. But their laughter is more forced, less triumphant and they get off at East Croydon without the torrent of abuse that everybody had been bracing themselves for. The woman who spoke up looks over at Claudio and smiles at him.

'That was a good speech,' I say to Claudio as the train crosses the Thames. 'I will kill you . . .'

'I meant it. I stopped getting bullied at school when I learned a simple lesson. No pain they inflicted on me was worse than the fear and humiliation of being a victim all the time. So I made them understand that I would die trying to kill them if that was what was necessary. I would attack them when I was on my own and they would have to knock me unconscious to stop me. Then I would attack them again. The alternative was to leave me alone which was finally what they did.'

'An interesting strategy,' I say.

'I have never understood,' Emily muses, 'why men are so obsessed with the pubic hair of red-headed women. Nobody else gets asked that strange question all the time.'

'Not all men,' repeats the generalisation-hating Claudio. I think of joking that he has binary strings in his veins instead of blood but remember his earlier reproach and decide to keep quiet.

'OK, not all men,' Emily grins and punches his arm.

The train staggers into Victoria and we collect our bags together. I suddenly feel an acute desire not to be on my own but Emily has hooked her arm in Claudio's and they are going to take a taxi to Wapping.

'You could come with us and take the cab on?' Emily says, but I shake my head.

'I'll take the bus, it'll be just as quick.'

I can tell they are both relieved.

'Congratulations again,' I embrace them. 'I'm so pleased for you.'

Cielo mi cielito lindo, I sing softly to myself as I stare out of the bus window on the way back to my empty flat. I still feel the impact of Claudio's criticism like a throbbing burn suddenly reminding me of its presence. I know that I am going to dream tonight and I am frightened at the intensity of my dreams that leave me troubled and sad. The Atlantic waves are rolling in from the ocean and breaking on the beach of Punta del Diablo. Soon my son and his young wife will be heading there for a honeymoon; they will stay in a hotel with a sandy tiled floor; they will sit on a balcony gazing out to the horizon. I have made the grand gestures in my life; I have loved a woman intensely and twenty years later I miss her and grieve for her with almost the same intensity. I have been part of a clandestine guerrilla movement. How romantic. Throw a faded rose at yourself. *Was it all for this? Some of his stories are really interesting. Where the fuck were your fucking Tupamaros?* I despise self-pity but at the moment I feel great waves of it combined with an unbearable dry-eyed heaviness of heart, an utter and terrifying solitude. I am conscious of my breathing. It is as if I am having to struggle for each breath, as if the oxygen is being very slowly sucked out of the bus, out of my lungs. I am going to start gasping. I wish I could talk to somebody. I want to cry out. I want to shout for help.

Cielo mi cielito lindo, danza de viento y juncal...

Only singing can help me now.

Prenda de los Tupamaros, flor de la banda oriental...

The city is very big and I am very lonely.

La noche en Montevideo está tranquila y no está...

I will keep singing and I will get off the bus.

Se están fugando los Tupas uno a uno del penal...

I will open my front door and turn the light on. I will pour a big glass of whisky and maybe watch a little TV. Tomorrow I will laugh with Pancho and tell him about Brighton. Things aren't so bad, Orlando, you will be OK. Come on now, pull yourself together, breathe deeply, everything is going to be all right. Just keep singing and you will soon be home.

every day i think of him

Nick had plenty of time in the days following his night at the Sublime Club to contemplate the events which had taken place and his own less than exemplary role in them. He had felt like death the next day, slumped in bed watching TV, endlessly blowing his nose, sometimes checking with disgust the blood-streaked snot on the tissue, trying to find something that he wanted to eat. He felt the numb disappointment and slight bewilderment at having slipped so easily back into something that he had been convinced he had left behind for good. Caitlin did not ask him anything about the evening; she had left him lying in bed and gone out with some workmates for a Turkish meal. Nick had been half-invited to this a few weeks before, but Caitlin had not even bothered asking him whether he would be accompanying her. Nick knew that things were going badly between them, things quite apart from his moment of interrupted infidelity with Joanne Sullivan. It was as if Caitlin were distancing herself from him and he could not think – or was not prepared to take the time to think – of any strategy to pull her back.

Over the next couple of days, he worked dully but intensively on the Ron Driver programme which was in its finishing stages. He was sure now that there were people who probably knew what had happened outside the Sublime Club on the night that Nathan Clemence was stomped to death, but that nobody would talk about it and certainly not on camera. Joanne Sullivan knew – by her own admission she was linked to it – but he realised that whatever she knew or didn't know, it would not be sufficient to prick her conscience into any kind of action. He was not particularly worried that she might say something to Terry James about their conversation because she was too compromised, would have too many awkward questions to answer. He could imagine James turning on her ferociously – *And what did you go and open your fucking mouth for*? It was far more in her interest to keep quiet and Joanne appeared to be a person whose own interest was paramount in all her considerations. She took risks out of boredom but they were risks which involved evading rather than engaging with Terry James, slipping the bars of her invisible cage. Perhaps this was what she had done with Chris Gayle. She had said that Richard Irvine's office would have been more comfortable. How did she know? Had she done it before? With a handsome bouncer who also liked playing games and taking risks?

Sitting in the office one afternoon Nick wrote on his computer, *This is a story about clubs, drugs and murder.* He stared at the phrase for a moment – the three buzz-words to spark the reader's interest – and then he deleted it with the backspace one letter at a time until he was left with *This is a story.* He thought of Penny the series producer in meetings and her constant reminders – *Let's keep it simple, what story are we telling here*? Did he want to tell the story of an innocent man serving a life-sentence? Or of a bored girl flirting with danger? Or of a corrupt order in which truth and justice became irrelevant? No documentary could deal with all of these themes – there wasn't room, there wasn't time. The most simple angle was Chris Gayle and his imprisonment: he had to follow that, he knew that he was at lease close to finding out what had really happened.

Will phoned to tell him about a job opportunity.

'I know you're finishing up on your framed trade-unionist so I thought you might like something completely different. It's a series on ex-communist capitals – Prague, Berlin, Budapest, Moscow, etc. It'll be looking at the nightlife, what the kids are into, the people who've done well out of it all, the people who haven't done so well. I know the producer – she's quite a smart girl. If you get your CV together I'm sure you'd have a good chance. Bit of travel would do you good, mate.'

'Yeah, thanks, Will.'

Nick put the phone down and stared at it for a second. He had stopped thinking recently about what he was going to do after the Ron Driver programme.

'You're working late,' Orlando had appeared silently by his side.

'I've got to go and see somebody,' Nick rubbed his eyes. 'I'm just finishing up.'

'How is your investigation going? Down at the club? I was surprised to see you again the other evening.'

'You won't mention to anybody about what I'm doing down there?'

The cleaner laughed.

'I don't talk to anybody apart from the other cleaners. They wouldn't be particularly interested. Also, I don't really know myself what you're doing down there.' He laughed again suddenly as if something had just occurred to him and then picked up Nick's bin and emptied it into the black bag. Nick glanced at him. He suddenly felt the need to talk to somebody about what he was doing, to explain some things, to see if spoken out loud they made any sense.

'The murder down there; I don't think that the bouncer who was supposed to have done it really did so. I think that he was either set up or he was just a fall-guy.'

'I suppose that is not uncommon. My son calls me a conspiracy theorist but there are great big conspiracies all around us. Some people are just naive or blind to them.'

'Is your son better?'

'Very much so. He is getting married as well which I am pleased about because I like his girlfriend. I am going to Uruguay with them for the first time in ten years. It will be quite strange for me . . .'

Nick nodded absentmindedly. Orlando took the bin from the neighbouring desk.

'So what is it about this case that interests you so much?' Orlando had turned back to face Nick.

'I guess . . . well, first I was asked to look into it by an old schoolfriend who I had not seen for a long time. And that was kind of important to me. Once I started looking, it became a little bit compulsive. I suppose it's pretty hard for us to imagine the feeling of being locked in a cell like that completely deprived of your liberty . . .'

'It must be,' the cleaner assented.

'The only problem with a case that isn't cut and dry – you know, like the Birmingham Six – and where you might want to look at some wider issues, is that it's pretty hard to make an hour-long documentary about it.'

'And what do you think the wider issues are?' The cleaner seemed genuinely interested although Nick was finding the interrogation difficult. But he realised that until this moment he had not even talked to Caitlin properly about it.

'Well . . . the way in which this society has been run for the last twenty years; the way people have lived. Sometimes with so little control over what happens to them. And if I hadn't met somebody by chance I would never have heard of this man in prison. Don't you think that's strange?'

'It's a coincidence,' the cleaner agreed, 'but how is it the wider issue?'

'Not the coincidence itself. But the way you can find out about the strangest things just running beneath the surface, these odd interactions, the way things are hidden. It's hard to find out what the real truth is sometimes . . .'

'Perhaps the question is what you do with the truth once you find it out. In your case you might make a documentary or write an article for the newspaper.' Orlando shrugged as if unconvinced as to the utility of such a task. 'One would like truth to lead to justice. But it rarely does . . .' He laughed drily, '*Verdad y justicia.*'

'I'm sorry?'

'Oh nothing. I was just speaking in Spanish. It means the same.'

'It can all be very messy sometimes,' Nick mused.

'It can,' Orlando agreed gravely, 'but it just takes some work. It doesn't mean that things aren't straightforward as well. You still have to believe that the truth is out there.'

Nick nodded and started gathering his stuff together.

'Did you say that you were going to stop cleaning at that club soon?' he asked.

'I think so,' Orlando replied. 'I would like some more time at weekends now. Especially with my son getting married. The journey's easier now because we have a van that we share to go home in.'

'I hope you won't take offence at this,' Nick said, 'but I would have thought you could find a more . . . well you know . . . a less tiring, more stimulating job than cleaning . . . your English is very good . . .'

The cleaner laughed. He did not seem in the least offended.

'It is a very democratic profession. I work with somebody who used to be a skilled welder, somebody who ran a
wholefood cooperative that went bust, somebody who was
unlucky in love. There are people who can barely speak a
word of English. There are others who speak it better than
those who were born here. I spoke English even before I left
Uruguay so I had a head-start. I have not been doing this the
whole time I have been here. But when I lost my last job . . .
at my age . . . there were not so many choices. Flexible
labour markets, you know.'

'Well, I might see you again down at the club if you don't
leave before I finish this thing I'm looking into. I've got to
shoot off now . . .'

The cleaner nodded and moved away to the other desks
in the virtually empty office.

'It weren't just Chris Gayle who killed Nathan. I know there
was more to it than that but at least I got the satisfaction of
seeing one of the bastards go down.'

Mrs Clemence sipped at her tea and glared across at
Nick as if he were another of the bastards who had master-
minded the death of the blond son whose thin rodenty face
peered out from various photographs on the mantelpiece and
shelf-unit. There was Nathan in a cowboy outfit pointing a
pistol at the camera, Nathan in striped school tie at secondary school, a teenaged Nathan with his arm around his mum
and Nathan with a couple of mates lying on a Mediterranean
beach in a pair of union jack shorts.

After leaving the office, Nick had driven across
London to the Newham street where Mrs Clemence lived
– a cul-de-sac whose three sides contained identical blocks
of low-rise maisonettes with UPVC double-glazing and

secondary cages across the front doors. There was a cut-off feel about the street, as if it didn't properly belong to the city, as if it just existed on its own according to its own semi-detached logic. The air had become still and oppressive, storm-threatening. As he had got out of his car he had heard a man's voice shout from an open window – *I'll fucking wipe that smile right off your face.*

Mrs Clemence lived in a ground-floor maisonette. It was immaculately clean and everything in the kitchen was white and scrubbed – fitted cupboards, work surfaces, microwave, washing machine. The French windows from the living room led out to a small overrun garden. Hanging from the handle of the living-room door was a small claret and blue West Ham pennant, a little cheerful splash of colour in an otherwise sterile environment.

'Who else do you think was responsible for Nathan's death, Mrs Clemence?'

'It was that Terry James of course. Chris Gayle killed Nathan 'cause Terry James told him to. But nobody's gonna speak up against him.'

'Why would Terry James want to kill Nathan?'

There was a pause. Mrs Clemence looked at the mantelpiece, at Nathan the cowboy with his toy gun aimed at imaginary Indians. She took a cigarette from her packet and lit it with a soft click from her gold-ribbed lighter.

'I'm not stupid,' she said finally. 'There were people laughing after what some of the papers reported me as saying at the trial. They must have thought I was a right mug or a liar or both. Everyone knew what Nathan was: he was a drug-dealer. I used to find the bags of pills in his room sometimes. I'm not stupid. But he wasn't that all his life. He wasn't born a drug-dealer, was he? He did used to go fishing with his dad. He bought me that . . .'

She pointed to a china slipper on the mantelpiece with a plastic flower tucked into it and *MUM* painted on the side.

'That's really . . . erm . . . that's lovely,' Nick lied.

'He bought me that when he went with the school to Margate.'

Nick remembered school trips to Margate, removing the lightbulbs from train carriages and throwing them from the windows. Watching Andrew Hughes disappear beneath a group of boys who were sitting on his head, taking his glasses, while Nick simply felt relief that it was not him. The school victims: whatever happened to them? What were they like as adults?

'Why would Terry James want your son killed?' Nick asked.

'Something to do with the drugs. And money. A week before it happened, a couple of 'em come round here shouting the odds, asking for Nathan.'

'Was one of them Chris Gayle?'

Mrs Clemence hesitated.

'No,' she admitted finally. 'Roger I think his name was. But they're all the same. I asked Nathan about it and he said it was just a mix-up and he would sort it out. He always thought he could sort things out.'

'But you don't know why the men were angry with him?'

'What I heard was that Nathan was supposed to have been selling other drugs in there. And Terry James didn't like that at all, obviously.' Mrs Clemence inhaled deeply on her cigarette. 'Then somebody got sick on something they bought in there and they blamed Nathan. The night Nathan died, they came round to get him. They picked him up to take him down the club. "Don't worry, Mum," he says to me as he leaves. "It's all sorted out now." The next time I saw him he was dead.' She stared at the photos on the mantelpiece.

'It must have been very hard . . .' Nick looked down at his pad. 'What about this girl Joanne Sullivan? She said that Nathan was hassling her and Chris took him outside because of that.'

'That's bollocks . . . if you'll pardon my French. They was going to get Nathan that night. When that cheap little slut said that, it was just an excuse to get Nathan outside.'

'Maybe,' Nick chewed the end of his pen. 'But why go to all that trouble? Why not just take him out to the country somewhere? I'm sure they've done it before.'

'I don't know. All I know is that Terry James got Chris Gayle to do that murder and that Joanne Sullivan was involved somehow. I said it to that copper. Kinch? Was that his name? But he didn't want to listen. He said there was no point in going down that road 'cause we had no evidence against James. He knew though; he knew it was Terry James.'

'Kinch said that?' Nick remembered that Kinch had told him that Chris had taken Nathan outside because of a girl. He had not even hinted that there was any trouble between Nathan and Terry James. Perhaps this was just an additional motive. It was as if fragments of the truth were lying all around like parts of a diamond scattered among broken glass. He had to first sort out what was true and then consider how it fitted together. What he knew was true was that James had brought Nathan to that club and had had a motive to kill him. Joanne Sullivan had complained to Chris about Nathan, and Chris had taken him outside. Even Chris admitted that. Then, either Chris had killed Nathan or somebody else had done so after Chris had been dragged off him. But it had suited everybody to blame Chris – he had become the fall-guy whichever way you looked at it. There could have been a collective silence but the other doormen had rushed forward to lay all of the blame on one individual. And this must have something to do with Joanne Sullivan in Terry James' case.

'What if Chris didn't do it?' Nick asked Mrs Clemence. 'You wouldn't be happy, surely, knowing that on top of the injustice of your son's death, the wrong person was doing time for it?'

'But he did do it!' Mrs Clemence exclaimed fiercely. 'He killed my son.'

The room suddenly darkened as a cloud obscured the sun and shadows fell across the garden. Mrs Clemence pulled her cardigan more tightly around her. Without her belief that, in some small way, justice had been done, Nick knew that she would succumb to total despair. She clung to Chris Gayle's guilt and subsequent incarceration like a small golden nugget, a gleaming truth – polished and wiped as clean as all the ornaments and all the bright white surfaces in her home. To admit the possibility that it might be otherwise would be to admit utter powerlessness and bitter defeat. Even the possibility of the wrong person in prison appeared preferable to nobody in prison. Mrs Clemence had per-suaded herself that it had been Chris Gayle who landed the blows and although she knew that the chief architect of his demise had walked scot-free, she also knew that somebody was paying for what had been done. Somebody had been punished. Justice had walked blindfold with arms out-stretched and had bumped into Chris Gayle. Now he sat behind bars weaving his protective philosophies, an angel on his shoulder.

'Would you like to see his bedroom?'

'I'm sorry?' But Nick had heard and he groaned

inwardly. *No of course I fucking don't,* his imp urged him to say.

'His bedroom. He didn't stay there that much of course. But it's kept as it was.'

'That would be really interesting,' Nick murmured insincerely.

Nathan Clemence's room was exactly as he had expected, the remnants of childhood still on the wall – a picture of Bobby Moore, a cut-out photo of Louise when she was still with Eternal, a photo of Nathan fishing with his dad, a battered Connect 4 box, the smell of chemical lavender from the cleaning polish used by his mother to keep the room spotless.

'Every day I think of him,' Mrs Clemence said. The words fell out into the stillness of the room. Nick looked at her. She had produced Nathan; he had grown inside her; her belly had been swollen with him. She had given birth to him, suckled him, fed him, clothed him, taught him, walked him to school, photographed him, laughed at him, slapped him, probably berated him when she began to realise the extent to which he was going off the rails. She didn't seem to be a bad woman or vicious in any way and now she must lie in bed knowing that after eighteen years somebody had stamped on her son's chest and face viciously enough to puncture his lungs with his rib and cause him to choke to death on his own blood. She must think back to him at twelve or thirteen and grieve for the short time he had left – even then – before a death which was both violent and sordid. Nick supposed that Mrs Clemence felt like this; he supposed that Nathan had been the object of her love; that she held her grief tightly to her just as she had held her cardigan when the cloud cast a chill across the room. But he had no means of even suggesting this theme to her; there were no words available to him, and so just the echo of her own brief lament was left hanging in the late-afternoon air. *Every day I think of him.*

'It's very sad,' Nick said turning from the room, anxious now to get out of this house. He did not really find it sad; he found it unsettling and depressing and he wanted to escape. The evening was warm; he wanted to sit out on the roof garden with a drink and relax from his long day.

'It's just as it was,' Mrs Clemence repeated as she followed him down the stairs.

When Nick arrived home, Caitlin was already sitting out, warming her legs with what remained of the sun, reading a book and drinking a Campari and orange which was almost the same colour as the sky to the West. Her swimming costume and towel were hung out to dry; she was flipping her goggles round and round on her wrist and fingers as if they were worry beads. The sight of her and the sound of birdsong from the park made his heart ache with a mixture of love and regret. He still felt no guilt about what had happened with Joanne Sullivan, although there was remorse for his lack of professionalism. People were often mocked for saying *It was just physical; it had nothing to do with us* as if it were the lament of clichés, the most pathetic of lax excuses. But Nick thought that it was often true. His desire for Joanne at that precise moment in that situation made no difference whatsoever to the way that he thought about Caitlin whether or not he had resisted it. And the scene already had a vague dreamlike quality about it as if it had never really happened.

'Hi,' Caitlin said when she saw him. 'If you want a drink, bring a glass.'

They sat out on the roof garden drinking, without saying very much, watching the children playing in the park, the dogs careering about after sticks, couples arm-in-arm, a dosser swaying on a bench like a drunken parrot on a perch. Nick felt the bittersweet taste of the Campari at the back of his throat.

'I watched a documentary tonight,' Caitlin finally said. 'It was about these travelling salesmen. They sold fish from a van. They claimed it was fresh and that it was cod or salmon when in fact it was some frozen crap. Anyway, a so-called investigative journalist was chasing after them in their van, waving a mike around, shouting that it was a scandal and didn't they feel guilty defrauding housewives. But it turned out they were these three unemployed factory-workers from Middlesbrough and it was the only thing they could think of to do. The journalist – who was just this little prick straight out of college – would shout "I put it to you that this is not cod; I put it to you that this is frozen fishpaste." And the guys would look a bit ashamed and just go "yeah you're right". It was so pathetic.'

'I don't do that sort of thing,' Nick said. 'Whatever else I do, I could never do anything like that.'

'I know you don't,' Caitlin replied seriously and took his hand. 'You're too insecure – I don't mean that as an insult by the way – and you have more empathy for people. But you can still walk away from it all. You're not the man in prison or the unemployed men selling fish or the framed trade-unionist. You're not even the dodgy copper or the bent club owner. You just rely on them all for your story.'

Nick thought about Mrs Clemence that day and the way that she had held her cardigan to her. He remembered his absolute inability to communicate as he had invaded her house, looked at her photos, and inspected her dead son's room. He picked off a sprig of rosemary from one of the pots on the roof and rubbed it between his fingers, sniffing at the aromatic oils as they were released.

'It doesn't make me a bad person though. It doesn't make me the enemy either,' he said thoughtfully.

'Of course it doesn't. But remember the bitterness of that guy at the party, the one that told you about the club and the murder. About the way you were able to just walk away then, from that school and from his friendship. He's not going to be happy with any dilettante approach on this case. You can't just dip your finger in the pool out of interest, make a few ripples and then just leave it.'

Nick blushed deeply. He could not see her expression and did not know whether she could see his face.

'I don't want to do that,' he murmured at last. 'But I have made it clear that this is just preliminary research; I haven't made promises. And, anyway, as you said before, I've still got a lot on my plate with Ron Driver. Also, Will phoned about some programme looking at ex-communist capitals . . .'

Caitlin's face darkened as he explained the project to her. He began to tail off as her disapproval became more and more apparent.

'Sorry, it just sounds like total bollocks to me,' she said.

'Why? It could be really . . .'

''Cause you just know how sissy and lightweight it's going to be already. What clubs are the kids into! Is drum and bass big in Prague now! A feature on the new Moscow millionaires with a little giggle at how vulgar they are and then an image of a beggar to cover the we-haven't-forgotten-poverty angle. A frown of concern at the rise of the mafia. Most documentaries just seem to be recycling clichés or they're completely made up. It's sad really.' She shrugged and spun her goggles round on her wrist. 'If you have to do it 'cause it's work then that's fine.'

'Well, yeah, it's a job you know. It would be a bit of a break from miscarriages of justice for a while.'

'OK,' Caitlin said. 'Anyway, I want you to be careful for your own sake as well on this bouncer story. One person is dead and one person is in prison already as a result of it.'

'Isn't that a bit contradictory?' Nick grinned. 'Don't dabble but don't get hurt.'

'I'm allowed to be contradictory,' Caitlin retorted.

They sat quietly for a moment until it was just too dark for comfort. Nick suddenly heard the phone ringing inside.

'I'd better take that,' he said.

It was George Lamidi and he was excited. Nick blinked as the living-room lamp dazzled him after so long in the dusty half-light. He could smell the rosemary on his fingers as he held the phone.

'The chicken has landed. He's come home to roost. You've got to meet him, man. Can we meet up at that hotel again tomorrow?'

'What the fuck are you talking about?'

'The Jock who used to work at the club. He'll talk to you but only if I'm there. We can do it tomorrow if you're free. The good news is that he hates that James geezer.'

'OK, I'll meet you there. But it'll have to be the evening. I've got a busy day tomorrow.'

'No problem. By the way, have you spoken to Trevor at all?'

'Well, I saw him at the club last weekend. But I haven't spoken to him since. Why?'

'No reason. I spoke to him in the week and he was just a bit weird when I mentioned you. I thought you might have had words or something.'

'No.'

'OK. Good. I'll see you tomorrow then.'

Nick put the phone down. Caitlin came back into the room carrying her dry swimming costume. She dumped it over the arm of the sofa and took the two Campari glasses with their pinky-orange dregs and fragments of ice into the kitchen.

'Come to bed,' she said holding out her hands to him. Nick did not want to think any longer about George or DM or Joanne or Mrs Clemence or a Glaswegian called Chick or Terry James. He did not even want to begin to wonder why DM might be acting weird when his name came up, although he could have a pretty good guess. He followed Caitlin into the bedroom and switched off the lights so that the flat was filled only with the soothing noises carried on the warm air of this early summer night – a distant motorbike, a car door slamming, a couple speaking in a language which might have been Italian, the faint sound of a TV from an open window. Nick slid into bed and closed his eyes.

viewing

And I just hope that what happened to me doesn't happen to anybody else. I hope that we've gone past that stage now because it destroyed me you know . . . it ruined my life . . . I hope it never happens to anybody else.

Ron Driver looked up from his hands at the camera and then his image crackled and distorted as the programme ended. Penny, Nick's Series Editor, leaned back in her chair and put her hands behind her head.

'Congratulations,' she said. 'I've got a few points but nothing that requires any major changes. Really, that's excellent Nick. Topical and interesting without being worthy. Get the VHS over to the lawyers so that they can run through it. This should stir up a few people. I especially liked the link you made with the Scargill case and all those false accusations about his mortgage without sinking into conspiracy theories. The prostitute was a star performer as well.'

'Mark did some very good work on it,' Nick said modestly. 'He really chased a lot of contacts. Especially when we thought we might have lost Mandy.'

Penny smiled at Mark who blushed deeply and scratched his head. He was absolutely terrified of her.

'Well, I'm glad at least one of the programmes is looking like the finished article. That bloody university lecturer case is turning into a can of worms. I think the guy probably is a raving pervert.'

They walked back into the office and Nick and Mark returned to their desks.

'We need to get the thank-you letters off to the contributors soon,' Nick said.

'Sure, no worries. It looked good didn't it?'

'Yeah it did.'

'It'll piss people off though. Nobody wants to hear about trade unions these days. It's not like this government has a higher opinion of Big Ron than the last one.'

'I suppose the point is whether it's legitimate to frame your opponents and use the security services to do so. I don't think this government would go that far. And it could have been anybody they didn't like . . . not necessarily just trade-unionists,' Nick shrugged as he searched through some papers on his desk.

'But it wasn't just anybody though. It wasn't like they were paranoid or over-the-top. They had a plan didn't they? They had a strategy. And it worked. It's probably still going on. We don't know the half of it. We think we're safe 'cause we can make a TV programme about it. They could do it again whenever they wanted. If they needed to. But they don't 'cause trade unions have no rights and this government isn't about to hand them back the rights that were taken away.'

Nick glanced up at his young researcher. Mark's main topic of concern that week had been Chelsea's chances in Europe and whether he was still in with a chance with Emma of the cone-shaped breasts.

'It depends on who you think "they" are I suppose.'

'I think "they" are the same fuckers who always have power and control over our lives. They might be government officials, spies, businessmen, criminals, bankers, you name it. There are people who run the show and we don't matter a fuck to them.'

There was silence. Mark glanced down at his desk and

then looked up again brightly.

'Still, there's no point in slashing our wrists over it. I'm off to get totally spannered tonight.'

Nick laughed. 'Well, that attack of concern for our democratic vulnerability didn't last long.'

'No, man, but what the fuck can we do? I ain't gonna do a one-man picket on MI5 headquarters. I can't walk around with a placard round my neck. Don't mean I don't know what the picture is. What about you? Got any plans?'

Nick tensed slightly as he thought of his interview arranged rapidly with DI Kinch that afternoon. He knew the gloves were going to come off, that he was going to have to push Kinch more on his knowledge of and involvement with Terry James.

'Nick?'

'Oh sorry, erm, I've got to go and see that copper again. Then I'm meeting someone who used to work at the club.'

Mark raised his eyebrows.

'I suppose that's how come you're a producer and I'm just a humble researcher. I get to go out in the evenings, have a really good laugh and get off my face. While you have to interview coppers and bouncers. Do you think you'll get to make a programme out of this?'

'I don't know,' Nick acknowledged. 'Maybe not. Maybe I'll do an article on it instead. But I want to find out what happened anyway. I'll see you tomorrow.'

'I'm not quite sure I see your pwoblem, Mr Jordan.'

Kinch had clearly not been happy at the idea of seeing Nick again, and the journalist's line of questioning was making him even edgier.

'The problem is this: I believe that there is at least

circumstantial evidence linking Terry James to the murder of Nathan Clemence and almost certainly a motive. It was just easier all round to nail Chris Gayle.'

Kinch walked around the interview room. He paused before an ageing poster warning of handbag theft and stared at it as if it were the first time he had ever seen it. He solicitously straightened a frayed edge with a frown on his face. Accusations of sloppiness clearly did not sit easily with him.

'You have nothing to show that Gayle didn't commit that crime while I had witnesses and forensic evidence.'

'All of the witnesses were linked in one way or another to Terry James. Most of them worked directly for him. The blood on his shoes proves nothing since nobody denies that Chris was outside with Nathan. Nathan Clemence's mother thinks that you knew that Terry James was behind it.'

'You've been speaking to her?'

'I saw her yesterday.'

There was silence for a moment while Kinch paced the room ostentatiously. Nick felt an urge to giggle. The detective was so humourless and self-important that he almost encouraged flippancy as a provocation strategy. *Your flies are undone. Only joking!* Nick tried not to grin as he imagined the reaction. Kinch stood across from Nick and put his hands on the table.

'What is it with you lot? We go to all the trouble of putting people away and you are desperate to get them out again. But if anything happens to *you*, it's us you come squealing to. If a member of your family was murdered you would be round here quick enough demanding to know what we were doing. In all other cases though you care more about the criminal than the victim . . .'

Nick had heard this refrain so many times that he felt a

tremendous weariness at its repetition: he had heard it from policemen, from politicians, from indignant citizens on crime programmes, even from his own father during one argument. What he really wanted to say provocatively whenever it came up was that he didn't particularly care about either criminal or victim.

'. . . You say you've talked to Mrs Clemence,' Kinch continued, his eyes hard with dislike, '. . . well ask her if she's unhappy that Chris Gayle is in prison.'

'I think that you're rather missing the point,' Nick replied drily. 'I'm all in favour of criminals being in prison as long as they actually committed the crime for which they have been sentenced. Whether Mrs Clemence is happy or not is irrelevant to that. I never thought that part of our legal system involved sending people to prison in order to keep other people happy.'

'Do you know what it used to be like down there?' Kinch demanded, suddenly shifting tack to Nick's surprise. 'It was a war-zone. It was Beirut. They've turned that club around. Chris Gayle was just the beginning of that, do you know what a breakthrough it was when we got that degree of cooperation from them?'

'Now that Terry James has imposed order?'

Kinch stared at Nick. 'Well you can sneer . . .'

'I'm not sneering. It's just that the order that you seem so pleased with rests on criminal activities. You must know perfectly well that James controls the drug supply in that club.'

'I couldn't possibly comment on that. But even if it were true, I would still like you to have seen the situation a few years back. Even if what you're saying is true – and I have no idea whether it is or not — say we was to go charging in there now. We definitely wouldn't get James; we probably wouldn't get any of his staff. The guy holding the gear will have it stashed somewhere that would make it pretty difficult to pin it on him. At the most we would get a few punters for possession and a few kids working the floor. And for that? To go back to the chaos of a few years back. Think about it.'

Nick realised that Kinch believed that the problem was one of incomprehension. For Kinch, Nick was not only the liberal who cared more for the criminal than the victim, he was also the naive fool who had no understanding of the ways of the world, of the compromises that were necessary in pursuit of the greater goal. There might not be an explicit bond – a cash relationship – between Kinch and James, but there was a bond of understanding which Kinch clearly felt did not exist between himself and the journalist. It was as if he were almost willing Nick to understand.

'Look,' Nick said, 'I can see your point perfectly. But my job in situations like this is to try and come up with the truth. I'm not particularly interested in who runs the drugs in there because that's not the main story. But I don't think that it is the truth that Chris Gayle went over the top with Nathan Clemence because he had been hassling a girl, who incidentally is the girlfriend of Terry James. And I don't think you do either.'

'Well a jury certainly thought so.'

'Your faith in juries is touching. I assume that you'll have the same attitude when a villain gets let off who you know is guilty.'

'OK,' Kinch was still leaning on the desk in front of Nick, glaring down at him. 'But be careful, son. I would mind how you go if I were you.'

'I hope that isn't a threat?' Nick replied.

Kinch laughed. 'Don't be silly. I don't need to make

threats to you. I hope you're not suggesting that I might. You poke your nose into somebody's business though and you might find you get it . . .' Kinch rather bizarrely made a loud snapping noise as if impersonating an alligator '. . . bitten off. Especially somebody with rather complex business interests like our friend Terry James. It's up to you though. It's a free country.'

Nick got up to leave. 'Thank you again for your time.'

Kinch half-laughed sarcastically and did not bother replying.

The squares of Bloomsbury were filled with people enjoying the early evening sunshine. They strolled about eating ice creams or formed little circles on the grass. A few solitary beings sat on park benches in sombre meditation. Men in suits loosened their ties and watched the women in light summer dresses, little gaggles of foreign students laughed and flirted with each other. The sun made the city feel more benign, more democratic, more at ease with itself – there was a kind of balmy peace and sociability about it all. Around the squares, the tall terraced buildings with their blue plaques testified to previous generations of eminent Londoners who had strolled or sat here; who had been in this very place; who had seen the same buildings as Nick was now seeing; who had felt the pleasure of the early summer warmth on their open faces.

Nick was early; he sat down on a park bench for a while and kicked out at the vile pigeons which began to cluster around his feet in the expectations of crumbs. He truly detested these strutting vermin — birds that spent more time on the ground than in the air; beady-eyed, chests puffed out as if they had something to be proud of. And perhaps they did; after all, they were the consummate urban survivors – like cockroaches and rats they adapted well to the particular conditions of the city, scrabbling for whatever bits and pieces that careless hands might let fall.

Nick thought about Chris Gayle in his prison cell; he wondered what Joanne Sullivan was doing at precisely this moment, and whether Caitlin was arguing the case for some victim of bureaucratic failure or gliding down the pool with her easy front crawl, the steady tilting of her head to snatch air. Nobody knew where he was. For a few minutes, he had the luxury of complete solitude and independence. Just as he contemplated this pleasure, however, his mobile rang. Nick sighed, took the machine out and stared at it for a few seconds as George Lamidi had done with his mobile when they had met for the first time. It was DM.

'Hey, Mr J.'

'Hi, Trevor.'

'You busy?'

'I'm sitting in a park. It's a really beautiful day.'

'It's all right for some. Listen, I was wondering if you was coming to the club again this weekend.'

'I didn't really have any plans.'

'Well, come down. I think I might have found something out for you.'

'Oh yeah, what's that?'

'I can't really speak on the phone about it. Come down Friday and we'll talk then. Catch you later, Mr J.'

Nick switched off his mobile and wandered towards the hotel where he was to meet George Lamidi. He was surprised to find when he got there that George had already arrived. He was accompanied by a broad-shouldered Glaswegian who George introduced as Chick. It was not the most appropriate name for somebody of Chick's appearance and demeanour. Chick's face was flat and broad-jawed, reminding Nick of the scene from *Tom and Jerry* when the chasing cat runs slap into an iron, moulding his features temporarily into the same shape. He also had a mumbling, murmuring voice which made him difficult to hear. His words seemed to fall out of his mouth and plummet to the ground like sky-divers without parachutes. Nick felt slightly embarrassed as he had to keep asking him to repeat things. He worried that Chick might be insulted and think that it was simply because of his accent — although admittedly, the addition of the heavy Glaswegian intonations did not help matters much. Nick bowed his head to put the minimum distance between his ear and Chick's mouth. Chick was not the sort of person Nick wanted to insult.

'Aye, I'm working up in Birmingham now,' Chick said as they were making preliminary small-talk.

'Oh yes I know Birmingham,' Nick replied. 'I had to work there for a while as well. Bit of a nightmare really.'

Chick glared at him unblinkingly. 'I like Birmingham.'

'Do you? Oh, right, yeah well it's got its good sides . . .' Nick lied. The only good sides of Birmingham as far as he was concerned had been Platform 4 of New Street station and all roads leading to the M6.

'I've got a mate,' George joined in, 'who was in Pentonville on an attempted murder charge. He gets bail but his bail condition is that he has to go and live with this relative in Birmingham and he can't come to London. And it weren't just Birmingham but some right fucking slum up there as well — sort of the Birmingham within Birmingham if you know what I mean. After two weeks in the place, he comes down and begs to go back to the 'ville.'

'You don't know what you're fucking talking about,' mumbled Chick. 'There's nothing wrong with Birmingham.'

'Yeah, well you're from Glasgow, mate,' George retaliated. 'Anywhere must seem like fucking paradise after that.'

Nick smiled nervously at Chick. It was all very well for George: he was big and hard enough to engage with Chick in this verbal jousting.

'I mean,' George blithely continued, 'I used to see this Scottish bird once. We got on all right but she couldn't fucking speak properly. She used to go . . .' he broke into a sing-song Scottish accent, '. . . "George, your jeans need washed." So I'd go "No, darling, my jeans either need washing or they need *to be* washed. Your jeans need washed just ain't English." '

'Heh heh,' Chick laughed. 'Right enough, but you see where you come from you've probably got twenty wives washing your stuff for you so it disnae matter. If you dinnae like the way one of the lassies speaks like, you can always get another of the wifeys in the tribe to do it.'

'When somebody asks me if I feel Nigerian or British or whatever,' George ignored Chick, 'I say that I'm a Londoner. That's my nationality. 'Cause if you're from London you're different from everybody else in Britain. It's a London thing . . . you wouldn't understand it,' he added jovially to Chick.

'What happened to your mate?' Nick asked George, anxious to steer the subject away from the racial, national and regional stereotyping.

'He got off,' George said. 'Which is funny 'cause he did it. He had no defence. He couldn't believe that he never went down. He said the foreman of the jury winked at him when he come back in.'

'Unlike Chris Gayle,' Nick said.

There was a pause and George glanced at Chick.

'Tell him.'

Chick studied his knuckles.

'Chris Gayle never killed that boy.'

'So what . . .'

'He gave him a beating. Broke his nose but he never killed him. He was stupid though. Brought it on himself.'

'How's that?'

'He was a bigmouth. He was shagging that Joanne lassie. And he couldn't shut up about it. In a place like that the word goes around. Especially with doormen . . .' he glanced at George. 'Especially the schwartzers. They can't keep anything quiet; everybody knows everybody else's business. It was the best-known secret. Only a matter of time before Terry James hears whispers. He has it out with her, there's screaming and crying, she denies everything, she says it's all Chris and she's been fighting him off. And he wants to believe her so he tells her what she's got to do.'

'She's got to get Chris outside with Nathan Clemence? Set him up?'

'Aye. She tells Chris that Nathan's been touching her, making comments. So when Chris takes him outside, he looks mad 'cause he *is* mad. He looks like he's gonna kill him. There are a lot of witnesses to that.'

'But he doesn't . . .'

'No. The other guys pull him off. Nathan's hurt. Most of them go back in with Chris. Then he gets finished off by somebody else. Two birds with one stone. The boy gets punished for trying to rip off Terry. Chris Gayle gets fingered and gets a life sentence.'

'And it was Terry James who finished off Nathan Clemence?'

Chick shrugged. 'Who else? Could've been him, could've been that Roger cunt. Probably both of them. I was in the club the whole time so I didnae see what happened . . .' he glanced again suddenly at George who looked down at the table. Nick knew that Chick was lying and that he had probably been one of the bouncers who had taken Chris back into the club. And Chris must have known this as well – *Find Chick* he had urged. Why did Chris think that Chick would be prepared to tell the truth though? What was in it for Chick? Why had he even agreed to meet Nick?'

'So Joanne had to betray Chris . . .'

Chick's face darkened. 'She had no choice, pal. She knew that she could make him believe her. She knew what might have happened to her if she hadn't: she'd seen a lot . . .'

Nick thought back to the dreamlike scene of Joanne Sullivan standing in front of him holding her dress. How frustrated she must be to take such risks. And yet she would always protect herself; she was not just the captive princess, the troubled soul longing to be free. She was not brave, she was reckless. Boredom made her foolhardy: she was still a hard-hearted mercenary for all her little party-trick of quoting from *The Merchant of Venice*. Chris Gayle sitting in prison would not betray her although she had screamed and cried his guilt to a man she knew would exact a terrible revenge. Nick was beginning to understand a little more about Chris now – he must know that Joanne had betrayed him and yet he would not speak about her; he knew that others had committed the murder for which he was accused and yet he would not do anything other than proclaim his innocence. There was something admirable there, a kind of stubborn morality to it all.

'Nathan had upset Terry James about the drugs?' Nick said. 'That's what Nathan's mum thinks.'

'He was another idiot,' Chick said, 'bound to get caught. One thing about the gear that James was providing in there, it was decent stuff. That boy starts selling shite, complaints start coming in . . . it's a matter of time. He was unlucky they needed a body though . . . otherwise he might have got away with a couple of broken legs.'

Nick considered this appalling thought. Nathan Clemence might not have been killed if it had not been for the fact that it dovetailed nicely with setting up Chris Gayle. He did not know if this were true or not. Perhaps Terry James caught up in a frenzy of violence just could not stop. The helpless face staring up from the ground either invited compassion or it invited a boot. Some people might hesitate because they could suddenly imagine the pain and fear of the other, imagine it being them on the ground. For whatever reason, there were others – the cold or brutal of heart – who did not have this restraint. Or perhaps he had really wanted to kill him all along. Intent was a curious concept – like sticking a knife in somebody and claiming you didn't mean to kill them. You couldn't shoot somebody in the head and claim that though. But maybe there was an instant where no thought of consequence intervened, just a moment of pure action.

'I hope you don't mind me asking,' Nick said cautiously, 'but what is it with you and Terry James? Why did Chris know that you would tell the truth?'

'I don't like him. He doesn't frighten me. And I don't like his business.'

'The drugs?' Nick was surprised. Chick did not appear to be the kind of person who would find this aspect of James distasteful. Chick laughed grimly.

'You think that's his main business? That's pocket money for him at the moment, pal. Girls, that's what he deals in. Some of them under-age. He brings them over from Eastern Europe, from Latin America. Some of them come through

271

Germany. Then they get their passports taken away . . .'
Chick shrugged: '. . . they're slaves. You could walk past the
house and think it's just some nice house out in Essex. I've
seen some things . . . they provide girls for certain events . . .
you wouldn't believe . . . they've done things . . .' he shook
his head, tailed off and lit a cigarette.

Nick contemplated him. Something Chick had seen had
disgusted him; he had seen the helpless face and it had
stirred pity and outrage in him, the basic ingredients of any
moral code not entirely based on self-interest. While Nick
had been sitting drinking Campari and orange on his roof
garden, there were Eastern European and Latin American
women being raped and beaten in suburban houses for the
pleasure of some and the profit of others. And men were also
filming this to create another subproduct from their human
currency. It was not liberal breast-beating: these were the
plain facts and you could make of them what you would.
Nick could go in and secretly film the men filming the
women and it would change nothing but might make good
television. He thought of Caitlin and her disapproval at the
triviality of the programme on ex-communist capitals. He
thought of the cleaner and his assertion that in spite of
complexity there was truth out there. And he thought of
Mark the researcher and his statement of powerlessness – *I
can't walk around with a placard around my neck*. And really he
was right, he was right. Nick might feel good if he turned
this project into a powerful indictment of the legal system or
the capacity of humans to transform other humans into raw
materials. But then he would sit on his roof garden drinking
Campari and orange, watching the sun go down, feeling
wistfully knowledgeable but basically decent.

'I have to go,' Chick said. 'The Chief here's got my
number.'

Nick watched him leave the bar and raised his eyebrows at George.

'It's interesting that he's got that thing about what Terry James does. The girls and everything.'

'He's seen some pretty wild things. And he was telling me that there's some psycho running around Glasgow knifing prostitutes. Some friend of his, some girl he went to school with got shredded or something. Anyway, he took it hard. I don't think it's made him very sympathetic to pimps or anybody involved with that shit, men who get off on the whole violence thing.'

'You don't hear that much about it do you?' Nick winced a little at the throwaway use of the word "shredded". It was so easy to say with that thoughtless flippancy, so divorced from the terrible reality of it. He remembered a dinner party where somebody was drunkenly proclaiming their desire to glass somebody. "Have you ever seen anybody who's had a glass in their face?" Caitlin had asked him quietly.

'It's only a Glaswegian whore,' George said ironically. 'Who gives a fuck?'

But some people did give a fuck, Nick thought. People might not be perfect but it didn't mean that everybody was a Terry James. George Lamidi cared about the fact that Chris Gayle was sitting in a prison cell for a murder that he did not commit – he thought that it was unjust. Chick tended his private corner of grief for a girl with whom he had gone to school, with whom he had shared certain things that made her important enough to matter, that made her more than just a photograph on *Crimewatch*. He knew these things about a girl whose life had been ended by one of those men driven by such dark imperatives; men who felt no pity or compassion; men who might on the surface be blandly pleasant, charming even, but who were utterly incapable of the critical imaginative leap necessary to loosen their grip around the neck and turn away staring at the hands that had been squeezing the life out of their terrified victim.

'So that's the story,' George said placing a pint in front of him.

'It's no great surprise.' Nick sipped at his drink. 'I had worked it out as something along those lines. I just wasn't sure what fitted where.'

'Well, now you know for sure,' George said.

pinocchio

Will refused to go with Nick to the Sublime Club at the weekend.

'No, man, I'm bored of all that cheesy music and over-dressed people. Besides, the last time you just fucked off and left me. I've been with you twice. You're a big boy, you can go on your own now.'

Nick knew that there was little point in trying to persuade him. He couldn't think of anybody else – there was no point in even thinking about Caitlin. As for Karl, Nick might as well invite him for a trip on a homemade rocket to Mars in an attempt to persuade him to go to a place like Sublime. *But why would I want to go there?* Nick could imagine him asking with genuine curiosity. Karl would not go to many places whose postcodes did not end in *1* or contain the letter *C*. He was also fairly suspicious of anything without a *W*. Nick considered insisting that Mark accompany him as a work outing. He suspected that Mark would probably enjoy it, especially the women on display, but then thought that Mark might end up getting a slap for overdrooling and that Nick would also have to listen to football trivia all night. He had snapped at Mark at work because of his incessant babble about who Chelsea might or might not sign over the next few months. Before he could outline the pros and cons of virtually every available player from each corner of the world, Nick's patience snapped and he told him that he would ensure that he never worked in television again if he mentioned the word

Chelsea once more. Mark had sulked for the rest of the afternoon.

So Nick accepted that this was something he would have to do on his own. He prepared to go on an evening when the heat had turned to a sticky humidity, windows were open in all the houses of their street and people wandered about slowly in shorts. He was getting dressed in what he considered to be reasonably appropriate Sublime clothes, while Caitlin sat on the sofa steaming through a biography of Yeats after finishing with Yuri Gagarin and the various space-dogs.

'Funny how such a conceited little prick could write such great poetry,' she mused.

Nick did not answer. He was too busy wondering at what DM might have discovered for him to think about Caitlin's protective wall of books. She knew about Peggy Guggenheim and Yuri Gagarin and W.B. Yeats. She read books that other people only knew the titles of and treated poorly-read people with contempt, especially if they made excuses about not having the time to read. But what real engagement did she have with the external world apart from her job? She could quote Marx extensively but she had less direct political involvement than Bella the Blairite. Nick thought all of this as he sprayed deodorant under his arms. He experienced a sudden thrill at thinking unkind thoughts about Caitlin – she was opinionated; she was self-regarding; deep down she was a coward. But then he watched her brush a strand of hair from her face as he eyes followed the words down the page and he knew that she was extraordinary and original. She had not been trained to read from an early age as he had: it was something that she had discovered and crafted for herself.

'I might not be in when you get back,' she said. 'It depends on how late you are.'

'Hopefully, I won't be late this time,' Nick replied, 'I'm just going because that bar manager has got some new information for me. Where are you going anyway?'

'For a drink with a few people from work.'

'You didn't mention that.'

'You didn't ask,' Caitlin said irritatingly. 'Like you don't ask me about a lot of things. Anyway, I hope you're not going to come home in the state you did the last time. I don't want to seem like a nag but you were the one who was so insistent about never doing it again.'

Nick sat down heavily. His surrender had depressed him intensely for the next few days. Caitlin was right that he had been insistent, and he had believed it; he had believed that it was something that he had left behind. And then suddenly, with no advance warning, he had slid back and made irrelevant all his months of abstinence. If somebody had told him the morning of the Shoreditch party that he was going to backslide so badly that evening, he would have laughed in their face. He had told and convinced himself that it was evil and insidious and vulgar and repetitious and expensive in terms of both time and money. And yet in the time it had taken Will to pass him the rolled note, these had seemed like trivial considerations, he had done it with a shrug of the shoulders. *I deserve it.*

Caitlin saw his look of discomfort and took pity on him.

'There's no point in crucifying yourself about it,' she said. 'What's done is done. As long as you learn the lesson from it.'

'The problem with the lesson,' Nick said, 'is that it's rather a depressing one. It doesn't matter how much I think it's gone away, there might always be a situation when I fall again.'

'Next time you'll be more aware,' Caitlin said and patted him on the head.

There was no sign of DM when Nick arrived early at the club that evening. He contemplated asking for Richard Irvine because the flattering little piece written by Will's friend in which Sublime was mentioned had appeared in the Sunday papers. Nick wanted the approval that he was sure Irvine would give him for the good publicity. When he wandered to the downstairs bar, he saw the silver hair and expensive suit of Terry James who was sitting drinking a bottle of beer. He was accompanied by Roger his oversized familiar.

'Ah,' James said when he saw Nick, 'here's our journalist. Sit down, have a drink. All on your own son?'

'Yeah, I might meet somebody later. Did you see the little piece in the paper with the quote and everything . . . ?'

Terry James stared at him rather disconcertingly for a second and then he laughed harshly.

'Yeah I saw it. Roger, does this boy remind you of somebody?'

Nick stirred uncomfortably. There were traces of mockery in James' voice that he had not heard the first time. Could he have found out something about Joanne Sullivan? Had she said something to taunt him? She wouldn't be that stupid.

'He does as it goes. Now who is it? It's something in the nose.'

'You're right, it's the nose. You got a bit of Jew in you? I suppose not, with the blond hair and everything. Although you do get blond-haired Jews. Only way you can tell is to have a look at their dicks. The Krauts did that, you know. If

278

they weren't sure . . .' James swigged at his beer with a contemplative expression as if in admiration at this piece of Teutonic cunning.

'I'm not Jewish,' said Nick stiffly, trying to conceal his distaste.

"Course you ain't. But there's something about you . . . it reminds me of . . .' Terry James slapped his forehead with mock-theatrical emphasis: 'Pinocchio! That's what it is. Don't he look just like fucking Pinocchio, Roger?'

Roger laughed. 'That's what it is. Pinocchio. 'Course Pinocchio ain't blond . . .'

'Nah, he ain't blond but the fucking nose is the same . . .' James leaned forward in his seat and wiggled Nick's nose. 'You've got Pinocchio's fucking nose, mate.'

Nick felt extremely agitated. He looked about again for DM but he was nowhere in sight.

'What are you talking about?' Nick asked shaking his head. 'I'm not with you.'

Pinocchio whose nose grew when he lied – was this what they were saying? Were they calling him a liar? *You poke your nose into somebody's business though, and you might find you get it bitten off.* Kinch! It must be. Kinch must have tipped them off. He had pushed Kinch too far and Kinch had quietly dropped the word. Fear coursed through his veins; he wanted to piss.

Terry James took a bag out of his pocket. 'Yeah, that's our new name for you, son. Pinocchio. 'Cause you like a bit of the old bugle, I saw your nose growing as soon as you clocked me.'

Nick felt the tension drain away to be replaced by a wave of euphoric relief. The worst they had him down for was a cokehead and possibly a bit of a scrounger.

'Here,' James said dipping his credit card into the bag

and holding it towards Nick's nose. 'Go on, get that up your
nose . . . Pinocchio.'

Roger laughed sycophantically as if his boss deserved to
be garlanded with awards for this piece of coruscating wit.

'Pa-pa-pa-pa,' James mimicked a bugle with his hands
and Nick laughed obligingly as well. He realised that part of
the source of James' power was that he invoked a desire to
please in those around him. Like most psychological terrorists, James offered two options: I can be charming and
funny or I can be a monster. You want me to be the former
and so you must always try and please me. But just to
complicate matters, I will also switch bewilderingly between
the two without any reason or explanation. Nick knew
people who used such tactics – to a greater or lesser degree –
within relationships as a form of power-play, a useful strategy in the struggle for dominance.

'Go on then,' James said still grinning, looking down at
the card.

'Actually, I'm . . .' a sudden change in James' expression,
a quick blink, warned him not to refuse, '. . . oh go on
then . . .'

'You ever banged this stuff up?' James asked him as
Nick was wiping his nostril.

'What?'

Roger grinned and mimed a needle in a vein. Nick shook
his head.

'You should try it,' James said. 'I think you might find it
very . . . pleasant.'

'Maybe he could try it later,' Roger said and both men
laughed again as if at some private joke.

'Is Trevor around tonight?' Nick asked, anxious to steer
the conversation away from a topic he had always found
very tedious and ultimately disconcerting. He could hear the

mockery creeping back into their voices.

'Trevor?'

'You know . . . the bar manager.'

'It's his night off,' Roger said. 'Was you expecting to see him then?'

'I thought . . . yeah, I thought I might.'

'He's probably gone to see his baby-mother . . .' James laughed. 'Ain't that what they've all got, Rog, baby-mothers. Stupid fucking expression if you ask me. Why do you want Trevor. We boring you?'

'No, it's really good to see you again. I wasn't sure you would be here.'

'Where did you think I might be?'

Out brutalising your sex slaves, you fucking pimp. Nick's imp had hopped catlike on to his lap.

'No idea, just out and about, you know.'

James nodded slowly. He jiggled his gold chain on his wrist.

'So, you're a journalist then? Don't make you all that popular does it, going around sticking your nose into other people's business?'

'I suppose not, but I'm not really . . .'

'They've never bothered me that much. Journalists that is. But then they haven't been poking their nose into my business which would be a different matter. What paper did you say you worked for?'

'I didn't. I'm freelance.'

'Oh, freelance,' James mimicked a posh accent. 'I say.' Roger laughed again.

'Leave it out,' Nick tried to say jokingly. James froze and blinked several times, cocking his head and fixing Nick with a sudden glare.

'What did you say?'

'I was only joking, I said . . .'

James got off his chair. 'Did you . . .' he jabbed his finger at Nick, '. . . just tell me . . .' he pointed at himself incredulously, '. . . to leave it out?'

Nick went pale and did not say anything. His throat was dry. Terry James suddenly roared with laughter.

'Look at him, Roger, he's gone white.' He slapped Nick's cheek a couple of times: 'That'll get the blood back into your face, I was only messing about.'

Nick grinned weakly while Roger laughed as if this had been a practical joke of such vintage quality that it should be bottled, corked and labelled.

'Anyway, we'd better make a move as well. See you later . . . Pinocchio.'

Nick forced a smile as the two men stood up and James adjusted his jacket. As they were leaving, James turned back to him, his eyes glasslike.

'Oh, there's another thing about Pinocchio that maybe you have in common. He was a fucking lying little toe-rag. Be seeing you.'

And they walked off leaving Nick sitting at the bar, one hand still around his bottle of beer.

Nick sat for a second trying to think rationally. They were definitely on to him in some way; they must have been tipped off by Kinch. But what had Kinch told them? What did they know? He had to try and get out of the club somehow. But perhaps they were watching him, waiting for him to do precisely that, so that they could drag him off into the alley and administer a similar kind of punishment to that received by Nathan Clemence. To his surprise, Nick felt calm. He called the barman over.

'Where's Trevor? Is he not working tonight.'

'He was meant to be. But he hasn't shown up. Can I get

you a drink? Maybe he'll be in later.'

'No, no, it's OK.' Nick was worried about DM. If they were on to Nick, then they might have also uncovered his connection with the bar manager. He looked around the bar. Nobody appeared to be watching him; there was no surveillance. But they had definitely been toying with him and the last comment was hardly ambiguous. On the other hand, it could just be a warning, an instruction to get out of the club and cut his losses. He finished his beer and walked up the stairs, pushing his way through the incoming crowds to the entrance of the club. The bouncers on the front door watched him as he approached. He could feel their eyes hot on him. One of them smiled and appeared to shake his head ever so slightly. Nick's courage failed him and he turned back.

He was walking back through the upstairs bar when he saw Joanne Sullivan. She was at the bar waiting for a drink. For an instant he remembered her as she had been when she stood in front of him and felt a sharp pang. Then he walked up to her and tugged at her arm. She turned in surprise but her face betrayed nothing when she saw that it was him.

'Oh it's you. What are you doing here?'

'I'm thinking about leaving as soon as possible. Your boyfriend knows what I'm doing here doesn't he?'

She shrugged. 'I don't know what he knows and what he don't. He doesn't talk to me about that sort of thing. It's none of my business.'

'Just like Chris Gayle was none of your business?'

She flushed and stared him in the face for the first time. Then she glanced over to where a couple of bouncers were standing.

'You be careful what you say. I could get one of those boys over here . . .'

'Like you did with Chris you mean? Only it was him you got to take somebody else outside and now he's sitting in a cell. I've seen him you know. I've talked to him. Do you want to know how he is? How life's treating him inside where he's doing life for a crime that was committed by your gangster boyfriend and the knuckle-dragging animal he hauls around with him? You set him up because you couldn't face the consequences.'

Joanne laughed bitterly.

'Oh well that's very easy for you to say isn't it? What do you know about consequences? You haven't got a fucking clue; you don't know what's at stake. You think you've got the fucking picture? You think you've got the story? You haven't even begun to scratch the surface. You should run home to your little girlfriend, stay out of things you can never understand.'

'That's just bullshit.' Nick could feel anger and tension unravelling inside him. 'It's not so complicated. In fact it's quite simple. Don't pretend that there's some big mystery about your instinct for self-preservation.'

'Ah, I still like it when you talk like that.' She laughed and looked at the rings on her hands. 'I can't help you if you've got yourself into trouble with Terry. I didn't ask you to come down and start nosing around. I didn't tell Chris Gayle to boast about me to every single person that he could find who would listen. I wasn't going to pay for the fact that he didn't know how to keep his mouth shut. If he's keeping it shut now then good for him. I don't hurt people and that's why you can stand here accusing me of all sorts, telling me how you would like me to be, but suddenly it's like I'm the villain; I'm the one to blame.'

A girl came wandering over. She had been observing the conversation and seen Joanne's growing animation. She was also attractive but standing beside Joanne she appeared awkward and clumsy.

'Are you OK, Jo?' She gave Nick a sharp look.

'I'm fine.' Joanne handed her a drink. She turned to go with her friend but Nick grabbed her arm.

'Just one thing. I'm worried about Trevor. The bar manager. I was meant to meet him tonight but he hasn't shown up. They haven't . . .'

Joanne laughed and stared him full in the face. 'Don't you worry about Trevor. That's one thing that Trevor and I have in common. He knows how to look after himself. You've probably got a bit too much on your plate to be worrying about anybody else.'

Nick watched her walk away, the way her body moved against her clothes, the slight arrogant swing in her stride, and he turned back to the bar. He knew that he was in deep trouble.

a package

'That *rubio* is here again,' Pancho says to me biting into a cheese and pickle sandwich as we sit in the shabby room upstairs at the back of the club where the cleaning stuff is kept. Pancho has become greatly enamoured with certain types of English food, especially convenience foods, preserves and spreads. It is a sign that he is getting over Sophie that he can acknowledge anything good about England. He holds forth on the virtues of fish fingers, steak and kidney pies, salt and vinegar crisps, pickled onions, scotch eggs. He particularly loves sandwich spread – "it's absolutely exquisite," he said to me once, which I thought was rather overstating the case.

'Which *rubio*?' I ask picking out some toilet rolls from the stack on the floor.

'The journalist. I saw him sitting on his own at the bar.'

I am surprised to hear this and hope that he will be more careful than he was the last time when he was saved by the bar manager. If he is investigating something down here then he was hardly behaving in a subtle and unobtrusive way by disappearing into this room with the girlfriend of the most vicious person in the club. Still, I can understand that most men would have found it hard to resist that particular temptation.

The night is humid and the club is hot. This is the last time that I will come down here to sweep up broken glasses, cigarette butts and sticky beer, the last time that I will mop out the toilets and fill black bags with the detritus of people's enjoyment. Pancho is going to carry on because he has decided to abandon Dr Sophie and return to Uruguay. He is saving all the money that he possibly can in his last months. Tonight, he appeared at Claudio's flat to pick me up in the battered old van which he uses to ferry us about and which he drives without a licence much to Claudio's fury. 'That thing could never pass its MOT,' he said contemptuously kicking a wheel. 'You'll get caught.' Pancho just shrugged and grinned at me. 'You've become more Gringo than the Gringos,' he told Claudio. I am going to miss Pancho when he returns but have told him that I will come and visit him when I return to the country with Claudio and Emily.

'My mother will treat you like a king,' Pancho told me. 'We'll have a big *asado* to thank you for looking after me.'

'What's an *asado*?' Emily asked.

'Oh you'll love it,' Claudio retorted with his eyes gleaming mischievously. 'Basically, it's great big pieces of very tender, very delicious dead animal cooked outside on a barbecue, washed down with lots of wine.'

Emily shuddered.

'Don't worry,' I told her. 'We'll find you an alternative.'

'I can have . . . what was an aubergine called? *Berenjena?* They're lovely barbecued. And so is sweetcorn.'

'Maybe,' Claudio said licking his lips. 'But not as lovely as sizzling steaks and crispy chicken and juicy *chorizos* in fresh bread. Eh Papi?'

'Sorry, Emily, I'm afraid on this one I must agree with my son. It's in our DNA.'

'Savages,' Emily shook her head sadly. 'People talked like you do about the slave trade. In fifty years time, they will look back in amazement at a time when humans ate meat.'

'I doubt that somehow,' Claudio said.

They wandered outside to see us off and Claudio too was reduced to shaking his head as he watched Pancho attempting to get the van started, the engine giving an unhealthy gravelly sound like the rattling lungs of an old smoker.

I take some more paper downstairs to the toilets. Two of the bouncers are standing chatting and laughing while they urinate. They do not notice me as I enter one of the cubicles to replace the paper.

'So they're taking a package out to Essex tonight?' One of the men says.

'Yeah, some cunt's been nosing around pretending to be a journalist or something. He's leaving with us tonight. He's already nervous. Knows something's up. They dropped him a hint just to make him suffer.'

I freeze and try and move further over into the cubicle so that the men will not know that I am there.

'What's he after?'

'Dunno. Nosing into Terry's business I suppose. He's gonna wish he hadn't though when they get him out to Epping.'

At this moment, I manage to drop a toilet roll. It unravels across the floor and out of the cubicle like in the adverts. Unfortunately, it does not bump into the velvety nose of a golden puppy but lands instead at the feet of one of the men. '*Hijo de Puta*,' I murmur. They turn round and look at me.

'Dropped something, Pedro?' The man bends down and picks up the toilet roll. The other one looks at me slightly askance.

'Was you fucking earwigging in there or what?'

When we arrived in Britain, Claudio's favourite TV programme was *Mind Your Language*. He – like many Latin Americans learning English – thought that it was absolutely

hilarious and was devastated when it was deemed to pander
to racial stereotypes and removed form the schedules. I cock
my head with an inane smile.

'Earwiggy? What ees . . .'

Both men laugh with the happy confidence that English
people experience when they have demonstrated their natural superiority over the foreigner by proving that he cannot
speak their language.

'See! He ain't got a clue. Here's your bog-roll, Pedro.
And don't go fucking earwiggy again. Or you'll get a slappy.
Comprende, compadre?'

He thumps me affectionately on the head with the toilet
paper and places it in my hand. In spite of myself, I feel a
brief spasm of irritation at being treated like a houseboy by
this lamentable representative of the British lumpenprole-
tariat. The two men zip up their trousers and leave the toilet.

I quickly make my way back up to where Pancho is still
lazing about and tell him what I have heard.

'Maybe it is not him,' Pancho says.

'I'm sure,' I say. 'We have to get him out of here. At least
I have to go and warn him.'

'Be careful, Orlando,' Pancho says. 'Why should you put
yourself at risk for some Gringo? I would stay out of it if I
were you.'

He looks at me quizzically, not troubled in the least by
his own frank admission of self-preservation as a guiding
principle to action. I think of the men in the cubicle and their
use of the word "package". I don't have the time to explain to
Pancho how that made me feel; how packages used also to
be bundled into the back of Ford Falcons; how packages
used to be dragged bloody and broken from their cells and
flown out to be dropped over the Río de la Plata. I remember the journalist in the office – his clumsy embarrassment

when he called me a Paraguayan, the mess he makes when he eats his sandwich, his curly-haired daughter rolling about on the desk talking about her cat.

'I'm going to find him,' I say impatiently.

I go all the way downstairs to the dance floor but he is not there. So I climb back to the upstairs bar and there I find him sitting dejectedly on a bar stool, as people push past him to purchase their drinks. I make my way to his side.

'You're in trouble,' I say to him quietly.

'I know,' he says without turning to look at me. 'I was going to use my mobile but it's not charged up and I didn't really know who to phone. I need the toilet but I don't want to go in there. I know they're waiting for me to do something. I'm trying to think what to do. This is ridiculous.'

I glance at him for a second, this tall blond journalist who usually seems to self–possessed, so authoritative. The thought of fists and boots landing on his body and face from the men who patted me on the head and called me Pedro fills me with pity and rage. I look around but there doesn't appear to be anybody watching.

'We'll get you out of here,' I say. 'Follow me upstairs. Make sure nobody sees.'

I walk back towards the stairs not turning my head to see whether he is following me. When I get to the top of the stairs, I turn round and he strides anxiously into the room. Pancho watched incredulously as he runs straight over to the sink and starts to piss into it.

'Christ, I was absolutely bursting,' he murmurs.

Pancho raises his eyebrows. I open the small window which looks out over the alley below. It is not so high but too high to jump. There are black drainpipes leading to the ground which might offer the possibility to shimmy down but they are slightly away from the window making it risky.

'Pancho, go and get the van and bring it round to the front,' I say in Spanish. He looks at me sceptically.

'Anda, boludo! Apurate, hombre!' My voice rises. Pancho scuttles quickly away.

The only option it appears to me is to get Nick through the back fire-exit doors out into the alleyway. But there is a bouncer standing on those doors. In which case, I will have somehow to get him away from the door. Suddenly, I hear footsteps on the stairs. A look of terror crosses the journalist's face. Quickly, I make my way to the top of the stairs where two bouncers are on their way up.

'Who else is up there? Is there anybody up there?' One of them snarls at me.

'Nobody ear. Only me. Who you look for?' I sound like some kind of Chicano from the Bronx.

They turn contemptuously on their heel without answering and retreat back down the stairs.

'Where is that slippery little fucker? I thought Lee said he was headed this way,' I hear one of the mutter.

'Maybe he's hiding on the dance floor,' the other says.

I return quickly to the room where Nick is waiting and explain to him that I am going to get the bouncer away from the door and then let him out into the alley.

'Are you sure the door opens?' He asks me nervously.

'No,' I reply. 'But I doubt whether they would have a bouncer on the door if it didn't.'

'How will I know if you've got rid of the bouncer?'

'You won't. Come down slowly in about a minute. It's our only chance.'

I make my way down the stairs and round to the back door where a big unshaven man is standing holding on to the bar of the door. He looks at me as I approach him.

'Yeah?'

'I have a message for you.'

'What is it?'

'They say you must go to front. They say package is there and they need help.'

'What?' He stared at me angrily with a total lack of comprehension. Obviously, not everybody is included in the plan to deal with Nick.

'To front. You must go to front. Package is there. I wait by this door. Hurry please. They say ees urgent.'

'Package? What package? What the fuck are you on about? Fuck me. The front you say? I'd better go and find out what they really want.'

He pushes his way through the crowd in the front bar towards the entrance. Where is Nick? Hurry up, hurry up. It must have been a minute by now. Then I see him peering nervously round at the door. I motion angrily for him to hurry up and push the drop-bar to the door. It doesn't open. For an instant I think everything is finished but when I push again and knee the door, it opens out into the dark alley. We both emerge into the sticky airless night.

'Wait,' I hiss at Nick who almost immediately begins to run for the main road. 'They might be waiting. Wait for the van.'

We stand with our backs against the wall. I cannot shut the door properly behind us and I know that it will only be a matter of time before the bouncer furiously returns. It is a curious parody of my past – *se están fugando los Tupas uno a uno del penal*. I can feel the blood thumping in my chest and veins. There is no van. Where is Pancho? What is he doing? Has he decided it is not worth risking anything for a blond-haired Gringo? I look up at the starless sky in exasperation and refuse to offer a silent prayer to a non-existent God.

'There he is!' The words cut into me like hot knives. Two men have stopped at the entrance to the alley and are staring at us.

'Hello, Pinocchio,' says the biggest and ugliest of them, grinning at Nick. 'Good try, mate. Now we're going for a little ride.'

Behind them, Pancho pulls up. He motions unhappily to me with the keys to show that he has had problems starting his wreck of a van. I gesture to him to get the passenger door open.

'You've got to try and get into the van,' I murmur quietly. 'I'll help you.'

As if sensing what is needed, Pancho suddenly blasts hard on the horn several times behind the men. 'Run!' I say as they turn with their attention diverted. Nick is already halfway past them when they turn back. Their reactions are not quite quick enough as they spin back towards the van. Pancho has the door open but one of them manages to grab Nick's arm as he tries to scramble in. I hurl myself forward and in that instant I am Claudio confronting the men on the train who were tormenting Emily. I have rage pounding in my head – these are the men; these are the men: they call people packages; they would leave a little girl without her father. I fling myself on to the man who is trying to drag Nick out of the van, and pull him back by the neck so that we tumble to the ground together. I start beating his head furiously with my fists. He grunts and moans more with surprise than pain. The door to the van slams shut but I do not hear it starting.

'Go, Pancho,' I yell and hear the engine spluttering. The man who is not on the floor with me throws himself at the van like a rabid dog, first trying to wrestle the door open and then launching a flying kung-fu kick against it.

'Get out of the fucking van, you slag,' he screams, hammering furiously on the window with the palm of his hand. Soon he will break the window. From my position on the ground I can see Nick's pale and terrified face. Pancho is still struggling with the ignition and then finally the engine catches and he wheel-spins away down the street. One of the men runs stupidly after the van and then gives up. Get help quickly, Pancho, I think as the man who I have been wrestling with stands up and straightens his jacket angrily. They turn and look at me still lying on the floor and the one I was hitting shakes his head.

'What the fuck did you do that for?' He asks and through his fury there is genuine bewilderment. Another bouncer appears panting.

'Where is he? Have you got him?'

'No because this . . .' he kicks me in my body '. . . fucking idiot went and helped him to get away.'

'I'm so sorry that I interfered with your plans,' I say in the most clipped English accent I can manage while I am still gasping for breath from the kick to my ribs. 'I can only say in mitigation that it was a categorical imperative.'

I look up at the three men above me and beyond them to the starless sky. *Cielo mi cielito lindo*, I start to laugh. How absurd everything is. One of the men licks his lips. *Danza de viento y juncal.* They look down at the laughing man on the floor about whom they know nothing. The laughter is making them more angry. I can still see puzzlement in the eyes of the one I was hitting. Nobody knows anything about me, not even the journalist I have just helped to escape. *Prenda de los Tupamaros.* They step towards me and one of them takes something from his pocket. You can't touch her any more, can't hurt her any more: she is safe. I am shaking with laughter. I cannot see their eyes, their eyes are empty while mine are filled with light. *Flor de . . .*

writing up

'Of course you can have the cottage for a week, darling.'
Nick's mother refilled their glasses with wine. They were
sitting in the garden in Chalk Farm, the sun beating down
on them. 'Will you go as well, Caitlin?'

'No, I don't think so,' Caitlin replied. Nick glanced at
her.

'You'll come down though? At the weekend?' He asked.

'Maybe,' Caitlin said, running her finger around the rim
of her glass.

'So,' Nick's mother clinked their glasses, 'it seems that
you had a terribly lucky escape. Do you really think you
should write this article?'

'Well, it doesn't make any difference now does it? They
know who I am,' Nick shrugged and sipped at the cold wine.
He watched a fat bee buzzing around the velvet throat of a
bright red tulip that was swaying slightly in the soft breeze.
The red of the flower reminded him of Joanne Sullivan's
dress the first time he had met her. He pushed the thought
from his head.

'And how is the man who helped you? He was in
hospital Caitlin told me.'

'Yes. He's got some complications with his kidneys.
Apparently, he had been tortured before in Uruguay. So, the
beating they gave him before the police arrived didn't help
matters. They're keeping him in for a while longer.'

Nick felt sudden tears pricking at his eyes. His mother
shook her head and tut-tutted.

'And are they going to charge the men who did it with anything?'

Nick smiled ironically. 'Well, who knows? Maybe with something minor. The main guy claims that Orlando attacked him. And he's got witnesses.'

'Orlando?'

'That's his name. The guy who helped me.'

'Are you going to write about what he did? Is that part of the article?'

'I'm not sure yet what I'm going to write.'

'You will remember to visit him and take him something, Nicky. Caitlin, dear, you will remind him won't you? He's terribly thoughtless you know . . .'

Caitlin smiled and nodded vaguely.

'Of course I'm not going to fucking forget,' Nick snapped irritably. 'I've already been to see him quite a few times.'

'Please don't talk to me like that Nicholas,' said his mother frostily.

'I'm sorry,' he took her hand, 'and thanks a lot for the cottage. I just need some peace and quiet so that I can write up and get my head together. I'll be starting this other programme soon . . .'

'Oh, the Eastern Europe thing? That does sound like fun. Your father and I went to Moscow you remember? Of course, it was so different then. Caitlin, darling, would you be an absolute love and fetch me my sunglasses . . . They're on top of the dishwasher . . .'

When Caitlin had trotted obediently off, Mrs Jordan turned to Nick.

'Is Caitlin OK, Nick? She seems very subdued. You haven't argued or anything.'

Nick shook his head. 'No we haven't argued at all.'

He was not lying but he was not telling the entire truth. Things were not right between them again but, instead of arguing, both had become more and more detached. One night, Caitlin had not returned home. When he asked her about it, she had said that she stayed with a friend because it had got too late to come home. Then she had run a bath and stayed there for about an hour.

'Good,' his mother said looking at him from under the palm of her hand. 'I should so hate there to be something wrong between you. Caitlin is such a treasure.'

They both watched her walking back down the garden holding Mrs Jordan's sunglasses in her hand. She smiled at them both and held the glasses out to Nick's mother.

'And your programme about the trade-unionist? We got the card about it this morning but I didn't check the date. It sounds very interesting.'

'Two weeks' time.'

'Well . . .' Mrs Jordan smiled benignly at her son, 'you have been busy haven't you?'

Nick turned off the road before Ipswich and drove down small lanes towards his parents' cottage. The evening was beautifully warm and he was almost tempted to stop for a pint in one of the pubs lining the route. He had said goodbye to Caitlin, holding her tightly in his arms, knowing that this week was the biggest test their relationship had yet faced. As he had got into the car, he had looked up from the street and seen her watching him from the window as she sometimes watched for his arrival when she heard a cab stopping outside their flat.

He had wanted to speak to George Lamidi before he left but his mobile was switched off. George had come to see him after the night at Sublime. Nick had been extremely anxious about DM but every time he asked George about it, he seemed to be evading the issue.

'It was him,' he finally blurted out when Nick was expressing his anger over Kinch's betrayal. 'It wasn't the copper. It was Trevor. I've spoken to him. He told me that it was him that grassed you up. That's why he wasn't there when you got there. They never done nothing to him. He fucking betrayed us.'

'What? Trevor did? Why? What had I done to him?'

George raised his eyebrows. 'Well, he said a lot of things. Some of it was quite mixed up. He said you was just doing research and you could always walk away from everything. That seemed to make him really mad. So, I think a bit of it was to make sure you didn't just walk away. I don't think he wanted you to get hurt as such, he just wasn't thinking properly. But I think it was also to do with that girl . . . '

'What girl?'

'I think you know what girl,' George said quietly.

'What, he had a thing for her?'

'Well, I don't know if it was just that. He said she was just getting herself into trouble. And he didn't want to see her do that. I think he really likes her. Something you did upset him big time. I don't really want to know about it and I told him that as well. He's always had attitude, Trevor. He ain't a mate but I never thought he would let me down like that.'

There was something in George's tone that troubled Nick slightly. George didn't seem sufficiently angry about DM's outrageous betrayal; it was almost as if he could see his point.

'So, I nearly get taken out to Epping and a cleaner gets

half-beaten to death because of Trevor's fucking jealousies . . .'

George looked at him sombrely. 'I never said that it was *just* the girl. I think there's a mixture of things. And it wasn't just that he fancied her; it was the way you went about things, he didn't like it. He kept coming back to that research thing.'

'Well, it was research that might have got somebody out of prison . . . did you talk to him before?'

'About what?'

'About us. About school and everything.'

George returned his gaze. 'What are you worried that I might have told him?'

Nick could not bring himself to pronounce the words; he could not articulate them; they stuck in his throat; they almost condemned him by their utterance. He stared angrily at George; he would not humiliate himself by confirming that he knew what George and DM might have talked about, what he stood accused of. George had protected him at school and he had just walked away. DM must have decided that this was what Nick would do again, was doing again. The two men gazed at each other in silence until finally George broke the silence.

'He wasn't happy you know. He didn't do it to get anything out of it. And he liked you at first.'

'Did you tell him what happened? How I got out of there? About the cleaner?'

George nodded.

'And?'

'He laughed. He laughed and laughed. That was it. He just laughed.'

'I doubt if Orlando sees the funny side.' But Nick knew that this was a clumsy defensive stroke; it wasn't the point at all.

'I don't think it's what Trevor was laughing at either,' George said.

Nick pulled into the driveway of the house and opened the front door. It was cool but slightly musty and something was off in the fridge. He left the front door open to let some air circulate. He took his bag from the car and a box of provisions which included two cartons of cigarettes, some wine and a bottle of whisky. He lit a cigarette and poured a glass of whisky and went out on to the front step, flapping at the midges that swarmed around his head. In the neighbouring garden a young girl was doing handstands and cartwheels as he remembered his sister doing when they were children.

Nick thought about Orlando whom he had visited in hospital with Rosa earlier in the week. Orlando had brushed off his thanks; he had seemed calm and happy. Before they left, Orlando's son had arrived and Nick was surprised to find that he was a rather serious – almost pompous – young man with little round glasses and his father's high forehead, carrying a lap-top in a travelling case. He was accompanied by a red-haired girl who gabbled rather nervously but who also spent a lot of the visit gazing balefully at Orlando as he tucked into the hospital beefburger that had been brought for his dinner.

'I'm going to start bringing you some proper food,' she announced and Orlando's son had laughed for the first time at his father's crestfallen face and said, 'So get out of that one.'

As they left the hospital, Nick had said something to the son about what Orlando had done for him, how grateful he was. The young man turned to face him and said almost passionately, almost as if somebody had argued contrary: 'That's what my dad's like. He's always been like that.'

Nick watched him walk away with his girlfriend down the corridor. Just before they disappeared through the swing doors the girl slipped her hand into his and started swinging his arm playfully as if coaxing him into good humour.

Nick stubbed out his cigarette on the step. The cartwheeling girl was being called inside for her tea and she ran back into the house, her laughter echoing in the hazy midge-filled air, a small dog yapping good-naturedly around her ankles. Nick got up, stretched and padded into the living room where he took the laptop from its bag and set it up on the big dining-room table. He rubbed his hands as he summoned up the blank document. All he wanted to do now was start writing, to get the barest of outlines down on the page. He thought of Joanne Sullivan standing before him, of Mrs Clemence pulling her cardigan around her shoulders, of Kinch and his cold dislike, of DM laughing, and of Orlando's bruised face. He thought back to his days with George Lamidi – round and round the hall, skating forwards and backwards, sometimes bumping into each other, tumbling on to the floor and struggling to get up and fly off again. He sighed as he thought of how they had changed, of how long ago it was that he had stood with his hands on his hips and watched a fourteen-year-old George lying on his back and laughing up at him.

Nick got up and refilled his glass. He looked at the phone and suddenly reached for it and dialled the flat in London. The answerphone clicked in and he heard Caitlin's brisk voice. *We're out. Leave a message.* Nick hesitated when the bleep sounded and then murmured. 'It's me, please call me.' He replaced the receiver and stared again at the blank computer screen. There was always this gap between what he knew and what the article demanded, between the truth and how it was presented. And there were still things that he did not know, connections he might not have made, half-truths and grey areas. *Think of your audience,* he heard the voice of his Series Editor in his head.

He wrote: *This is a story about clubs, drugs and murder.* He paused and looked at the words again for a moment. Then he continued: *It is also a story of betrayal.* He stopped, rubbed his hands again, lit a cigarette and settled down to his work.

the silver river

There is a song I remember about a river. I think it may be based on a poem. It tells of somebody walking by its banks and thinking that the river descends clear and singing from the mountains but quickly becomes cloudy and enclosed in restrictive banks. Then the river disappears from view like the poet's illusions. Only when its waters become salty with the approaching sea does it sense the recuperation of its liberty. I suppose that the religious symbolism is rather obvious, but I like the poem in spite of that.

I lie in my hospital bed where I have been for the last few weeks. Many people have been to visit me – Zamorano from work brings a bottle of whisky and tells me that a referee had his nose broken at the last football tournament. Pancho brings me spare pyjamas and sandwiches with sandwich spread to make up for the hospital food. I open them up, look at the little bits of green and red vegetable lying on margarine and give them to the nurse to distribute around the ward. Nick the journalist comes to see me with his little daughter. She has drawn me a picture of her cat with felt pens. 'My granny is in hospital as well,' she tells me sorrowfully. During Nick's visit, my son arrives and it is strange to see these two young men together slightly wary of each other – the computer expert and the journalist. Nobody can choose the time they live in; nobody can alter the circumstances of their birth, but I am glad that I have known a different time from this one even if I might mourn the disappearance of my youth.

The blows that the men gave me have aggravated some old injuries which means I have to stay in this place for a while but I don't really mind. I think that it is perhaps time to put a stop to my invisibility and hang up my mop once and for all.

In the warm afternoons, I doze in front of the TV as images of riots in Indonesia mesh with my dreams. *Ya viene Jakarta* they wrote twenty-five years ago on the walls of Santiago as a brutal taunt at the impending torment. Now in the Indonesian capital, black smoke billows from the shimmering buildings that rose themselves over the bodies of dead communists, and students place flowers in rifle barrels as they once did in a different era, in the time when I was young and black-haired and vibrant with hope.

I dream that a dragonfly was blown into my room on the warm air-currents; it is hovering above me and it hangs on whispering wings. And I dream of Silvia, that we are on the beach at Punta del Diablo looking out for her cousin, her first great love who was swept away by the tide. And when she turns away from the horizon she is smiling; she is smiling at me just as she did when we first met in that small flat so long ago crowded with young people. Before any other familiar terrifying images can intervene I wake to find Claudio and Emily are sitting squabbling by my bed.

'Smoky-bacon crisps don't even have meat – it's just flavouring so shut up and leave me alone,' Claudio is saying as he holds a bag of crisps between two hands ready to pop it open.

'That's not the point,' she hisses. 'Anyway, shhh, your dad's sleeping.'

I open my eyes and smile at my children, Claudio my beloved moody son who used to chase papers on the roof-top of our house in Montevideo, Emily with her soft red curls and her vegetarianism and her kindnesses. And I smile and feel my spine tingle because I know for every Suharto and Astiz and Pinochet, for every heartless sadist who drops to one knee and shoots a fleeing child, there are others, there are always others; there will always be others. I know that the river leaves the mountains clear and singing, even if it is telling a tale of bitter endurance. I close my eyes again listening to the murmuring and laughter of the children at my bedside and I do not see the hemmed-in river, nor the river with its murky waters filled with corpses. Instead, I see a great silver river, a river of silver, and it is glittering as the wind blows across and ruffles its surface. Its waters are salty, yes its deep waters are salty, but it is twisting and turning like thousands of bright mirrors spinning in the sunlight and it is flowing towards its liberty, pouring from the estuary and out into the sea.

acknowledgments

Especial love and thanks are due as always to Rossana.

Many other people helped me to write this novel either through help and advice or putting up with impromptu readings. Thanks also to: Harry Lansdown, Javier Hauret, Niki Johnson, Rachel Sieder, Alison and Lydia Richards, Vivien Bradford, Ernesto, Juan and Sonia Leal, Ernesto Leal (Snr), Sonia Riquelme, Louise Phillips, Simon Hinton, Andrea Purcell.

The story of Orlando and Silvia is fictional but is obviously based on real events which were shared by many thousands of people. There is a massive literature on the experience of the Latin American southern cone countries during the 1970s including many personal testimonies which have influenced the writing of this book. In relation to the events depicted in the book, accounts of Harald Edelstam's role in freeing prisoners from the National Stadium as well as eye-witness accounts of the coup in Chile can be found in *Storm Over Chile* edited by Samuel Chavki and published by Lawrence Hill and Co. A version from the Uruguayans who were released from the stadium can also be found in *Chile Roto: Uruguayos en Chile* by Eleuterio Fernandez Huidobro and Graciela Jorge, published by TAE. This book also gives a fascinating account of the experience of Uruguayans during the Allende years. Information on the principal activities of the Tupamaros during the early 1970s is taken from *manual de historia del Uruguay 1903-1990* by Benjamin Nuham. An account of the situation in Argentina following the coup and the case of Dagmar Hagelin can be found in *The Disappeared: Voices from a Secret War* which is edited by John Simpson and Jana Bennett and published by Robson Books.